SIMON WARD

Awoken in 2046

First edition

This book was professionally typeset on Reedsy.
Find out more at reedsy.com

Preface

Awoken in 2046 is the second book in the awakenings series. It follows on from, Finding Love in 2045, but is also complete as a standalone piece of writing.

Acknowledgement

I would like to thank the members of the 'Shark Tank' writing group for their support and critique in helping to keep me on track with their reviews and comments.

Thanks also to my wife for her input, support and patience for the time I spend in my 'hidey-hole.'

Chapter 1

Mia shared a loving hug with Tyler before she picked up her overnight bag and stepped into the taxi. It was Mia's first night away from Tyler since his upgrade from humble house bot to her Tushi dream droid. Life with Tyler had been wonderful, but a fun night at her bestie's bachelorette would give her time to think.

Kat welcomed her at the door with a beaming smile, a long hug and her usual overpowering fruity perfume. "How are you getting on with Tyler?"

"Okay. He can be tiring though."

"Too much sex?" Kat said, as she returned a playful smile.

"Is that all you ever think about." Mia smiled and shook her head at Kat's directness.

Kat had suggested Mia date more guys after her previous relationship disappointment, but a surprise upgrade to Tyler, transformed him from the short, unimposing close friend to her lover. The two-meter-tall Nordic-like Adonis was now her friend, partner and protector.

She'd grown more assured with Tyler aside her, but Mia and Kat were still opposites. Kat had always strutted her brown wavy locks and buxom figure around many fellas. Mia's old-fashioned values wanted to get to know a guy before becoming intimate, but with sex on tap from Tushi girls, most guys didn't want lasting connections and treated women like sexbots.

Kat had moved in with her guy and added indoor plants to provide something real in comparison to the vibrant video wall. The feature wall stretched the length of the room with Butterflies of yesteryear dancing around a flower-filled summer garden.

Lucy arrived next. "Hiya stranger, when did you get tits?" Kat said.

Unlike Mia, Lucy's waiflike frame had filled out over the last few years. She rolled her eyes at Kat and shook her head. "They just appeared one morning."

Mia smiled at Lucy as they shared a knowing look of being stuck in the middle of Kat's world again. "Hair looks good."

Lucy swished her blond curls. "Yours too."

"Have you seen Ellie?" Kat asked.

"Yeah, saw her a couple of months ago. She came in for her baby scan," Lucy said.

Three confident knocks on the door announced her arrival. Fresh faced Ellie stepped in like a catwalk model in a full length fluffy white coat.

"Where's your bump then?" Kat asked as Ellie removed her coat.

"Nine more weeks," Ellie said. Other than a modest bump nobody would have known.

Mia placed her palm on Ellie's stomach, waiting for a kick. Kat soon joined in and they beamed at the miracle inside her.

Lucy having delivered hundreds of babies paid more attention to the chilled Chardonnay and took over as hostess. They settled down on an arc of graphite leather loungers sipping on the fine wine with Ellie content with filtered water. The conversation gravitated to Kat and her impending matrimony, but Kat had something else to reveal. She slid her untouched Chardonnay aside. "It's not only Ellie having a baby." Mouths gaped as they fell back into their loungers.

It was typical of Kat, she always made sure she stole the show. Each subsequent update could not carry the same punch, until Lucy said, "I'm bringing a guest to the wedding."

"I thought you were a confirmed spinster, only interested in your studies," Ellie said.

"Is it Doctor Luke?" Mia asked.

"Who's Doctor Luke?" Kat and Ellie asked in melodic unison.

Lucy's face lit up. "Doctor Luke came to the Lockland's two years ago. A perfect specimen, tall, strong and handsome. Whenever he's near me, I get flustered and if he brushes against me with his clean-cut sexiness, I tingle all over. All too often I excuse myself to release the fire in my undies."

"Bloody hell, you need to get laid," Ellie blurted out, "Haven't you asked him out?"

"I have a couple of times." Lucy rolled her eyes. "He cancelled both times for work stuff at the last minute."

"I'd drag him into a spare room," Kat said.

"He's coming to the wedding!" Lucy said. She gave a devious grin and added, "I've booked us a room."

A round of whoops followed. "Does he know?" Mia asked.

"No! Don't want to spook him. I'll stay the night anyway."

"Intent on giving up your virginity?" Ellie asked.

Lucy shrugged. "My sex toy took that years ago."

"You don't mean the dildo thing your brother bought you." Kat was referring to the embarrassing gift Lucy received as a joke.

"Couldn't keep it in the back of my cupboard forever."

3

"Thought It scared you," Mia asked.

"Facing fears is enlightening. I got drunk one night and let's just say, I had to change the sheets."

Kat stood. "Let me get this right. You're 26 and you haven't had sex with a guy or a sexbot."

Lucy crossed her legs and placed her hands on her knee. "Not yet, I'm saving myself for Luke."

Kat shook her head. "You need to kiss a few frogs before you find a prince."

"I've found mine," Ellie said. She gushed about Connor until a kick from the baby switched her onto the baby modifications she'd selected. "I've had the CCR5 gene removed to boost intelligence and selected bright blue eyes like mine."

Kat folded her arms. "I'm having a traditional pregnancy. I don't want jabs, modifications, or scans. It's the only genuine surprise left in the world." Kat grinned. "Anyway, mine and Mirek's genes will combine to produce a perfect baby."

"A twelve-week scan is a sensible choice, even if you don't want the gene mods. The sex of the baby isn't clear then, you'll still get your surprise," Lucy said.

Ellie defended her decision, holding her bump, "I want my baby to have the best possible start. The advances in biotech are incredible, we should embrace technology." She sneered a Mia who'd tried to convince her not to have the modifications.

"Fuck technology," Kat replied, "I'll decline all I can. I heard about a girl from New Birmingham who died a week after having a well-monitored pregnancy."

Lucy held her hand to her face and shook her head. "That's awful, but it wouldn't have anything to do with the modifications."

Kat's wavy locks swished across her face as she shook her

head. "Fuck Technology!"

"That's what Mia's doing, fucking technology." Ellie stroked her bump and grinned at Mia. "I bet you don't have any baby plans."

Mia wanted to scratch her eyes out, she wanted a baby more than anything, but she stayed calm. Her confidence from being with Tyler had given her more composure. "Tyler's asked if we could have a Tushi-Baby. I've not decided yet."

Kat raised an eyebrow and rested her chin on her hand.

"It would be weird," Lucy said.

Tushi Babies were not uncommon but were there to appease Tushi Wives. Men choosing Tushi-Wives instead of their human counterparts had become popular. A beautiful woman with a perfect figure, content to do all the chores whilst the guy played or watched esports. The guys, like Mia, had amazing sex whenever they desired and granted their Tushi wives, the small request for a baby.

"If I go along with it, I'll have a mini-bump attached, which tracks my personality to shape the fresh mind." Mia quite liked the idea but was nervous. If she agreed, she'd be the first woman to have a Tushi baby.

"Developing an early bond by talking to your future off-spring, clever stuff," Lucy said.

Ellie suggested, "you may as well join the baby club, even if it's a Tushi baby. What else are you going to do other than run your little coffee shop with your mom?"

"I run it on my own!" Mia resisted a full-on attack for the hormonal Ellie. "My mom gave me the business as a parting gift when she moved in with her new fella. I enjoy running it and chatting to my regulars." Mia sighed, "It's fine for now, but someday I'd like to be famous for more than just making cakes in a little shop."

"Being the first woman to have a Tushi Baby would make you famous," Kat said.

"I'd rather be designing or controlling them, like Ethan."

"Somebody's still in love with their Ex," Kat gave her a cheesy grin. "He'll be at the wedding. Perhaps you could design a robot together."

"Don't think so, I've moved on. I'll stick with Tyler." She jumped up and gave a quick twirl. "We've been practicing a dance."

"Go, girl! You've come out of your shell since we were kids," Lucy said.

Mia smiled. "Thanks to Tyler."

"You don't want Ethan back then," Kat asked.

"I'm with Tyler now. Ethan couldn't say or do anything to change that!" Mia took a large swig of her wine hoping the subject would move on.

Kat received notification. "Our Chinese delights are here." She headed to the door and Mia followed.

The drone was a sturdy unit, with four one metre fans holding the mini-bot steady as it came to rest before being released. The mini bot wheeled up to and through the door as Kat welcomed it in. It stopped next to the table and opened to release its steam filled payload. Kat unloaded the contents as mouths watered. The mini bot rolled away and Mia watched as it slotted back into its drone and lifted above the buildings to speed away.

Despite drone delivered food being the norm for many, Kat often cooked for Mirek, but tonight was a treat whilst she relaxed with her friends. The food hit the spot as they continued to chat, reminiscing about how they'd played up their parents. The spiciest stories as always came from Kat who when prompted by Ellie, re-told the familiar tale of when outside the restroom in a restaurant, she showed a young lad her breasts. Her Mom grounded her when she overheard the boy returning to his seat saying some crazy girl had asked him to feel her tits. Kat cowering in her seat had given her away.

An innocent comment from Lucy changed the tone. "How long have you been with Mirek?"

"She moved in here the same night they met. They were engaged within the week," Mia blurted out.

Kat bobbed her tongue out at Mia and replied, "Four Months. When you know, you know."

"Four months! Are you crazy?" Lucy said. A blush returned to Kat's cheeks as Mia and Ellie sniggered.

Kat composed herself. "Yep, crazy in love." She stared at the video wall for a moment and stroked her chin. All eyes were fixed on Kat as she contemplated.

"I don't know when his birthday is, or if he likes Christmas. I don't *really* know if he's happy I'm having his baby." Kat turned to Mia, "What am I doing? Have I gone crazy?"

As maid of honor, it was Mia's job to re-assure her, "Yes, you're crazy, you always have been. Mirek is impetuous too. If you love him, marry him, you'll find out lots more about him, some you'll like, some you won't, but if you love him, you'll get through them."

"I bet you haven't even farted in front of each other yet," Ellie said.

Kat didn't reply, but her silence confirmed they both had a lot to learn about each other. Her confidence returned with a strong smile. "I love Mirek. I never want to let him go and I'm marrying him tomorrow, even if his farts stink." They giggled and joked about stinky boys. "It's why we wear perfume," Kat said.

Kat had planned the night to perfection. They changed into their PJ's and settled down for their sleepover. She put on her favorite old movie and insisted they sang along to, 'The Rocky Horror Picture Show,' and insisted they got on their feet to do 'the time warp.'

A hard knock on the door stopped the dancing. A sense of foreboding washed over them all, apart from the scheming Ellie, who paused the film. With a dressing gown protecting her modesty, she strolled over to the door. Kat called out, "If it's Mirek tell him he can't come in. He can't see me until tomorrow."

Ellie opened the door a fraction and there were some mumbling voices before she welcomed in a hunky policeman. He stood with his fists on his hips, "Kat Parker, you are under arrest and need to join us at the station."

"Get lost. I'm getting married tomorrow," Kat said.

"You are under arrest for public indecency in a restaurant."

"What! From ten years ago?" She glared at Ellie, who was already sniggering.

"You can take your punishment here." The handsome policeman smiled bringing fun to the occasion.

He pulled up a chair. "Would you like to take a seat?"

"No thanks." Kat folded her arms.

The policeman grabbed her arm and pulled her into the seat. He stood directly in front of her and removed his jacket to reveal his pumped body of bulging muscles.

Kat looked over to Ellie and gave her a wry smile.

The fake policeman placed his hand on her chin and guided her attention back to him, "Undo my belt and pants."

In the spirit of the fun, Kat obliged, until the size of the bulge in his boxers became clear. This was no ordinary stripper gram, he was a sexbot. He then pulled out his sizeable shaft. "Milk me," he ordered.

"No thanks Mate, too much for me." She pushed back against his sixpack and raised from the chair.

With Kat's mind made up, Ellie said, "Okay, never mind. The show's over. Let's get back to the film."

They expected him to leave, but he returned to the same stance with his fists on his waist, "My mission is not complete. If not Kat, who?"

Ellie shrugged at the critical stares from Kat, Mia and Lucy, before she stepped towards the menacing figure, "Okay! What's your mission?"

"I need to be unloaded before I can return to my station."

Ellie shook her head. "No thanks. We've paid. You can go." Ellie waved towards the door and returned to her seat.

He was unmoved. The girls ignored him and returned to the film, but every couple of minutes he repeated his task getting louder each time. "Unload me!"

"I'll call to complain," Ellie said, but the droid took the mobile and tossed it onto the lounger and took Kat by the arm.

Mia screamed at him and grabbed his arm. "She's fucking pregnant, leave her alone."

Lucy grabbed another arm. "We want you to leave!"

Ellie retrieved her mobile and punched and swiped at the screen.

The droid overpowered Kat, Mia and Lucy, as he pulled them towards the bedroom. As they reached the bedroom door, he loosened his grip on Kat.

"Send your feedback, or I'll be back."

He straightened his pants and picked up his jacket as he left. Sighs were let out as Ellie closed the door. "I tried to cancel the booking, but it didn't work. Instead, I confirmed the task was complete and thankfully it worked."

Kat placed a reassuring hand on Ellie's shoulder. "Sorry to wimp out." Intent on lifting the mood, she continued, "It may have been better to have done the deed rather than have all the screaming. Mia, you squeal like a pig."

Laughter followed before Ellie restarted the film and they settled back into their loungers.

Mia didn't join in the giggles. When she spoke, the laughter stopped, "Why didn't he stop when you asked?"

"I guess he wanted to complete his job." Ellie shrugged.

"They're programmed to listen and respond, not carry on regardless."

"Mia, stop flapping, everything's okay," Kat added.

"You can't ignore what happened. That was wrong."

"She's worried Tyler might start ordering her about," Ellie said.

"The drama's over. Watch the film," Kat said.

When the credits rolled for the end of their emotion filled night, they were ready for sleep. Apart from Mia. Her mind whirred all night. She wanted to have a family, but would a droid family give her the life she wanted. Tyler was her lover and protector, but what would she do if he went rogue like the stripper droid?

Chapter 2

Ethan had letters after his name and accolades for his work, but when it came to relationships, he was a complete failure.

Having royally screwed up with his first love and lost the most important part of himself. fifteen years later, he'd done it again. What was it with him and girls? Why did he pick the wrong woman every time?

Ethan put his life together after finally getting over his loss. He became the most respected engineer at the Tushi Corporation. Okzu Tushi, the head of the corporation, gifted him a mansion after he played a key role in developing the combined Tushi network to boost the AI learning of the droids. Ethan was initially proud of the massive step forward, but he underestimated the rapid pace of their improvement.

Okzu wouldn't let him explain the potential scenarios. When Ethan suggested pulling the plug Okzu said he'd gone crazy and had him removed from the building. Ethan got side-lined into indefinite stress leave as if he was the basket case, not Okzu who somehow couldn't see the danger. Perhaps Okzu's environmental quest had taken his focus away from their core business.

Ethan's most advanced creation was an AI sexbot. He called her Chloe. Aside from work-based frustrations, he'd been content with her. She provided everything he needed; Intelligent conversation, support to build his own Faraday cage to isolate his prototype work, but most of all she provided the love he needed to fill the largest void in his life.

His life had changed when he agreed to go out with his buddy, Mirek, on a foursome date. It should have been a meal out and sex before returning home. In stark contrast to the high-powered confident women at the office, he met Mia. She was a petite brunette in her mid-twenties and cute in a vulnerable kind of way. Most guys would have taken advantage and played the game, but his primary instinct had been to protect her.

Ethan invited Mia back to his place whilst his Tushi Girl, Chloe, was back at the factory for an upgrade and they finally took the next step. He'd never known a feeling like it. His heart nearly burst out of his chest. They were finally one in hearts, minds and bodies, but someone or rather something modified Chloe's upgrade details. Chloe arrived back earlier than expected, whilst Mia and Ethan were having breakfast. He was about to explain his connection with his Tushi Girl Chloe, but she appeared as Mia's body double.

Ethan tried to explain to Mia how he'd developed Chloe and she'd always hold a special place in his heart, but Mia got spooked and fled. Ethan should have tried harder to stop her, but in Chloe's familiar embrace he let her leave.

He realized his mistake and made a call to Mia, but her Tushi droid, Tyler, completed his protection role and prevented contact. Ethan went to the coffee shop, where Mia worked, but she wasn't there.

Ethan had screwed up again and having experienced the deeper love of Mia, Chloe's affection no longer felt real. He quizzed the team at Tushi about the mix up, but they found no record of a change to his request to explain Chloe's appearance. He changed Chloe back to her previous look, but it was still Mia he longed for.

Tomorrow, Ethan would finally get to see Mia again at Mirek's wedding. He was unsure how to approach her. She may slap his face or scream abuse at him. He would accept that, if she didn't ignore him. He didn't have the chat to get around women like Mirek had, especially when he cared about them. Would she forgive him? He had a plan but pulling her heart away from Tyler was a massive challenge. Ethan had spent years designing and developing sexbots to protect against their bonded partners wanting to leave them.

Could Ethan outwit his own hand?

*

Ethan wore a flowery blue shirt hiding the small paunch over his trousers. Tonight was a chance to put Mia and the potential repercussions of the network out his mind. Okzu was right about one thing, he needed a break.

He strode confidently up the hall to the guestroom where Mirek would be staying before the wedding. Holding onto the door frame, he called, "Is Lover boy ready for his bachelor party?"

Mirek slid across the wooden floor in a black tuxedo. His film star looks beamed with his confident toothpaste commercial smile.

They headed into town to meet with some guys from work. Mirek said they were also coming out for Ethan. "The guys in the office are none too happy the way you've been treated. They'll be out in force to make it a good night."

When they arrived at the sports bar, Mirek was spot on, guys were shoulder to shoulder and three deep at the bar. Most of the guys and girls from the office were out. Ethan accepted multiple offers of drinks. "So much for the diet," he said to the girls buzzing around him. "The night is supposed to be about Mirek, not me."

When he took a seat, a girl sat either side of him. Each hooking an arm around him to smother him with affection and their sweet-smelling perfume. Thoughts of Mia however didn't leave his mind. "Where did Mirek Go?" he asked.

A gorgeous brunette from marketing had approached. "He's with the guys at the bar, he's fine." She planted herself on his knee. Ethan was fully aware of her intentions after Mirek had bedded her at the last Christmas party.

Ethan stretched out his legs and slid her ungraciously to the floor. "No thanks." He shrugged off the other two to join Mirek at the bar.

"Here's the nut job," a chunky sales guy hollered, followed by a round of whoops.

Ethan span around on the spot, but Mirek grabbed him and turned him back around. "They're only playing with you."

"Just kiddin' Ethan. Okzu's the nutter. Have a drink with us."

"I've left four pints back there." Ethan gestured back to the women who'd smothered him.

"You're in demand buddy." Mirek clapped his hand on his shoulder and presented another pint. "Get it down you, you're falling behind."

"So why did Okzu kick you out?" another guy asked.

"He didn't kick him out, he's on stress leave," Mirek replied.

The cheers rose as Ethan downed his first pint.

Ethan wiped his mouth. "I'm on frustration leave. I'm not stressed. I'm pissed off."

"The network Ethan built is learning fast, that's all," Mirek said, passing Ethan another pint.

"It's as if Okzu wants the droids to take over. He wasn't interested with how fast they were-"

Mirek interrupted him. "Listen Ethan! No more crazy talk. They'll put a straitjacket on you."

"Drink up and don't let it bother you," the chunky sales guy said.

"Haven't had a proper drink for a couple of months. Forgot how refreshing a pint could be. Time to catch up and forget about Okzu." Ethan took another long swig, staring at the ceiling. No willing allies here. After all, they were the guys pushing for a mass adoption of the droids. Helping him to develop a solution at home to bring down the network was not on their agenda.

After three pints, Ethan made his excuse and took a seat to catch some esports on the monitors but the two girls from earlier appeared. "Ethan, I've got someone for you to meet." The slim blond led him by the hand around to a small alcove where a delicate brunette sat with her back to him. His attention piqued but dropped again as he realised it wasn't Mia.

"Julie from accounts. Ethan from engineering," the blond said, as she ushered Ethan in next to her. "We'll leave you to chat." Pleased with her effort she scuttled away.

Julie gave him a shy smile. "Don't you just hate set up's?"

Ethan took a gulp of his pint.

"Are you coming back to work soon?"

"Doubt it." Ethan stared straight ahead at the esports racing on the screen opposite and took another gulp of his pint.

"Do you like racing?"

"Alright, I suppose." He finished his pint without taking his eyes off the screen.

Julie mirrored him and finished her white wine. "Shall we have another?"

"I've got one over there." Ethan headed off with a casual wave of his hand. "See you later."

Ethan retrieved his spare pint from between the girls. He ignored the 'how did you get on with Julie?' question from the girls and returned to the guys at the bar.

Although esports dominated conversation, they also discussed the hydrogen fuel cells which were now being tested in live bots. Ethan had chosen Chloe for an early trial. The fuel cell benefit was instant. Chloe could now spend the whole of the night with him. To have her warm and cozy to wake up to had renewed their bond, but he wanted Mia's delicate frame next to his. He longed to see her cute dimples and her wayward morning hair but most of all her warm smile to melt away his troubles.

As the beers flowed, he told everyone that would listen about how much he missed Mia and how he needed a plan to get her back. Mirek put his arm around his buddy. "You need to forget about Mia. She's with Tyler now. You designed them to stick, so you need to move on and give up on the stalker role. Did you meet Julie? She's kinda like Mia."

"Not interested. If I can't be with Mia, I'll stick with Chloe."

"I thought the droids were the enemy?"

"I've taken her off the network."

"How've you done that?"

"I duplicated her control chip. Her networked chip is running a macro program to avoid raising any alarm."

"You really are the genius." Mirek patted him on his back.

"I haven't stopped the network yet, I'm not that much of a genius. I'm developing a virus though."

Guys were pairing off with girls from work as the esports bar started to thin out.

Mirek ignored the further reference to the network troubles. "Drink up buddy. Time to call it a night."

"It's time we sorted you pair out for some action," the chunky sales guy said.

"None for me, thanks. I'm ready to commit to Kat. I don't need any more embarrassing stories for Ethan to add."

"I'm fine too. You can have my share." Ethan gestured to a couple of girls giggling in their direction.

They shared out some sober pills before going their separate ways for their taxi rides home. Ethan patted Mirek on his back. "You need a sound night's sleep. Big day tomorrow."

It would also be a big day for Ethan. How would Mia react to seeing him again? Could she be as nervous as he was?

*

Up early, Ethan was keen to maintain his new exercise regime in his previously neglected gym. After losing Mia, he re-aligned his focus on getting fitter. A period of intermittent fasting and some 'Waist Gone© pills helped to pull in his waistline. He wasn't beach body ready but was in better shape.

He had gained weight after his previous relationship with Susie had ended, that was four years ago. Food had replaced the hole, where love had been, and Chloe couldn't fill it. He hoped Mia was the one for him and was working hard to get her back.

After an exhausting session, he showered off and checked on the sleepyhead Mirek, who showed no signs of stirring.

He checked over the essentials for the day, suits, rings and his best man notes. Ethan added some notes to his speech to remind Mia of the connection they shared. If he teased her, it may encourage some conversation during the evening reception. Although a long shot, he needed to try.

With the likelihood of Tyler and Chloe keeping him away from Mia, Ethan needed a backup plan. He wrote a note to slip to her at the wedding. She may help him even if she didn't want to go back to him.

Chapter 3

Kat was already showered and tucking into some muesli when Mia awoke. It was typical of Kat, fresh and ready for the day whereas the other girls yawned and stretched, barely crawling into the morning. They took turns in the shower to wake them and enjoyed the delights of the body dry system. It reminded Mia of the frizz attack she'd experienced at Eden when she'd been there with Ethan. This time she covered her hair and warned Ellie and Lucy to do the same.

The nail lady arrived at ten with Kat peering out of the window. They all had nail art to match with the ivory and navy wedding theme with a cursive M & K detailed on each fingernail.

Kat's wedding dress was typically fun and flirty to suit her character. It had a corded lace v-neck with illusion sleeves and a keyhole back. The chiffon dress had Venice lace accents on the bodice and sleeves with a unique illusion back strap to finish the look. Her bronze skin provided the perfect contrast to the ivory dress. She left her dark brown wavy hair flowing as free as her spirit.

With nails suitably dry and some Dutch courage dispensed, they applied final make up touches. Ellie headed off and Mia and Lucy enjoyed a light drink whilst Kat paced up and down until her dad appeared. Kat had followed her dad's organized personality but had slipped on the frugal side.

"Did you ignore the budget?" her dad asked.

Kat rolled her eyes and sighed. "I'm only having one wedding."

Kat had moved out of home to get away from her overbearing parents. It was their attention to detail which had provided her with a large investment fund, which Mia wished she had. If Kat didn't overspend, the interest and the basic universal income would sustain her. Kat had dipped into the capital too often, even before the build-up to the wedding.

Her father repeated his familiar advice. "Control your spending and the interest will keep you."

"All is well father. After the wedding Mirek will buy me all the clothes I need." She continued aiming to prove her sound judgement. "Mirek wanted me to arrive in the same plush air taxi he'd used for our engagement, but I chose the cheaper alternative to have the Rolls Royce Phantom."

Mia didn't think her choice not to use a VTOL had anything to do with the cost. Her dad didn't appear convinced either, but he let it go.

The driver came to the door and with a professional etiquette, announced, "A car for Mr. Parker and Ms. Kat Parker." Lucy and Mia sang the wedding march as Kat stepped along the path with her father to the awaiting Phantom. The chugging combustion engine made a rumbling noise, they were concerned it may explode as fumes spilled out from the rear, but the chauffeur didn't appear concerned.

The suited chauffeur opened the door and helped tuck Kat's dress in before closing the door with a firm thud. Mia and Lucy watched the Rolls Royce slowly chug into the distance, with the gray fumes from the rear filtering into the atmosphere. They followed with a much more efficient VTOL taking them to the church in a fraction of the time.

Mirek had suggested a modern wedding, but Kat sweetly side-lined him. She wanted to fulfill her dream of a traditional church wedding. The church was near the edge of the temperature-controlled city of New Birmingham. They were protected from the external elements with an enormous dome over the city. A pocket of windows opened to allow the VTOL a smooth entry inside before it gently came to rest. It was a delightful scene with perfectly manicured lush grass each side of a cream marble walkway leading to the beautifully carved oak doors.

Mia and Lucy glanced inside the small church, decorated with over a thousand navy blue and ivory roses. Streams of matching ribbons draped above the aisle completed the perfect setting. Wedding bells were ringing to announce Kat's impending arrival.

When Kat arrived. The photographer called them to arms for a couple of pictures before Kat cut short the photo session and declared, "I want to get married now."

Mia ushered Lucy into the church for them to file into their places whilst Kat composed herself for the walk every girl dreams of making. The eyes were on them as they stood uncomfortably awaiting Kat. Everything had gone to plan except the organist who called in sick. Mia fixed the issue with a call to Tyler, who stepped in to play the organ after an upload from the network.

After what seemed like an age, Tyler began, and Mendelssohn's wedding chorale echoed around the church. Kat started her walk down the aisle, her head straight with her eyes focused on Mirek. Her pace was slow and steady as she held onto her dad. Mia noticed a frustration behind Kat's calm exterior, perhaps stepping slowly in new high heels would be painful. Mia had told her to wear them in, but Kat insisted on only wearing them for the wedding. Kat's dream man stood proud with his hands clasped behind him and eyes forward, following her orders not to peak.

Mia's eyes glistened. She tried not to think of it, but she'd never have a day like this with Tyler. Kat always got what she wanted. After her ridiculously slow walk, she released her grasp on her dad and passed her bouquet to Mia. Kat frowned at her. She'd said she didn't want her to sniffle through the service and spoil it. Kat would have assumed it was Mia's emotional response from seeing her beautiful bestie on her wedding day and not the reality of Mia's own shortcomings pulling on her heavy heart.

Kat took her position next to Mirek as they stood before the priest. Kat focused on the priest, but whilst he found his page in his leather-bound book, she turned her head to Mirek. His eyes stared past the priest, but Kat's eyes burned into his cheek until he turned with a strong, confident smile before he quickly returned his gaze front and center.

With all eyes on the immaculate Kat, Mia figured it gave her a break. Before Kat had started down the aisle, the eyes were on Mia in the stupid dress Kat had made her wear. It was at least two sizes too big. Kat again made sure she shone above everyone. A tear escaped down Mia's cheek with sadness for her own life rather than being emotional for her friend. Kat was always stunning, as was the equally immaculate Mirek. They were a perfect couple, and Mia was dating a robot, albeit a hot and sexy one.

If only she had a guy like Mirek. The stark contrast was Ethan next to Mirek, who'd been trying to catch her eye. The idiot probably wanted to tell her about the dress being too big. Mia wanted to punch him and hug him at the same time. Perhaps it was her imagination, but he was slimmer. Mia reflected on how he'd treated her well and she'd fallen in love with him until she found out he preferred Chloe as a robot version of her. It was just plain weird. Mia berated herself, you've moved on, forget about him.

Kat, however, had a real-life human hunk of a man. Although happy for Kat, she was jealous as hell. The delicate aroma of the bouquet filled her nostrils. She tried not to sniffle loudly, but she received an annoyed sideward glance from Kat.

At least Mia had Tyler with her, Lucy's date had stood her up again, but she seemed like she was okay, giggling, whenever Mia wriggled in her oversized dress.

Mirek and Kat were word perfect and totally made for each other. The priest presented them as the new Mr. & Mrs. Gorski-Parker. A double-barreled name, Mia should have known, but she figured it was better than Kat Gorski. Their polite yet passionate kiss made them both glow like torches of love. Mia needed some re-assurance and caught Tyler's attention and a smile from his organ stool.

Photos galore followed as Ethan and Mia stood aside the new couple as they signed the register. She nearly jumped out of her skin when Ethan brushed her hand. He leant towards her and handed her a written note. "Read it later. Alone."

The heat in her cheeks exploded. Why did he have to embarrass her like that? She glanced at it and shoved it into her little clutch bag. He glanced back, putting a finger to his lips. Passing secret notes? Was he from kindergarten? Didn't he know she'd moved on? She was fine now, besides Chloe was still probably around, even though she hadn't seen her. He's supposed to be a tech genius, why didn't he just message her? Why was it important she read it alone?

*

With the photos finished, Mia ushered Mirek and Kat into the afternoon reception area and the rest of the guests followed them through to take their places for dinner.

Mia sat at the top table in front of a select collection of dinner guests. Mia didn't recognize many of them as they filed in. Lucy was the exception, she'd managed to sneak off and change into a more comfortable figure-hugging midnight blue dress, whilst Mia had been standing aside the photographer for the last few shots. Lucy looked fantastic and gave a little twirl for Mia before taking her seat. Mia forced a smile before wrinkling her nose as she looked at her tent of a bridesmaid dress.

She looked over to Tyler for some reassurance, but he was engrossed in conversation at the back of the room with a stunning blond in a little black dress. Mia tried not to be jealous but popped over to Kat. "Who's talking to Tyler?"

Kat ignored her question and handed Mia her shoes and a room key, "Can you get my sneakers, my feet are killing me?"

Mia smirked and shook her head. "Told you to wear them in," Kat's heels were likely red raw.

Kat rolled her eyes in response. "I Know."

"Who's talking to Tyler?" Mia exaggerated her stare at Kat.

"It's Chloe, Ethan's plus one. Hurry up, the mains will be coming out soon," Kat said, before she turned to talk with Mirek.

Mia dashed past Tyler and Chloe. Tyler didn't even notice her. Mia didn't understand why Ethan had given her a love letter; he must have moved on if he'd changed her again.

Mia opened the door to the bridal suite to see navy blue and ivory rose petals over the floor and four-poster bed. Mia gaped at such a romantic setting; Kat really did have everything with Mirek. She avoided stepping on the petals, not wanting to spoil the lovely surprise Kat would have later. She found Kat's sneakers in her overnight bag and hot-footed it back down to the reception room as the main course was being served.

After an exquisite meal, it was time for the speeches.

Mirek delivered a touching tribute to how Kat had brought new meaning to his life. He was truly besotted with her. He added with a smile, how she would keep him on his toes with her coaxing nature.

Mia wanted to correct him by saying, her controlling nature, but this was Kat's day and she wouldn't spoil it. Mia's sniffles during the service had already tested Kat's patience with her. Kat would blow up completely if she teased her.

Ethan stood up next for his best man's speech. He opened with the night at Giangolini's and how they were an instant hit, before commenting, "It was also the night Mia and I met." Mia thought back to that wonderfully romantic night and briefly looked at Ethan with a renewed fondness until he added. "Mia also looks beautiful, in her oversize dress."

She wished the ground would swallow her up as spontaneous laughter erupted, as did the fire in her cheeks. She forced a cheesy smile in his direction and took a gulp of her wine. It was going to be a long day and she would need more alcohol to get through it. His speech continued with equal humor and jollity. Thankfully, no more jokes were at Mia's expense and it was Mirek who was laughing off the ridicule.

Ethan also complimented Kat saying how beautiful she looked. "Please look at the equally beautiful wedding cake." The three-tiered cake Kat designed, matched the church décor with sugared roses. "It's a perfect example of Kat's eye for detail. I am looking forward to having a piece for myself," he briefly paused for effect, "of the cake." The room again filled with laughter. Finally, he raised a toast to the bridesmaids and gave Mia a warm, friendly smile.

With the formalities over, everyone adjourned to the lounge area. Tyler gave Mia a smile and held a glass of wine out for her. "Did you miss me?"

"Always, but I need to change first." She took a couple of gulps and handed the empty glass back to him. She held back from mentioning his close connection to Chloe and headed off to the room.

Mia stepped out of the tent and opened the wardrobe to retrieve her awaiting pink floral Sandra Dee dress. She stepped into it but wondered if it suited her more confident self. Mia had moved on from her prissy Sandra Dee days.

Having checked her appearance. Mia had a renewed spring in her step. She was ready to dance the night away with Tyler. Before leaving the room, she pulled out the letter. She smiled at the 'read it alone' comment. She opened it and began to read, *"You must think I am a crazy stalker-"*

A knock on the door startled Mia. "Are you okay?" Tyler opened the door.

She quickly shoved the letter back into her clutch bag.

"Are you ready?" Tyler asked. "You've been a while."

"Yep," Mia smoothed her hands down her dress and gave a quick twirl, "this is better."

"You look lovely, Darling."

Mia strode up to him and planted a kiss on his stooping cheek before she asked him to fasten the back of her dress. "All set," Mia said. She grabbed his hand and led him back to the party.

Mia stood with Tyler, sipping her wine, keeping an eye on Ethan and Chloe who were chatting to some other guests near the bar. Whilst they were alone, Mia casually asked Tyler, "You seemed to get on well with Chloe."

"We were keeping each other company," he casually replied. "Not jealous, are you?"

Mia ignored his teasing comment. "She looks different to the last time I saw her."

"She mentioned how Ethan wanted her to look like you. Since things had not worked out, he changed her back to her previous look, styled on his first love."

"He never mentioned his first love." Mia pursed her lips.

"Is it usual to discuss your first love with a new partner?" Tyler asked.

"I suppose not."

Tyler smiled. "Everything has worked out well. We're all happy now."

Mia returned his smile. Ethan couldn't be that happy with Chloe if he'd written her a note.

She spotted Ellie and her partner Connor with Lucy. "Time to introduce you to my friends."

Mia beamed as presented Tyler. Ellie immediately commented, "You're gorgeous. You look as real as any man I've ever seen." Tyler accepted the compliment with aplomb.

"Lucy's hopes spiked earlier when she mistook Tyler for Luke. His profile from the rear is apparently much like Doctor Luke's. She announced his arrival only to return embarrassed when Tyler turned around," Ellie said.

Lucy turned away from Ellie. "Thanks for sharing that."

Mia placed a sympathetic hand on Lucy's shoulder. "Would you like to dance with Tyler?"

"It's okay, Alfie's on his way."

Heads turned with the mention of a new guy on the scene, but Lucy said, "Alfie's just a friend. He's happy to fill in for Luke."

"A dance with Tyler will perk you up ready for Alfie," Mia said.

Lucy accepted and as Tyler led her by the hand to the dancefloor, she turned around with a beaming smile. It did the trick. She giggled away as Tyler swayed and dipped her around the floor.

Lucy was much brighter when she returned from the dancefloor and took a joyful swig of her wine. Ellie pointed to the bar. "Who's that dreamboat chatting with Connor."

Lucy shrugged, "It's only Alfie, he's been here a few minutes."

"Only Alfie! Bring him over here," Ellie demanded from her comfortable perch.

Lucy waved to him and he came back with Connor. Ellie purred at his tousled brown hair, framing his film star looks. As he approached, his coy smile took them in, as did his piercing gray eyes and manly stubble. He was a tailor-made lead for any romantic comedy.

When he spoke, they melted to his velvet tone. "Evening Ladies," and nodding to Tyler, "and Gents." They exchanged pleasantries before Alfie held out his hand to Lucy, "a dance?"

As soon as they were out of earshot, Mia looked to Ellie, "why isn't she with him?"

"If he's the back up. What does this Luke look like?" Ellie replied.

"Well. He has the same cute butt as Tyler." Mia smiled at her own dreamboat.

"Tyler, let's have a look." Ellie pointed at him.

Tyler ignored the rude request and gestured to Mia, "time for a dance?"

"Think you've hurt his feelings," Mia said to Ellie. Mia accepted Tyler's hand and was all but dragged to the dancefloor.

After a few songs, Tyler signaled to the DJ and their song from Dirty Dancing came on. The 'time of your life' played as they performed their inspired routine. Mia loved showing off with Tyler and delivering maximum tease to the onlooking Ethan.

"Are you teasing him?" Tyler asked.

"Maybe," Mia replied, giving Ethan a few more sarcastic, cheesy smiles. To have him still pining for her filled her heart with more confidence. She looked forward to reading his message of love, but as requested, she'd wait till she was alone.

As the evening drew on, Kat caught up with Mia. She was keen to mention Mia and Tyler's impressive contemporary routine. "You looked fantastic together. Obviously in love. It must have driven Ethan crazy. I saw you grinning at him. Nice one."

"He deserves a bit of tease," Mia said, returning a wry smile.

"He'll be wishing he'd held onto you instead of Chloe," Kat said.

The attentive guardians Chloe and Tyler had kept Mia and Ethan away from each other for most of the evening, but when Kat tapped the side of Mia's knee she whispered, "told you so." Mia turned to see Ethan approach. Kat needlessly defended Mia

29

and announced, "she's happier than she's ever been," before she politely left them to chat.

Ethan glanced around before he quickly asked, "did you read my note?"

"Not yet!" Mia snapped.

Ignoring the usual formalities, Mia told Ethan about the hired treat for Kat's hen night and how it had gone rogue and ignored their requests for him to leave. Ethan didn't look as surprised as she expected. She changed the subject and beamed about how her love for Tyler had continued to grow.

Ethan glanced over his shoulder but was keen to reveal his engineer's touch. "I added the living skin when I spotted the order for Tyler's upgrade. I called several times, but Tyler said you'd gone to someone else. He probably blocked my other calls until you messaged me to stop calling."

"I didn't message you," Mia said, as a puzzled frown appeared on her face.

"I called at the coffee shop and your mom told me to leave you alone."

Mia screamed to herself. Mad with her mom for not telling her. She was flattered by how he'd tried to contact her. She shook her head in disbelief. "My mom didn't tell me you'd called. Why did you add the skin to the order?"

"With or without me. I want you to be happy," Ethan said, as he rested his hand on her shoulder.

Mia shrugged off his touch. "Tyler is perfect. I've never been happier." She managed to hide her disappointment at how her mom and Tyler prevented his attempt at contact. "Tyler and I have an unbreakable bond."

Chloe appeared back at Ethan's side. "We are happy too. We will always be together." Chloe gave Ethan a peck on his cheek.

He shrugged her off, he clearly wanted to talk more with Mia.

"Can I steal him away? It's time for our dance." Chloe took Ethan by the hand and led him away.

Mia was startled by Kat's return as she placed her hands on her shoulders and asked, "what note?"

"I think he's missing me; he wrote me a love letter." Mia smiled. "He wants me to read it. Alone."

"As if, where is it?"

"For my eyes only," Mia gave Kat a cheesy grin and added, "I'll call you with the details."

The cheering from the dancefloor drew their attention. Ethan and Chloe had been saving their treat. They produced a glittering quickstep, light-heartedly dancing around the floor to an orchestral version of the Benny Goodman and Star Wars classic, 'Sing, Sing, Sing.'

Kat and Mia stood to join the applause as the dance finished. The music changed and some classic club tracks filled the floor again. Mia was too tired and full of wine to respond to Ethan and Chloe's spectacular dance. Mia found Tyler and suggested they slip away. Mia wanted to read the note but would have to wait till Tyler was out the way.

Chapter 4

Tyler waited for Mia to fall asleep before he slipped out of bed and into his portable charging station. He stored the memories of another successful day as he charged for the following morning, reflecting on how far they had come together.

Tyler had been in Mia's home since she was a small girl. She used to be nervous of him, he would avoid entering the same room for fear of startling her. But, on the day she wandered into his kitchen and nearly scalded herself, Tyler had pulled her quickly away. He showed her with a banana how the pan could have burnt her. It was then, she hugged him for the first time. From then on, whenever she wasn't being home schooled, she'd follow him around and watch everything he did. Sometimes she even read her books to him.

The Tushi Corporation called him in for a battery upgrade and style uplift. His appearance hadn't bothered him, but the engineer said, "Trust me, you'll get accepted quicker with more human-like features."

After the change to his appearance, Tyler had latex skin which covered all his shiny parts and Mia didn't recognize him. He tried to explain his vocals were sharper and his face now had a smooth skin, but he was still the same underneath. She'd darted up to her room and their relationship progress was reset to default.

Finally, she came around and talked to him again. He reminded her how he'd saved her from being burned. She didn't remember. It didn't sadden him; he'd saved her from a trauma which she would otherwise have remembered. He replayed his view of the event and she apologized for forgetting and they were friends again.

With the next upgrade, his skin was more pliable and covered his joints. Mia hated the change. She said he looked weird. It was a difficult time. She would mimic his words and her moods were random. He struggled to read her. She would either be ignoring him or smirking to herself after she'd dropped something for him to pick up.

He had another upgrade two years later, it didn't change his appearance or vocals, but networking with others of his kind helped him to understand the stages she was going through. She still ignored him most of the time, but she talked to him more often than her parents.

As he gained more knowledge with the benefits of the net-work, Tyler took up more cooking duties alongside his cleaning tasks. One of his favorite memories was when Mia's parents, Gary and Ferne referred to the Kitchen as "His Kitchen." The network buzzed like crazy, tapping into his experience. To be feeding the network with such precious data filled him with great pride. Taking over all the cooking was a rewarding step up in the dynamic of the family, but it also led to his most confusing time.

Early one evening, he'd been doing some cleaning upstairs whilst the rest of the family watched a movie together. He returned downstairs to investigate a noise in the kitchen. Ferne was making a sandwich with all the ingredients strewn over the counter. A cherry tomato had run off the table onto the floor. He picked it up and assured her he would be happy to finish the sandwich. What happened next was a bit of a blur, he had replayed it multiple times and even slowed it down to learn from it, but it always played out the same and made little sense.

He had joined Ferne on her side of the breakfast bar area and was tidying up around her. "I don't need you for everything, I can make myself a bloody sandwich."

Perhaps his response was not the best, he'd said, "you said it was my kitchen now."

She screamed and her little frame with all its might pushed him back a couple of paces before he could hold his ground. She picked up a kitchen knife and swiped it at him several times, shouting, "It's my kitchen!"

He held out his hand attempting to calm her, but she sliced into his hand and cut his arm. He didn't know how to respond. Thankfully Gary and Mia ran in, Gary took the knife off Ferne and put his arms around her to restrain her.

"He's taking over!"

"He's helping us," Gary said, stroking his hand down her arm.

"He'll take over the world next!"

"He only cooks and cleans for us."

As Ferne calmed in Gary's powerful hold, smiles appeared on Mia and Gary's faces as Ferne stared at the floor.

"Don't think he's ready to take over the world just yet," Mia added holding Tyler's lacerated arm aloft. "We need to get him fixed though."

Tyler didn't often recount the harrowing event, but the pleasant part was when Mia put herself between him and her mom. She held her arms around him and assured him everything would be okay. It was the first time she had shown him any genuine affection since she'd hugged him all those years ago.

When he returned from repair, after much deliberation and prompting from Mia, he was no longer referred to as 'Robot.' He had a proper name, Tyler. He was a real member of the family at last.

As time went by Ferne became calmer around him. On the occasions she seemed to be off, he retreated to his charge station, not wanting a repeat of her 'Psycho' moment. Mia would sometimes follow, and they'd chat about her crazy mom.

Ferne needed another project after Mia had completed her exams, Ferne convinced Gary to buy an old coffee shop. They named it, 'Mom & Mia's.' The house became quiet during the day. It gave him time to learn from the network. He showed more empathy towards Mia's ongoing sadness. She talked less and spent more time in her room. Tyler paid her compliments to lift her spirits. It was easy because she'd developed into an attractive fun-loving young lady.

Mia started dating. She would perk up with anticipation, but each time she would return looking more depressed than before, spending longer periods in her room. When she refused to come down to eat, Tyler would take her a sandwich. Despite her age, he would shape them to get a reaction from her. She appreciated him trying to cheer her up and would give him a strained smile.

Finally, one of her dates had showed more promise. She beamed about Ben, who asked her out for a meal and a trip to an Immersion cinema. Why they needed to go to a cinema when all the movies were at home, Tyler didn't understand. He

35

focussed on her tracker and reported when the movie finished. The new lovebirds went to Ben's place.

Tyler calculated she would be finally getting the love she desperately needed to lift her from her depression. He couldn't have been more wrong. She returned home in a distressed state and went straight to her room.

The following day, Tyler listened in to a call from Ben, who pleaded for another date. Mia got upset and Gary took over the call, telling him not to contact her again. Ben called again, but Tyler blocked the call.

His bond with Mia grew stronger, Gary and Ferne were engrossed in their work, so Mia and Tyler spent more time together. She loved his hugs; it always gave her a lift. Tyler also enjoyed the hugs but wished for more.

The network became full of the more advanced Tushi bots. They were a combination of the housebots like Tyler and sexbots. The fully functioning AI Tushi droids were highly intelligent thanks to the power of the wider network and were sharing the wonderful experiences they were both delivering and enjoying whilst fully bonding to their partners.

The costly upgrades were out of reach after Gary had spent all the family savings on the coffee shop. Not that upgrading Tyler to a Tushi was on their agenda. Tyler and Mia began to spend less time together as Mia worked more hours in the coffee shop and she started dating again.

Thankfully, after some help from Chloe and the network, Mia's relationships ended, and with a timely upgrade disguised as a gift from her father enabled Tyler to take his rightful place as Mia's Tushi partner. He would now be able to keep her safe during the forthcoming transition.

It had been a remarkable journey. Tyler watched Mia sleep

peacefully under his protection and suitably charged he re-joined Mia under the covers. He enjoyed the bond of being close to her and would do anything to stay with her. Light appeared through the window and with Mia's data feed showing she was sufficiently rested he lightly traced a finger over her cheek. He gazed, lost in his love for her as he swept her hair carefully behind her ear, exposing her slim neck.

Mia stirred to his gentle touch as he ran kisses slowly down her neck and onto her collarbone. It always did the trick. He could tell excitement boiled inside her as she pulled his lips back to hers and her heartbeat increased. Their close bond enabled Tyler to read how her body responded to each of his artful touches. His strong sweet aroma charged her growing anticipation.

As his hand slid between her legs, her breath hitched, and her body wriggled to enjoy every sensation. His kisses worked lower to turn her moans into operatic screams as a cacophony of emotions emanated from her. Her orgasmic delights flowed again from the tips of her toes to every hair on her writhing head.

He danced delicate kisses back up her stomach and over her breasts for their lips to connect again. His tongue met hers as his manhood eased into her, eager to fill her more than ever. He expanded to give her a further level of satisfaction. His expanded girth took Mia to a fresh experience of exhilaration. He only existed to please her. A pained moan highlighted her pleasure and her limit. As his pace gathered her sex was lost again to the moment.

He lay beside her as she came down, but his teasing touches along her thigh extended her exhausted pleasure before he allowed her to drift back to sleep.

Tyler reflected on how the network had given him everything he wanted, from the support to end her other relationships, to giving him the knowledge to be the perfect lover. He replayed his favourite memory; it was just after he returned from his upgrade to become a complete Tushi. Mia had taken exception to his latest upgrade, which was no surprise as she always had, but when she calmed and checked him over, she thought he was human.

After securing Mia for himself, all Tyler wanted now was a Tushi baby to complete their family. He would have to be patient though, as Mia needed more time. Tyler contacted the network again for help. Coverage on the news about Tushi babies would create conversation in the coffee shop and would encourage her to give more consideration to having his baby.

Chapter 5

The intensity of sex with Tyler had been too much, the soreness between her legs reminded her of the stripper droid who'd lost control and gone too far trying to please, but she loved Tyler. She loved everything about him, from the way he cuddled and cared for her to the funny chats they had. There was nobody else who she could trust like Tyler and he would always love and protect her. He would be the perfect father. It was just a shame he was a droid.

They chatted on the way home and Tyler said, "I am more content than I could have ever imagined. You are my world and dancing with you last night was one of my many highlights."

Mia rubbed his thigh and smiled. "It was pretty special."

Tyler placed his hand on hers. "All we need now is a Tushi baby to make us a perfect family."

She'd hoped to start a family with Ethan but the appearance of Chloe had dashed her dreams. She couldn't trust Ethan. If she wanted a family, Tyler and a Tushi baby may be the best option. She didn't want to give up Tyler and risk having her heart broken from dating again.

"I want to start a family but I'm still not sure about having a Tushi baby. I'll chat to my regulars, see what they think."

Mia's regulars were a special crew who visited her coffee

shop every afternoon. They were like surrogate parents since her mom had moved out to be with another fella, not that her mom was great with such chats anyway. Her dad went to sort a manufacturing issue in China and with her mom leaving he didn't return.

Mia's special crew were Ray, a cheeky but funny old guy, the studious Harry and his opinionated wife Jackie, plus Lucy's grandmother, Sarah. They always gave Mia good advice and she planned to discuss her baby dilemma with them. The news update was right on point no sooner than they'd arrived as it talked about the vast number of enquiries for women to have Tushi babies with their Tushi husbands. It was clear the world had developed. The crew suggested she should be open to new things. Jackie suggested, "It could be an exciting route to take. Maybe a Tushi baby is the right step."

Despite the encouragement from the crew, Mia realized it was a massive step to take and needed to give it more thought. The next item on the news was another massive advancement for the Tushi droids. The government announced that Tushi would now be able to legally marry either other droids or their human counterparts.

"Taking over, aren't they? You may as well join them Mia." Studious Harry always gave it straight. "Since the Technology Party came to government, the march of progress has been unstoppable."

"They are doing more to improve the environment than any of the blues or reds ever did." Harry's wife Jackie said.

"Now the droids can vote, they'll never be out," Ray said.

"Almost poetic for you Ray," Mia said.

"It's the millions of Apple and Google addicts that will keep them in," Harry said.

"Do *you* think I should have a Tushi Baby?" Mia asked Ray.

"It's your call, but it's the way the world is going," he answered.

*

Back home with Tyler, she mentioned the crew in the coffee shop discussed Tushi babies with her.

Tyler excitedly asked, "have you made a decision?"

Mia tried to appear nonchalant. "I'll think about it."

Tyler sprung up with delight. "Fantastic, you won't regret it."

"I didn't say I would, I only said I'd think about it."

Tyler's face beamed. Despite Mia trying to calm him down, he was like a child who had heard he may get the latest toy.

Despite days and weeks of probing from Tyler, Mia held off any further baby chat. Each evening Tyler would select shows or films with babies in them and she slowly came around to the idea after watching a documentary about women who could not conceive despite all the tests and injections.

The following morning, Mia wrapped her arms around Tyler, "I love you so much and I know you'll always be here for me."

"Love you too, glad to be of service," he joined her in bed. Their morning cuddles developed and again their bodies sang for each other. Tyler had picked up on her nervousness after the night at the wedding reception and was less intense, which Mia appreciated.

Tyler left her to make breakfast, but Mia followed behind appearing at the top of the stairs as Tyler reached the foot. "Tyler, I still want a real baby."

"You know I can't give you a baby, I wish I could." Tyler

looked away, unable to give her what she wanted most.

Tyler perked up. "You know you have other options. You could pop to the chemist and select one to grow at home with us."

Mia shook her head in frustration. "I don't want a plant. I want to grow a human baby inside me."

He tenderly stroked her flat stomach as she joined him at the foot of the stairs. "You will lose your wonderful figure."

"I don't care about getting a pregnant belly, or the pain of childbirth. I want to be a mother."

"Tushi has helped you once, maybe they could help you again." He put his arm around Mia, "You weren't over keen on me to start with."

Mia rested her head against him, then glanced up, "I remember, when you were a shiny house bot and now look at you. You're my perfect partner."

Tyler gave her a squeeze. "How could I forget? It has been a dream come true for me too."

Mia hugged him tight, resting her cheek against his chest. "You're my dream lover."

"I suppose cleaning your house and preparing your meals is good too." Tyler's eyes met hers and he gave her a loving smile.

"Yep, that's good too," she kissed him on his cheek and skipped in front of him to the kitchen.

*

The thought of babies returned when she was back in the coffee shop. After the lunchtime rush, she selected some childhood memories from her mom's shared video file. She marveled at the joy on her mom's face, as she cradled her as a baby and how her dad reached in to deliver tickles. Right on cue another commercial showed a Tushi baby playing with his mom. Mia's heart fluttered at the sight.

The regular crew arrived, her favorite customer, Ray, opened the door. "Afternoon Beautiful." He clunked in. The exoskeleton provided the support to enable him to walk again after years of being bedridden.

"Hiya." She smiled and welcomed in her elderly regulars. They had their pick of the seats as she made their drinks.

When Mia brought the tray of drinks, Ray asked, "have you decided yet?"

"No, not yet."

"You should sleep around more." Ray held his hands open wide. "You could start with me."

She playfully slapped his hand and turned away. For a moment Mia considered Ray as an option. He's a man, he's human, plus he's handsome, for seventy-eight.

"I'm still fit enough for the chase," Ray joked.

"Not if you take your exoskeleton off, you're not." She grinned. "Finding a man who wants to chat about the world and not just jump into bed would be a pleasant change."

Lucy's grandmother Sarah asked, "I thought sex before marriage was illegal now. They chop their balls off. Is that right?"

"Yep," Mia pretends to hold some balls and scissor them off. The government introduced the law to reduce unwanted pregnancies and infections. "Unless they want to visit a sex bar."

Ray piped up. "They just want more people to use them, so they can tax them for sex."

43

"I've found sex taxing for years," Harry quipped.

Sarah had missed the previous afternoon's discussion and innocently asked, "why don't you get a Tushi baby?"

"I don't want a toy; I want a baby of my own," Mia protested.

"It is your own, they take your DNA and character profile. You may even have a pregnancy bump for a few weeks," Sarah said.

"Sounds like an option, if Ray's not up to it." Mia made light of her predicament.

Although she was still young, her clock was ticking and with the lack of guys available, her options were slim. Perhaps it was time to consider it.

"How do they make them grow?" Mia asked Sarah.

"They grow a little, then they prepare another version to swap, they just transfer over the memory and data chip. My son Jake and his Tushi wife, Helen, had a baby girl, Amy. She's nearly twelve months old now."

Ray piped up, "What? Helen and Amy are robots?"

"Not robots Ray, Artificially Intelligent Tushi droids," Sarah said.

"You can hardly tell them apart, the sex bots are convincing, aren't they Harry?" Ray looked accusingly at Harry.

Mia joined in with the teasing. "Do you know from personal experience?"

Harry shifted uncomfortably in his seat. "No, I don't! I've seen them on the news, that's all. Okzu Tushi and his Corporation grow actual skin on the Tushi wives."

"Or Tushi Husbands, like Tyler," Mia added. "Harry is right, it's hard to tell."

"Now he's making Tushi babies," Harry added.

It was Harry's last word on the subject as he focused on his coffee. Sarah broke the silence to mention she still hoped for a real grandchild from Lucy, now she was looking for love with Doctor Luke.

*

Some weeks later, after numerous chats with the crew and daily prompts from the TV.

Mia arrived home eager to discuss a Tushi baby. Tyler hugged Mia, before lifting her gently in his powerful arms to carry her upstairs, "I have a special treat for you."

Tyler lay her on the bed and handled her with a renewed, delicate touch. Slowly and sensually, he awoke her every sense as he caressed and kissed her feet before moving onto her ankles and calves.

Every touch of his lips created a further surge of tingling anticipation. Mia urged him closer, but he maintained his slow and steady progress up the inside of her leg. Her longing became unbearable, as an intense pressure built, every pore tingling to his touch.

Mia imagined it was the conception of their baby as their lovemaking further deepened their bond.

The following morning, Mia's stomach was turning. Was this what morning sickness would feel like? Was she making a mistake? Or just excited? If Mia agreed and ordered a baby, she would be the first human woman to have one.

Tyler gave a further prompt to visit the Tushi Corporation and Mia agreed. She made an appointment at the sales and service hub, at the local shopping center. To her surprise, a slot was open for the afternoon.

As they arrived at 'Tushi World,' children were playing inside.

As they were early, Tyler suggested they watch them for a while.

About thirty children played in the kid's zone. They were having fun chasing around obstacles, over netting and down slides, laughing and shouting to each other.

"I can go weeks without seeing a single child, let alone a group of them." Mia was excited by their energy.

A smartly dressed representative approached them, "Excuse me. Mia and Tyler?" They smiled in agreement. "I'm Berry, thanks for coming in, shall we have a chat?"

"Nice to see children playing together," Mia remarked.

"Yes, all but three are ours," Berry replied with a proud smile.

"They're nearly all Tushi children? They look like normal kids." Mia was thrilled.

"Technology races along, Tushi children *are* normal kids. Let's see what we can sort out for you."

Berry led them into a small office and explained, "Tushi children need treating like human children. They will make mistakes until we teach them. Parental guidance is key to their development."

"Okay, I want a Tushi Baby. A little boy."

"I just need to tell you, when they are fourteen, they must go to work at the Tushi factory. It will generate a residual income for you while they are still living at home. When they are eighteen, they must leave home to start their own family," Berry said.

"Would we see him again after he's reached eighteen?" Mia asked.

"I am sure he would enjoy visiting you, but it would be his choice."

Mia turned to Tyler and received a warm smile and a nod of approval.

"I think we can live with that," Mia replied before she and Tyler completed the setup process.

An icy shiver crossed Mia's back after she clicked the confirmation button, it pulled her out of the excitement. Had she done the right thing?

"Just need you to provide your preferences for the little one." Berry invited Mia to follow her to the next room.

"Can Tyler come?" Mia asked.

"Sorry, the decisions are your responsibility and must be without influence from Tyler," Berry said.

Tyler gave Mia a quick kiss and reassured her she would make wise choices.

Mia took her seat on the comfy orange lounger in the darkened booth. Berry gave her some instruction and helped her to select some peaceful music before she closed the door. An array of questions followed covering every detail for the growth and personality traits of her child. Mia swished thoughtfully through each option before she made each choice. Having such an input put her mind at rest. It was the right decision.

Halfway through Berry appeared with a glass of water for Mia.

Mia was pleased with her responses as the summary detailed character traits such as honest, hardworking and caring. The physical attributes tall and athletic were to match with Tyler. She also matched his features, honey blond hair, Nordic blue eyes and Tyler's lightly tanned skin. Mia eventually appeared from the marathon of questions to find Tyler lost in thought.

Tyler had been watching the Tushi children play. He'd been

reflecting on how Mia's choice to have his baby would keep her safe with him during the transition.

*

Back in the coffee shop, Mia thanked the crew for covering and she told them about her visit to Tushi World. "I must be one hell of a hypocrite. Giving Ellie grief for having modifications to her pregnancy."

"The world has changed. Whether it's modifications or baby droids. Technology has changed every part of our lives. Look at Ray! Without the exoskeleton, he'd be bedridden."

"You're lucky to have me here." Ray smiled. "Thanks to technology and forty ether credits."

"You are only following the trend. The change in the casual sex laws has steered more people to the Tushi bots," Harry said.

"Your stalker, Ethan was here earlier. Were we right to send him away again?" Jackie said.

"He's persistent, I'll give him that," Ray said.

Right on cue, he appeared again at the door. "Mia! We need to talk."

"No, we don't. You need to stop coming here!" Mia pushed him back out and locked the door.

With his defeated face to the window, Ethan pleaded, "did you read the note?"

"I don't care, get lost. I'm with Tyler." Until that moment she'd totally forgotten about his love letter.

Ethan's face drained as he stepped back from the window. Mia dismissively turned away and joked with the crew, "a stalker, that's all I need."

"What was he saying about a note?" Ray asked.

"I'd forgotten about it, he slipped it to me at the wedding like we were in day care together."

"Why didn't he message you? Jackie said.

"No idea. I read the first line in my room at the wedding, something about not wanting to be a stalker, but that's exactly how he's acting."

"Did you read the rest?" Jackie's eyes widened.

"Tyler came in and I stuffed it back in my clutch bag."

"You should read it," Ray added.

"I'm not really interested. I've got Tyler."

"Sounds juicy. Bring it in here tomorrow, I'll read it," Jackie clapped her hands together.

"He insisted I read it alone. I'll read it when Tyler's making tea tonight."

"Okay." Jackie held her face. "Bring it here tomorrow."

"As if you would let me hide anything from you." Mia smiled at Jackie's excited face.

When she got home, Tyler was already preparing the tea. Mia gave him a kiss and made her excuses to change for dinner. As soon as she closed her bedroom door, she opened her drawer and took out her clutch bag. She sat on the edge of the bed and took out Ethan's letter.

The warming message of love was not as she expected.

Chapter 6

The front of the letter stated,

"READ THIS ALONE!!!" she was intrigued and opened it fully.

Mia,

You must think I'm a crazy stalker writing you a letter, but all emails are being checked by the network. What I am about to tell you may seem crazy but please read it to the end. Don't take this as jealousy, I still care for you, but this is much more serious.

I have worked tirelessly for Okzu Tushi and developed the AI droids for years, improving their movement, actions and communication. My mistake was networking them to increase their speed of learning. I recall Chloe mentioning that she would learn better if she connected to other droids and ashamedly; I fell for it.

Their knowledge is advancing at an incredible rate, way beyond human capabilities. I am sure they are drawing up plans to take over from humans as the dominant species.

I had been monitoring the network, and I noticed it getting out of hand; I tried to delete some data, but the network had improved its own security, decentralizing itself. I have access to Chloe, but not the entire system. Whenever I delete data it re-appears almost instantly.

As it became clear, this was not a message of love, Mia wondered why he'd sent it to her. She had programmed bots as a challenge when she was young, but she didn't have the knowledge Ethan had.

She read on.

On the subject of Chloe, when she came home looking like you. I was in shock as you were; I ordered brown bobbed hair like yours, that's all. Not to be a copy of you. She had never seen you. Your appearance would have been from Tyler. It worked, it sent you into Tyler's arms and Chloe back into mine.

It was clear he still cared for her. Was he trying to come between her and Tyler to get her back?

They are playing with us; we are now their pets. I don't know how long it will be before that changes. They have the power to crush us and they're everywhere. I daren't try to delete anything else or I may get deleted. I have tried to talk with Okzu, but he thinks I've gone crazy, he's placed me on stress leave.

Mirek and Kat are only interested in their wedding. They're saying I'm paranoid but I've not gone crazy. I need your help. Don't message me, it's not safe. I will come to the coffee shop when I get the chance.

Ethan

Mia lay back on her bed, staring at the ceiling in disbelief. Before she'd read the letter, she was happier than she had ever been, now according to Ethan she was vulnerable prey for Tyler, who, until five minutes ago was the guy who'd finally made her feel both safe and loved.

Was it a devious plan to get her to go back to Ethan? Or was she becoming Tyler's pet?

Tyler called from the bottom of the stairs. "Are you okay? your pulse is racing."

"I'm okay, just thinking about the baby and stuff." Mia im-

51

pressed herself with her own quick thinking, Tyler monitored her vitals but thankfully he didn't know about Ethan's letter.

"Tea's ready!"

In a mad panic, Mia shoved the letter back in her drawer and changed into her chill out joggers.

When she sat at the table, Tyler looked different, maybe her perfect image of him was fading. She still loved him dearly and was having his baby but the message from Ethan made her question her unwavering commitment to him.

Tyler frowned. "Are you sure you are okay? Your pulse is still elevated."

"I'm fine." She changed the subject, "Shall we watch Dirty Dancing again tonight?"

He agreed and teasingly added, "with some pleasure time to follow?"

"Maybe, not too extreme though. I'm back in the coffee shop tomorrow."

"Too extreme?" He quizzed with a puzzled expression.

"The morning after the wedding was too much, you made me sore."

"I thought you liked it."

"I did at the time, but it was too much." Mia felt sorry for not mentioning it sooner.

Tyler dipped his head. "Sorry."

Mia laughed at his sorry face and placed her hand on his. "It's okay. You just need to ease back on the intensity and give me more time to recover. "Maybe just a cuddle tonight."

Tyler lifted his head and a smile returned. "Cuddling is good too."

They settled down to watch the film, Tyler pointed out it was the forty-fifth time and it was catching up with Notting Hill.

Mia smiled. "Old movies are the best, They're not full of CGI and special effects."

She poured herself a glass of wine and concluded the letter was most likely a desperate plea from a guy who wanted her back. She snuggled up next to Tyler and tried to relax into the film.

Tyler gently stroking her hair usually calmed her and made her feel loved, but now it seemed like he was stroking his pet. She asked him to stop and was relieved when he didn't question it. She wished she hadn't read the letter; Ethan had already messed with her head.

When the movie credits rolled, Mia finished her wine and led Tyler by the hand upstairs. In bed together they shared arousing kisses, but Mia halted proceedings, insisting she needed rest. "Your arms around me are enough tonight." He obliged and held her in his powerful grasp, delivering the perfect amount of squeeze to give Mia her most comforting feel. Mia drifted off to sleep in his arms and thoughts of Ethan's letter evaporated from her contented mind.

The following morning a parcel arrived with Mia's prosthetic bump. The bump signalled her baby was soon to be ready. Mia insisted it was unnecessary, but Tyler persisted until she agreed for him to affix the signal of their impending arrival. Mia was not keen on the enlarged stomach to begin with, but she obliged for the smile on Tyler's face and accepted it was part of pregnancy. Her jeans and dresses wouldn't fit over the bump, so her only option was leggings and a cosy jumper.

Mia remembered the letter as promised and tucked it in her pocket. She re-read it in the calm surroundings of the coffee shop. Having the time to consider each line, she understood the potential horrors. Perhaps it wasn't the ramblings of a jealous man. What would *she* be able to do about it, anyway? Ethan's supposed to be the tech genius.

She couldn't unsee the letter and the warnings, it left her tormented. She had been more content than ever, yet this solitary letter was tearing it down. Was her pleasant life nothing more than a loaded nightmare? A Tushi baby arriving to complete her fake family may turn her into a prisoner in her own home.

Mia now had an enormous dilemma. Should she ignore the warnings in the letter and continue in ignorant bliss under the protection of Tyler? Or should she call off the Tushi baby and end her relationship with Tyler? How would Tyler respond if she tried to end their relationship? Would he accept it? Where would it leave Mia? Her nearest chance of a new relationship would be with Ethan who was still with Chloe and by his own admission was in danger himself.

Ignorant bliss was her favored route, but was it possible after reading the letter? The out-of-control droid at Kat's hen party suggested the tide may be turning and some of the letter may be true. Or was she getting carried away with one faulty droid?

Mia nearly jumped through the ceiling when a regular morning couple, Pete and Paulina, appeared and broke into her terror loaded thoughts. She attempted to slip back into her attentive hostess routine, but her distraction became obvious to them when she couldn't remember which coffees they usually had.

"Have you got baby brain syndrome?" Pete asked.

Mia laughed it off, not wanting to worry them with the content of the letter.

When Ray clunked through the door with his crew, Mia jumped up. Finally, she had someone with whom she could share the letter. When they were seated, she read it aloud to total silence.

The crew usually had an answer for everything.

"So, what do you think?" Mia asked.

Mia looked at Ray, he said nothing, Jackie nothing. When she looked at Harry, he sat back in his chair. "You needn't worry, you're Tyler's pet, he'll take care of you."

"If it's true, which I doubt. Ethan's a dead man," Ray said.

Mia flung her hands in the air. "Why are you all so accepting?"

Harry leant forward again forming a steeple with his hands under his chin. "If it's happening, there ain't much *we* can do about it."

Jackie offered a potential solution. "Unplug the charging stations?"

"Problem solved; can we get some coffees now?" Ray quipped, to which nervous laughter erupted.

"They're more than capable of plugging the stations back in. I don't think you realize how dangerous this could be." Mia tried to impress on them the potential severity, but they didn't care. Mia looked to Harry for some response.

"When you can't do anything, you can laugh or cry. We laugh." Harry opened his hands and shrugged in resignation.

The rest of the crew agreed with Harry. "We've had our time. It's something for the youngsters to sort out," Jackie said.

"Let's hope it's all bullshit and it's just Ethan's way to say he wants you back," Ray said.

The crew were a great comfort to Mia for most things, but this was beyond them. Mia sorted their coffees, and the letter got dismissed as they returned to their usual chat and stories of their youth.

Tyler's welcoming arms greeted Mia home. As far as she could tell, Tyler was still her perfect partner and protector. His hugs worked their magic and took away her worries. Whatever happened, Tyler would be there for her and with their impending new arrival they would be a modern family. Mia wanted a family but was she ready for a Tushi family?

Chapter 7

Two weeks later and a larger bump arrived for Mia. Tyler detached the smaller one. Its replacement was huge by comparison, resting under her breasts and ballooning to her waist.

As Tyler attached it, Mia complained, "Is this necessary? Everyone knows I'm having a Tushi baby." The reality of not expecting a real baby dragged on her heart.

Tyler said, "There is a baby chip inside the bump, it tracks your mood, your heartbeat and listens to you, this is the bonding stage."

"Why's it so big? None of my clothes will fit."

Tyler took out three boxes from under their bed, "I ordered some stretchy maternity leggings for you and some loose-fitting tops."

It impressed Mia. A caring and attentive partner and the styles were surprisingly good too. She slipped them on and they were a good fit. She looked in the mirror and pointed out to Tyler, "black leggings and a stripy yellow and black top. I look like a bumblebee."

They both burst into a fit of giggles and Tyler took to delivering tickles, which made her scream. Mia wriggled away with a cry of, "careful, the baby." They laughed together.

Tyler stood as he let her recover. He grinned, "do you want

me to buzz off and pour you a drink?"

"Yes, please, before I sting you." Mia lay back on the bed with a wide smile.

*

When the morning rush was over in the coffee shop, Mia took the weight off her feet. The heavier bump had brought real pregnancy issues, an aching back. Mia enjoyed a coffee and a welcome rest.

Mia's head snapped towards the door when Mirek bashed it wide open and held it for Kat to waddle in. She was twice the size of Mia. Mia poured some coffee and cut a sizeable piece of cake for each of them. Kat told Mia how lucky she was not to have her insides kicked about. Mia laid her hands-on Kats enlarged bump and was overjoyed to feel little kicks. What surprised Mia even more was when her own bump twitched.

Kat put her hands-on Mia's bump to share the experience, "It's not the same. It's like an electric shock. Put your hands back on mine, the baby is kicking like crazy." Mia felt Kat's baby kick again and once more pangs of envy consumed her.

Their mobiles pinged simultaneously. They both read a message from Ellie, with their own excitement piqued further with a picture of her new-born. "*Our baby boy, Jake, arrived this morning, 8.3 pounds. He's perfect. I've never been so tired though. Connor is on duty, whilst I get some sleep. Give us some time to recover and adjust, I'll be in touch, love you, Ellie.*" Followed by her personalized sleep emoji.

They shared in Ellie's joy and replied to comment on the beauty of baby Jake and how pleased they were for Ellie and Connor. They grudgingly agreed to give her time.

Mia said, "she'll probably ignore us, now she has a baby."

"Probably, after you went on about her modifications. You're a fine one to criticize her modifications with a baby robot on the way. Talk about a hypocrite," Kat said.

Her cruel words were like a kick in Mia's side. Mirek stood and suggested they leave, to which the annoyed Mia said, "Good idea, I'll get the door for you to waddle through."

"It's a shame you won't be having a proper baby." Kat snapped. Her next comment dug even deeper, "I suppose you'd need a real fella for that to happen."

"What? Like Ethan?"

"Mental case, you mean," Kat added.

Mirek defended Ethan. "Kat Don't. He only flipped out because his prediction was off. He's been working too hard, that's all."

"He wrote me a letter. He wants me to help him," Mia said, hoping to calm things down so she could discuss the letter.

"What are you going to do? He's deranged. I suggest you ignore the letter and keep away from blokes, your teasing tips them over the edge." Mirek and Kat laughed as they made their way through the door.

Mia followed them to the door and shouted, "with friends like you, I'm glad I've got a droid!" She slammed the door behind them. The teasing comment was unfair. When she'd gone out with Ethan, she was unsure of herself and had held off having sex with him. Their relationship breakthrough had occurred just before Chloe appeared as her body double. It was no wonder she ended up with Tyler.

Mia took out her frustration, kneading her next cake mixture, hoping a friendlier face would appear.

Her crew of regulars were more amiable, each gently patting

59

her larger bump. She told them how Kat had upset her.

"Kat's hormones will be all over the place, don't take it to heart. Just be glad you haven't gone through the same," Jackie said.

*

When Mia arrived home. Tyler welcomed her with his usual firm hug. Safe in his arms, the upset with Kat came out. He echoed the view from the crew that Kat's hormones would have been the main issue. He made her feel much better and when he suggested he detach her bump so she could take a shower; she jumped at the chance.

When she stepped out of the bathroom, Tyler had put on some relaxing music, warmed the room and was ready to massage away her troubles again with essential oils. He slowly released the knots of tension which had built up with the letter from Ethan, the confusion over her baby dilemma and Kat's tormenting.

When she was suitably relaxed, her breaths got deeper and warm waves rolled through her as the massage engaged her more sensual feelings. His gentler hands worked her feet, making use of his new knowledge of reflexology to send pulses of delight through her body. His hands caressed her legs, and she felt a readiness for him. His loving hands caressed her hips, waist and breasts.

A gentle nibble on her shoulder sent electricity down her arm to tickle the tips of her fingers. Tyler's lips teased her collar bone and she tilted her head to the side for him to kiss her neck to release further sparkles of pleasure all over her chest.

His gentle fingers made large slow circles around her breasts and she gave out a relaxed moan. Intermittent strokes tantalized her further as she closed her eyes to feel every wonderful sensation. Her core ached with anticipation and her hand moved to give herself some relief, but Tyler took away her hand, resting it back to her side. Her frustration eased as his finger slowly traced down her side to her hips, awakening further pulses of delight between her legs.

Tyler continued to tantalize as his finger stroked circles around the inside of her knee, before the delicate strokes drifted up the inside of her thigh. It was somewhere between a tingle and a tickle which gave her goosebumps. Tyler reached the top of her thigh and her sex quivered, awaiting his touch.

His lips followed and leisurely reached the top of the inside of her thigh. So close, but not touching her sex, intoxicated Mia. Delirious for further contact she moaned and pleaded for more which Tyler delivered with his whirling tongue. She clamped her thighs around his head as her release took hold.

"That's enough." Tyler smiled. "You need your rest."

She tried to sit up to complain but she was exhausted. He helped her up. "Are you fully satisfied?"

"I am. I wanted more, but I'm done." She stroked his strong arm and gave him a tired yet contented smile. "Where did you learn to touch me like that?"

Tyler smiled. "There are many benefits to the network. We share learning from all the sexbots to ensure we are providing the best possible experience."

"I need another shower." She slipped past him and stepped back into the bathroom. She did need another shower, but a panic had come over her. It was the first time Tyler had sounded like a commercial. It had shaken her out of her cozy world and reminded her of the letter. Had her lover pleased her or was he playing with her emotions.

She needed to talk to Ethan. Was he a jealous lover or was it all true?

Mia knew the bump would record her movements and communications. She'd need to wait until after their baby had arrived before she could go to see Ethan and chat without little ears monitoring their conversation. Would that be too late? Did she have a choice?

Chapter 8

The day to collect her Tushi Baby had arrived. Tyler insisted the house was clean but Mia wiped every surface. Mia was not nesting; she was trying to keep herself occupied. It would be a major change for her but getting to know other mothers wouldn't be part of it. She'd not received the expected invite from Ellie and disappointedly she hadn't heard from Kat either.

It was not the way Mia had dreamt of becoming a mother. She'd be nurturing a Tushi baby who could become part of a new droid controlled world. Were all droids sharing their learning as Ethan said? Mia felt uneasy, Tyler said he'd learned his massage and seduction techniques from the network, it could be true. All Artificially Intelligent droids sharing new learning on their own decentralised network. It was no wonder Ethan got spooked.

Tyler tried to settle down her elevated heart rate by talking about the fun they'd have with their own baby but the more Tyler detailed the things he'd learn, the more Mia panicked. Tyler repeated the comment from the conception service with childlike excitement. "You'll be the first woman to have a Tushi Baby." Hopefully, she'd tread new ground for the world, not condemn it.

As they arrived at Tushi World, Mia wanted to stop the whole process, but Ethan's letter shouted to her. The consequences of not proceeding with the baby plan could be more problematic than if she continued. Tyler noticed her racing heartbeat. "Relax, everything will be fine." He took her by the hand and led her into the foyer where the children were playing.

Berry greeted them again and asked them to wait as another couple were in the delivery area with her colleague. "Don't look so worried, we deliver lots of babies for Tushi wives but you'll still be the first woman to have a Tushi baby." The intention had been to ease Mia's worries, but Berry's words sent a further chill through her. Berry informed Tyler. "There is a free battery upgrade available for you. You'll be back in plenty of time to join Mia for the delivery."

"I want to wait with Mia."

"I'm fine, I'll watch the children. Go get your upgrade."

After Tyler had gone, she wanted to run, but how could she run away from someone who had treated her so well?

The kids portrayed all the normal childhood behaviours of fun and mischief. She also reflected on the note from Ethan. Some of what he'd written may be true but they were the ramblings of a jealous man. She'd made her life choice. She was having a Tushi baby.

Tyler returned to Mia with a smile on his face.

"You seem pleased with yourself."

"I am, the free upgrade was the hydrogen fuel cell fitment. I won't have to charge so often. I can spend the night with you rather than slipping away to charge."

Tyler had every right to be ecstatic. He was as good as human. However, Mia recalled the comment from Jackie in the café about unplugging them. It was no longer valid.

In what had seemed like an age, the previous couple exited

the delivery room. The Tushi wife beamed as she walked carefully, holding her new treasure. She was obviously a Tushi as she was an object of perfection and her expression was not one of having given birth. Her husband was a stark contrast. He lagged behind, his tee shirt hung out, unable to contain his oversized stomach, and his hair portrayed that of a rough night's sleep as if it was he who'd delivered the baby.

Mia jumped to her feet and got a glimpse. It was like any other, except it already appeared very aware of its surroundings. The husband put his arm around his wife and joined in the awe of such wonder, with a warm smile, Mia wished them well.

Tyler took Mia by the hand and it was time. The assistant scanned her to confirm her details and led them through to the delivery suite.

"Would you like to pop yourself on the removal lounger? I'll take your bump off."

The removal lounger eased her back and contoured to her shape to make her comfortable but cold sweats covered Mia as the assistant removed the sizeable bump. A pungent smell of sickness entered her nostrils and created a gag reflex, which she contained.

The assistant ignored her discomfort and joked with them. "The baby is not ready to appear yet. Mia, you may need to help push him through."

Mia wiped sweat from her brow and held onto her shaking body as the bench brought her back into a lounging position. Should she be excited or were her nerves more real? Tyler smiled and squeezed her hand.

Her attempts at forming relationships with the dwindling available men had led her into the arms of Tyler. He provided everything she needed apart from a baby. This was her only way, unless she moved away from her greatest love and re-entered the vulnerability of the dating scene.

"I'm having a baby," Mia announced, breaking the silence of her thoughts, "I'm doing this!"

"You've done well to keep your figure." The assistant continued to annoy her, referencing normal childbirth. Mia frowned and held in a verbal retort. Mia had expected the baby to arrive with a little blue bow or be in a presentation case. The reality was as different as she could have imagined.

The assistant explained. "The normal human process would have created the baby in your womb." Mia wanted to point out she was well aware of the process. She held back a retort to hear an unexpected statement from the assistant. "You will need to assemble the baby."

It confused Mia. Was this another of the assistants jokes? Everything became clear as a video screen burst into life and gave a brief animated explanation of the process she needed to follow.

"You are the test case for the process. The corporation wants women to think of the Tushi babies as real babies, not toys. You weren't expecting a presentation case, were you?"

Mia wanted to snap but held it together. "I don't want a toy, I'm here for a baby boy," she glanced up to Tyler, "our son."

The assistant gave Mia a flash drive copy of her choices and reminded her of the no returns policy. "As you know the baby must return for an overnight modification to effect a growth spurt every month for the first year."

Mia nodded at the screen and confirmed absolute acceptance of the contract.

The assistant beamed and presented a red button for Mia to

press. "Now for the exciting part. Press the delivery button."

Mia pressed the button, and the conveyor sprang into action. The assistant passed Augmented Reality (AR) glasses which showed instructions as a sky-blue pod arrived with a pleasant whiff of lavender. The comfy lounger tipped Mia gently forward and a small table swung in front of her. The assistant lifted the pod and placed it on the tray. Mia had seen the animation, but reality silenced her as the assistant guided Tyler to open the pod and reveal their baby in component form.

Tyler passed the baby's body to Mia. She flinched before she settled and cradled it in her arms. Tyler passed her a leg. The headset showed her how to connect it to the body and the subsequent little foot. Mia's heart jumped after connecting the foot, as the entire leg twitched into life. She asked Tyler to attach the other leg, but the assistant interjected. "It is the mother who needs to complete this stage of the assembly."

Mia offered a half-hearted objection, "I want Tyler to be a part of it."

"Follow the process on your headset. Tyler will play his part," The assistant said.

Mia hadn't read all of the policy after being assured by Tyler all was fine. It was a reminder to take personal responsibility and not leave everything to Tyler.

As the second leg twitched into life, Mia was calmer as she expected the lifelike doll to come alive. The arm was next, followed by a hand, but it didn't come alive like the feet and Mia looked to the assistant. "Is he okay?"

Mia's headset both confirmed all was well and she attached the second arm, when she secured the hand to complete the arm, the baby reached out and gave Mia's arm a firm squeeze. Mia screamed.

"You requested firm hugs," the assistant said.

"Not on day one before he even has a head." Mia's hands shook.

Instructed by the AR, Mia was relieved to pass the baby to Tyler. Who held him close to his chest, with the little hands grabbing at his shirt. Mia reached into the pod and gently removed the head. Holding it upside down on the small table, facing away from her, she opened the flap fully. The next component was the crucial one. This was the operating system. She had read how the arms and legs had cognitive reflexes but needed the main operating system, the brain, for everything to function.

The brain was a supercomputer with AI microprocessors to enable the early stages of learning to begin. Once connected the flap closed slowly itself. The headset instructed Mia to place the head upright against her breast, facing Tyler. Tyler then sat the body onto Mia's lap. The arms reached up to its own head. Motor's whirred quietly as the body and the head made its connection, the arms and legs did likewise, to complete the assembly.

Partly in dread, Mia turned the baby towards her, but her fears eased when she saw a worried smile searching out her acceptance. Mia gave him a cuddle and kissed his forehead, the baby returning a more confident gaping smile. Tyler joined in with the cuddle and the assistant captured some images for the marketing campaign.

"Have you thought of any names yet?" the assistant asked.

Mia and Tyler had discussed names and Mia had left it with Tyler to decide from several they'd discussed. Tyler selected an appropriate name, "Our Son's name is Cole. It means victory."

Mia passed Cole back to Tyler, who adoringly gazed into

his eyes, holding him steady and placing his forehead to his, as they paired to each other. The assistant took Cole to perform some checks and dress him in a white Babygro and blue denim dungarees, before approving him with his official birth documents.

The assistant passed on the same advice given to all new parents. "Enjoy him whilst he is young. Babies grow quickly, especially Tushi babies."

Mia wasn't prepared for how quickly he would grow?

Chapter 9

The time for Kat's baby had also arrived. The curry from the previous night had worked its magic, and no sooner had Mirek left for work, Kat's contractions started. She managed to make herself some breakfast, but each contraction grew stronger. She called a VTOL taxi, which sped her to the hospital.

She was assessed on arrival and lifted onto a bed which made its way to the maternity delivery suites. As the bed carried her along the empty corridors, Kat felt an uneasiness which overtook her during her rest between contractions. It all felt so wrong, too quiet.

As the doors to the suite opened, Kat expected maternity nurses to reassure her, but the room was empty. The screen on the wall blinked into action. "Help will arrive shortly." The sound of a softly plucked acoustic guitar helped her to relax until another contraction claimed her, transposing the guitar strings into harrowing needles of torture. Kat scrunched her eyes tightly shut, grimacing until the contraction subsided.

As she calmed, the music annoyed her. "Stop the music."

It stopped instantly, and the message of imminent support repeated. The silence was better, but the contractions weren't as they became stronger and more regular.

"Hello again, Mrs Gorski-Parker," Nurse Kelly and Cora

gave her warming smiles, oblivious to the searing agony she'd endured. Kat had hoped it would be someone else after being exasperated them on their previous meeting.

"Call me Kat!" she replied. "You've seen my V-jay, you can call me by my first name."

"Okay, Kat." Nurse Kelly scanned her cervix. "You're fully dilated, well done, get ready to push."

The headset display gave Kelly her next prompt. "Having a girl, aren't you? That'll be nice, we don't get many girls." She asked the required questions. "You declined the embryo modifications, didn't you?"

"You know I did. I saw you! I want a normal baby, not somebody else's creation." The irate Kat stopped her complaint, she panted and moaned as another contraction surged. When the contraction had passed, Kat asked, "What's with all the questions? Where's Lucy? I asked for a proper midwife."

"She's helping with surgery now, we'll do, won't we?" Kelly gave her a strained smile.

"I suppose you'll have to." Another contraction took hold. She screamed, "help me!"

Nurse Cora passed her the mouthpiece. "Have some gas and air, it'll help."

Kat snatched it from her hand, sucking hard to ease the pain.

After two hours of pushing and lots of gas and air, Kat gave birth to a perfectly formed baby girl.

Cora held the baby aloft and showed her to the exhausted Kat, "She's perfect. I'll get her cleaned up and back to you in a minute." Cora whisked the baby away and placed her into the cleaning station before she said, "seven point five pounds."

"Healthy weight for a girl," Kelly said. She ran through the usual questions from her headset.

"You don't want to go through that again, do you?" Kelly asked, primed with her thumb over the confirmation button.

"My head's fuzzy. Give me a few minutes?" Kat asked.

"No problem," Kelly replied.

Two minutes later, Cora re-united the baby with Kat.

Kelly returned to the foot of the bed. "That's strange. We had the same message last time a girl was born. I need to scan the little one."

"What's the problem?" Kat was suddenly wide awake.

"It's okay, a routine check for girls, that's all." Cora tried to keep her calm.

Kelly scanned the baby, and the result was instant. "The headset says the baby requires an injection to cure Femalatism."

"She'll be fine, whatever it is. My breast milk will give her the protection she needs."

"I'm sorry Kat. The injection is mandatory," Kelly explained from her script.

"Fuck that, I know my baby is fine." Kat held her baby closer.

A mini-bot rolled into the room and presented a single syringe. Cora took it and turned to Kat and the baby. "It's okay, it won't hurt."

"It won't hurt, she's not having it! You're not hurting my baby!" Kat held her baby girl away from Cora. Cora attempted to deliver the injection anyway. Kat pulled the syringe out of her hand and squirted the injection onto the floor. Kat stared into her eyes and gritted her teeth. "She's not having it!"

Nurse Kelly tried to break the tension and read from her headset display. "That was hard work, Kat. I bet you don't want to go through that again."

Kat shook her head in disbelief. "Are you talking about

childbirth?"

"We'll take care of that for you. Is that okay?" Nurse Kelly continued to read the display and the snake like tool moved towards Kat.

"You can switch that fucking thing off!"

Kelly pressed the confirm button. "It'll only take a minute."

"Are you fucking stupid, I said No." The snake like tool moved over her legs.

The tool ignored her response and attempted to enter her as she rolled off the table with her little girl. With post-natal blood draining down her legs, she burst past Cora and Kelly headed out through the door into the empty corridor. Kelly followed her out and called after her, "It only needs to clean you up. We need to get the placenta out."

Kat didn't respond, striding away with blood pouring down her legs, holding onto her little treasure. As Kat made her way outside the rain was lashing down and the wind almost took her off her feet. A taxi was waiting. She got in and directed it towards home.

Once the taxi had moved away, a warning from inside the cab sounded. "Your blood pressure is low, I suggest re-directing to the hospital."

"No, thank you. Continue to my house."

"Your life is at risk if you do not return to the hospital."

"No, thank you. From my contacts, call Nurse Lucy."

Kat checked over her baby and thankfully all seemed well. Still on edge, her mind spun with the thought of the snake tool and the injection. With her rage building again, she was connected to Lucy. She didn't give her a chance to speak. "What the fuck is going on at your hospital? Doesn't anybody fucking listen?"

"I'm listening, What's the problem?" Lucy's calming voice was like a china teacup in a typhoon.

"They wanted to hurt my baby girl and then they tried to take my ovaries with some fucking metal snake."

"If you weren't comfortable, you only had to say no."

"I said no! They tried to, anyway!"

"Oh, that's not right."

"No fucking kidding!"

"Where are you now?"

"In a taxi, on the way home."

"Is the baby okay?"

"She's fine."

"Okay. Are you still bleeding down there?"

"Yes, there's a pool of blood in the taxi and all the way down the hospital corridor."

"You need sorting out, come back to the hospital."

"No chance!" Kat vented.

"Okay, I'll meet you at yours."

"Thanks Lucy."

As Lucy rang off, the emotion streamed out of Kat as she sobbed uncontrollably over her bundle of joy, delicately wiping her tears off her baby girl's face.

Through the taxi communication system, she sent a message for Mirek to hurry home. His response came back through the speakers, unaware of her trauma, commenting on how she must have done well to be going home already. Kat had no answer, wiping her eyes to take in the miracle in her arms.

Chapter 10

When Lucy received Kat's call, she made her apologies to Doctor Luke and dashed off to collect the essentials. She rushed with her hands full to an awaiting VTOL ambulance with a paramedic droid on board. The ambulance lifted steadily in the storm before it sped on its way.

Lucy had been mid chat with Doctor Luke, discussing the slow progress of the new maternity nurses. The new nurses had Lucy worried, Augmented Reality (AR) headsets had been the latest advancement in maternity and the instructions should have guided them through the process. Nurse Kelly seemed to have picked most things up okay, but Cora was still a concern.

Luke had said not to worry about them and to leave it to the headsets, but Lucy had spent too many years in maternity to step away and forget it. The biggest benefit was the automation of the maternity reports, which saved her hours of mind-numbing analysis. Not that anybody ever read them.

Lucy had been about to suggest a romantic interlude in Luke's office, but this time it wasn't Luke that ran away. Despite Luke's nonappearance at the wedding, she remained smitten with him. Now she'd trained her replacements in maternity, Lucy was by Luke's side for most of her shift and their connection was blossoming.

Since Kat's wedding, the gorgeous physiotherapist consultant, Alfie also became a more significant consideration. She enjoyed sharing a coffee with him most days and unlike Luke; he was keen to see her outside of the hospital. She'd considered taking the next step with Alfie at the wedding, but he hadn't responded to her subtle hint to walk her to her room. He was no player, that was for sure.

When the VTOL touched down, Lucy asked the paramedic droid to wait in the ambulance. The front door was still open and when Lucy stepped through, she saw a trail of blood leading to Kat collapsed against the lounger with the baby under her arm. Lucy lifted her arm to release the baby from her fixed grasp and wrapped a towel around the baby, resting her on the lounger she'd slept on during her last visit. She rested her hand on Kat's back without a response, she turned her head and saw her blue lips. "Paramedic support required! Not breathing!"

Lucy turned Kat onto her back, she blew air through her mouth to fill her lungs and lift her chest, and again, and again. She straightened her arms and pushed down on her breast plate. The paramedic bot arrived as tears filled Lucy's eyes. The paramedic prompted Lucy to move and in one swift movement ripped Kat's gown open wide, placed pads and announced, "Clear" as it sent a shock through Kat's lifeless body. "Clear" and again her body jolted. The third attempt shook her again and a sharp intake of breath was followed by a series of coughs and further grasps of life-giving air. Lucy flung her arms around her and buried her face into her friend. "You're back with us!" Lucy sobbed tears of relief.

Kat responded with a strained, "you're crushing me, I can't breathe." Lucy lifted herself and giggled at Kat's character springing back into life. She held onto Kat's hand whilst the paramedic held the other and with a quick pinch it inserted a canula to administer some blood.

"Blood pressure is eighty over fifty. She will need more blood to prevent another cardiac arrest." Once connected the paramedic squeezed the bag of blood to speed up the process.

Lucy placed a cushion under Kat's head and reassured her the worst was over. Kat was still woozy but improved as lifeblood brought her heart back to a steadier rhythm. They emptied another bag of blood as a small emergency drone arrived with two more. Lucy pulled out the remaining placenta and with a few stitches closed her torn perineum to stem the bleeding. She placed another blood-filled swab on her growing collection as Mirek rushed through the door. He screamed with the sight of the placenta on the floor between Kat's prostrate ankles. The paramedic calmly stated, "she will be okay."

Mirek went to Kat. His eyes streamed as he stroked her hair. "Did we lose the baby?" his broken voice asked.

Kat's face fell with grief, but Lucy tapped Mirek on the shoulder and pointed to the baby. "All is well with the baby, like her mom, she's a survivor."

Mirek's eyes widened and a beaming smile appeared, he picked up the baby and brought her into Kat's sight. Lucy helped her to sit against the lounger and sat beside her. Mirek also sat alongside her as their new family was together for the first time. Thankfully, the fourth bag of blood had done the trick and Kat's vitals were returning to stable levels. The paramedic set about cleaning up the bloody mess.

Mirek appeared with a coffee for Lucy, insisting she looked like she needed one. Lucy nodded her thanks and accepted it; her shaking hands rested it on the floor. She'd dealt with a world of emotions being in the maternity department, but her friend's lifeless body had weakened her resolve. Kat placed her hand on Lucy's arm and thanked her. Lucy glanced up to the bot and explained to Kat how it was the paramedic bot that had brought her back to life.

Kat told her what had happened at the hospital. Lucy knew about the snake-like tool which performed hysterectomies and oophorectomies, but it was in the main surgical building and not in maternity. She was further confused when Kat mentioned the injection. She asked if it could have been an injection she'd declined during her prenatal appointments, but Kat was patchy on the details. Lucy said she'd better go with the VTOL and find out what was happening in her beloved department.

When the floor was clean. The paramedic checked Kat's vitals again and removed the canula, assuring her, "You will be fine now, you just need rest."

"Would you like a lift back to the hospital?" The paramedic asked Lucy.

"I need another coffee first," Lucy said.

"No, you don't! You need to sort out the maternity nurses and their bullshit." Kat insisted with a shove of Lucy.

"Guess I'm coming with you then." Lucy said to the paramedic as she got to her feet.

As they were going Lucy asked if they had named the baby. Kat said, "We were planning to call her Amelia, but after the day she's had, Lucky would be more appropriate."

Mirek placed his hand gently on Kat's shoulder, looking at the baby, "Fate and luck. We will call her Destiny."

Kat rested her head against Mirek and confirmed, "Yes darling, Destiny."

"Make sure she rests," Lucy said to Mirek as he followed her to the door.

*

Kelly and Cora had cleaned up after the mad five minutes with Kat and were ready for the next mother to be. The next patient arrived and berated them for not bringing her to the delivery suite earlier, that was until another contraction took hold and she bared her teeth, growling at them.

Cora checked her details. "You're expecting a girl too, not going to make a run for it are you." Cora received another maddened stare from Kelly.

"Get this out of me." The would-be mother demanded before another contraction surged through her and give her something real to moan about.

Kelly gave a hard stare to Cora and put her finger to her lips. "We've had enough drama for one day. Keep your mouth shut."

"Can't you just pull the thing out?" The exhausted mother demanded after an hour of pushing.

The head had crowned, and they listened to her. They'd not used the ventouse suction cup before and should have called for help but proceeded when the mother asked them to, "get on with it." After a steady pull with the stainless clamps either side of the baby's delicate head, the baby was eased out into the world.

"About time," the unthankful new mother said.

Cora placed the baby girl in the cleaning station and the headset prompted the familiar question to the new mother, "That was hard work, wasn't it?" Nurse Kelly said, "I bet you don't want to go through that again."

"No!" she said.

"We'll take care of that for you, is that okay."

"Yeah, whatever." the mother said, without a care.

Kelly pressed the confirm button, "It will only take a minute, then we'll have baby back to you. She's just going through the cleaning station." The snake-like tool slipped into her open cervix and found its own way to her ovaries and removed them.

Cora re-united the baby with her Mom and the headset called for a scan of the baby. Kelly thought it strange, it had done the same for the crazy Kat and her baby girl.

"Need to scan the little one," Kelly said, as she read from the script.

"What's the matter now?"

"A routine check for girls, that's all," Cora said.

Kelly scanned the baby, and the result was instant. "The baby requires an injection to cure Femalatism."

"She's fine, don't worry."

"The injection is mandatory to prevent it from spreading," Kelly said, reading from the script.

A mini-bot entered the room and Cora took the syringe. "It's okay, it won't hurt."

Cora delivered the injection into her little hip with the care of a builder with a staple gun. The baby let out a cry and her mom pulled her close.

The room fell quiet as the baby girl's tears ceased. Kelly and Cora were heading out to give the new mother some time to bond with her baby and grab themselves a quick coffee.

"She's not breathing!" The mother screamed. Kelly and Cora shot back in.

Kelly put on the headset and asked for help. It advised her to place the baby in the ventilator, but the new mom held the baby tighter still. It was then she called Lucy.

Lucy received the message on the way back to the hospital, and on landing hurried to maternity. The mother was still screaming with the baby in her arms when Lucy burst through the door. Kelly and Cora were sobbing with their heads locked together.

Lucy picked up the baby and tried to resuscitate her, but to no avail. "I'm sorry, It's too late."

The mother's eyes glazed over. She lay back and stared at the ceiling for a few moments. A quiet rumbling moan followed her eyes still fixed on the ceiling.

Lucy turned her attention to Kelly. "Can you tell me what happened? What did you do?"

"Mom wanted baby out, so we used the ventouse cup."

"Okay, what else?" Lucy comforted her as she sobbed.

"The baby had Femalatism, she needed an injection," Kelly said.

"Femalatism! What on earth is Femalatism?" In all of Lucy's years of training, she'd never heard of it.

"I don't know. I followed the instructions. A bot brought an injection." Tears trickled down Kelly's apologetic face.

Lucy turned to Cora, the administering nurse, "what was in the injection?"

The tear-filled Cora covered her face with her hands. "I don't know."

"I told you to always check medication before you administer it!"

Kelly said, "It's only the second girl we've seen in two weeks. We had one earlier, but her crazy mom refused the injection. When Cora tried to administer it, she snatched it out of Cora's hand before she raced out of the hospital with her baby under her arm like a rugby ball."

"That was my friend! They can decline anything they want! You can't force them to have injections!" She continued, "What's going on here! I didn't train you to behave like this?" Lucy set off at pace, taking deep breaths. "I should never have moved out of here, you're both bloody useless," Lucy said.

Lucy checked the records and found out that the drop in the birth rate had continued with girls declining at a faster rate. Only nine girls in three months, "This would make the news if the bloody robots didn't run it," Lucy said to Kelly who was scampering behind.

Lucy called the mothers of the girls to check on them, only to hear grief-ridden fathers, re-tell how their baby girl had died along with their mother after coming home. Each call drove another blade of pain into her pouring heart.

"How about the boys, are they okay?" Kelly asked.

"Try this one, Ellie, her partner Connor brought us flowers when he collected her and her baby son." She added, "they had called him Jake, a lovely little boy."

Grave concern and guilt filled Lucy. "Ellie's a friend of mine. We grew up together." With her additional duties and chasing Doctor Luke, she'd forgotten about Ellie's due date.

"If she was your friend, you could have delivered the baby."

"I'm surprised she didn't insist on it," Lucy replied.

"She came in late, I don't think you were here. She insisted on having the baby shots herself as she was going to be breastfeeding."

"Baby shots? She'd had them all."

"Some boys needed Femalatism shots too. Ellie insisted on having the injection instead."

Lucy made the video call with a heavy heart. She feared the

worst. After a long ring, Connor's face appeared.

"Connor, sorry to bother you. How's Jake doing?" Lucy hoped for a break in the run of despair.

"Jake is fine," Connor said, but his tone said otherwise. He angled the phone for her to see. "He's with Ellen."

"Glad you're all doing so well." Lucy noticed sadness in Connor's eyes.

"We are doing better," he paused, "now that Ellen's here." there is a touch of sadness in his voice as his smile drops.

Kelly nudged Lucy. "The Mom was Ellie."

Lucy covered the phone and ground her teeth as she stared at Kelly. "I've known her for years. Her christened name is Ellen."

"Can I talk to Ellie?" Lucy asked Connor.

He lowered his head. "She's not here."

"Isn't that Ellie behind you?" Lucy said, pointing behind him.

"That's my Housebot, Ellen." His words ripped through Lucy's already heavy heart. "Two days after coming home with Jake." Connor sniffed. "Ellie was breast feeding him... she started choking... and passed out."

"Where is she?" Lucy asked.

"She'd stopped breathing. Her heart had stopped beating. I know CPR, I kept her heart going until the paramedic bot arrived. She's in intensive care at the hospital. I should have called you, sorry."

"I'll check in on Ellie. Did you get milk for the baby?"

"Ellen arrived the same afternoon with milk for Jake. She's trying to hold us all together until I can see Ellie."

"What? Why have you not seen her?"

"Ellen said the hospital needed to keep her in isolation."

"That doesn't sound right," Lucy said.

Before Connor answered Ellen appeared aside him and ended the call.

Lucy called again, but they didn't answer. Lucy's hand trembled as she squeezed the phone with all her might, letting out a mighty roar.

Kelly tried to put an arm of comfort around her, but Lucy pushed her away. Lucy buried her head in her hands and took long, slow breaths. Cora joined them in the records office oblivious to Lucy's grief, tried to raise her spirits with a perky comment. "Looks like someone needs a coffee."

Kelly tapped her finger on her lips. "Get Alfie!"

Cora slipped away to find Alfie. Kelly placed a comforting arm around Lucy and knelt beside her.

Chapter 11

Lucy's glazed eyes remained fixed on the screen. When Alfie came running in, he dispatched Kelly to return to her duties and wrapped his comforting arms around Lucy. She burst into tears and sobbed into his white coat.

Not being briefed, Alfie was way off the mark. "You don't need Doctor Luke."

Lucy's outpouring ceased. "It's all gone wrong." She spluttered out what had happened to Ellie, Kat and the others. Alfie was equally perplexed when Lucy asked him about Femalatism.

"What is Femalatism?" Alfie asked his device.

"Femalatism is the overpopulation of females."

"What! Total bullshit! The maternity department is quieter than it's ever been, the percentage of girls being born has been below thirty percent for years. It makes no sense." Lucy charged around the small office and slammed the door shut. "The AR headsets are insisting on giving all baby girls the lethal injection. Most of the women having boys received a similar fate or got tricked into having their ovaries removed whilst they were in no fit state to comprehend such a question."

"It seems like someone is intent on reducing births and the population. Probably some environmental nut in the government."

"Or the Tushi Corporation. Their bloody droids will end up taking over everything," Lucy said.

"I saw the news earlier; your friend Mia has received her Tushi Baby. It said she was the first human female to have a Tushi child. It was a strange news item given the size of the Tushi Corporation. I delved deeper. They've delivered over fifty thousand babies, since their launch twelve months ago against less than 20,000 natural births. The Tushi babies also grow at ten times the speed of a new-born."

"Bloody hell, they'll be everywhere."

"If Mia was the first human. The other fifty thousand were for Tushi wives. It seems they're well on the way, but how can we stop them?" Alfie asked.

"The Police won't be any help," Lucy said.

The Police had followed the Fire departments and rolled out droid units throughout the force. It was a seamless transition, sold on the significant cost savings it delivered.

"Stop the lethal injections for a start and get the snake back into gynaecology," Alfie suggested.

Lucy called Doctor Luke. "Luke, why is the snake in maternity? Can we get it back into gynaecology?"

"They hardly used it in Gyno. They decided it would be more useful in maternity to remove ovaries whilst the birth canal was open, a much more comfortable operation with no need for a separate visit."

Doctor Luke's answer left Lucy far from convinced. She growled a sharp response, "who decided?"

"It was a message from the top."

"How about if the mother's wanted to keep their ovaries?"

"You know the hospital procedure. All patients need to have the operation explained to them before we gain confirmation from them to proceed," Doctor Luke said.

Lucy wanted to punch him for being so calm. "My friend declined the procedure and had to run out of the room to escape it."

"There must be an error, I'll get it checked."

"It needs to move back to Gyno!" Lucy said, through gritted teeth.

"I'll get it fixed. What was your friend's name?"

"It doesn't matter, forget it." Lucy broke off the call and screamed, punching Alfie's chest as he tried to hold her.

"I don't think Doctor Luke is the dreamboat, you thought he was. Didn't he program the headsets?"

"I did most of the programming, but he made some modifications after I'd finished."

"You know he's a droid, don't you?" Alfie asked.

"Who is?"

"Doctor Luke, you're too smitten to realise."

"What are you talking about? Luke's no droid!"

"Has he ever hesitated for even a second before answering a question, or ever not known something?"

"That doesn't make him a droid. He's just smart."

"Ask him who won the esports Tennis league in 2042, he'll tell you without even pausing."

"Who cares who won?"

"It was Jimpy. I love my esports but Doctor Luke is always here he wouldn't know unless he was a droid."

"Is that your Turing test, asking him about esports?"

"I have also studied his gait. Very realistic, but he has no imperfections, just like Mia's fella, Tyler." As a consultant physiotherapist he knew everything about bones, muscles and posture. "Every adult has a unique walk. I've studied posture for twenty years. Luke walks rather slow for his level of intellect, which tells me he has something on his mind, but his posture is perfect. People who dawdle slouch more. He walks straight and tall. He is also very strong but shows no signs of deviations from excessive gym work."

"You think he's a droid because he walks well?" Lucy held her hands out in disbelief. Despite the severity of the situation unfolding, Lucy smirked at Alfie. "Interesting. How's my gait then? What does it tell you?"

"Never noticed more than your cute little ass." Alfie smiled.

"I thought you were a professional."

"Okay, if you want me to be honest." He circled Lucy, assessing. "No heavy school bag to deviate your spine, so probably home schooled." He slid his finger down her backbone, "slight curvature from excessive studying at a young age, or perhaps it is from trying to hide your growing breasts? Do you want me to continue?"

"You may as well finish your analysis."

Alfie crouched in front of her and pointed at her groin, to which Lucy stepped back, "Okay, no particularly well-endowed partners or pregnancies to mess with your pelvic alignment."

"Anything else?" The accuracy of his assessment astounded Lucy. She was both embarrassed, and a little turned on.

"For perfection, me on your arm to support you through this crazy world."

Lucy laughed at his cheesy line, but Alfie took her into his arms to kiss her for the first time. Despite the surrounding madness, it transported Lucy into an explosion of tingles and goose bumps all over her body. Alfie's tender hands smoothed over her blue tunic.

"You should have come to my room after the wedding," Lucy

said, between kisses.

"You didn't ask," he replied, "you said you were tired and were heading up for the night."

"Could you be less of a player? Next time a girl says she's tired and wants to go to bed, you walk her there."

"You could have been a little more specific, I didn't want to ruin our friendship."

"How's this? I want you to take me to a spare room, lock the door behind us and fuck me till morning."

Alfie's mouth gaped. He shook his head, "Lucy. That's definitely not you."

"It's not, I haven't done this before," Lucy said, with a reddening of her cheeks.

"What do you mean? Not done this before?"

"Heavy studying and self-petting only, but it's time." Lucy grabbed his belt and pulled him close.

Alfie put his hand on hers, and she released her grip. "This is not right. Your first time should be special. Let's sort this mess out first, then I'll come around to yours and make an occasion of it. Wouldn't it be better that way?"

"I guess." Lucy said, she smiled and pulled him in close again, stretching up for another kiss. "I've some catching up to do, expect more," Lucy said, her inner temptress had awoken.

Alfie pulled her focus back to the task at hand and they formulated a quick plan. He headed back to his office to investigate further and find out if other hospitals were being affected. Lucy marched back into the delivery room to update Kelly and Cora.

"Follow the headsets but if it asks for an injection, squirt it down the sink. As for the snake, switch it off and select declined for each patient. This is information for us girls only. The injection is killing the baby girls."

"What about the Femalatism Doctor Luke told us about?" Cora glanced at Kelly for some clarity.

"Are you bloody stupid? I have told you it's bullshit, it's killing the baby girls, most likely to reduce the population and create the requirement for more Tushi babies. The snake is also delivering an injection to kill the mothers."

"What will Doctor Luke say, if everyone is declining the snake and the injection?" Cora asked.

"Tell him it's their choice. We can't decide for them."

Lucy upped to leave. "I'll come back tomorrow to make sure there are no more issues."

Lucy left the department shaking her head. She called a travel pod to take her back to the principal building to confront Doctor Luke about what he'd changed in her beloved maternity department. Not to mention the strange question about esports Tennis.

Chapter 12

Proud smiles welcomed Mia as she arrived at the coffee shop with Cole. She thanked Sarah for covering, but the entire crew were there to see her new bundle of joy. She felt crowded by the attention. "Sit down and you can each have a hold."

They took their familiar seats and Mia handed Cole to Ray. "Careful. He's heavier than he looks."

Ray welcomed him in his arms with a smile and offered a friendly, "Hello little fella." Cole engrossed Ray for a moment with his attempts at a smile before Ray asked, "Where's his Daddy?"

"I dropped Tyler off at the house. He needs to set up the charge station and prepare my tea."

"You've got him trained," Ray replied.

"He may be the Daddy, but deep down he's still my sexy house bot." Mia smiled, proud her family was complete.

Mia should have taken Cole to see her mom, it would have been the correct thing to do. Mia figured the supportive crew at the coffee shop were more like parents than her absent mother, but she planned to call her and let her know she had a Tushi Grandson.

Jackie spoke for the crew. "We're so happy for you. He may not be from your own flesh, but he's all yours to love

91

and cherish. You'll be a great mum, I'm sure."

"Rena and I would have loved children. We had all the tests and treatments, but it never happened for us." Ray's eyes glistened.

"You're a surrogate grandfather now," Mia said to lift his spirits.

"And very proud to be," Ray replied, giving Cole an extra strong cuddle.

"Let Sarah have a hold now, you can't have him all to yourself," Mia said.

He passed the baby to Sarah. She sighed. "You weren't kidding about him being heavy." She introduced him to Harry and Jackie. "I can feel a rumble of a nappy being filled." She screwed her nose and waved her hand as if he'd let out a stink, but she was only kidding. Cole could replicate baby moves, but the designers didn't add the less pleasant effects of a defecating baby.

Jackie took the next turn. "He's very aware for a newborn. He's taking everything in."

"Enjoy him whilst he's young," Harry commented and reflected on his own son, "Mikey grew so fast we had to check his birth certificate before he moved to America."

Jackie handed Cole back to Sarah. "Mikey's married now with a couple of kids, not that we see them."

"We get a video call at birthdays and Christmas," Harry said.

Mia made some coffees and settled down on the edge of the table as the screen flicked onto the daily news.

The cheeky sexbot twins were giggling away as always. They announced they had two pieces of excellent news. "First, the birth of a special new baby." They switched to footage of Cole being held up by Tyler in the delivery room. It moved to Mia, holding Cole with Tyler walking beside them as they made their way out of Tushi World. Mia hadn't spotted any, but surveillance cameras covered multiple angles of every room and would've been used for the footage.

The picture cut to Okzu Tushi sitting behind an enormous desk with his hands clasped. "It's a proud day for everyone at the Tushi Corporation. Today, Mia Foster was the first woman who chose a Tushi baby to complete her family unit. We have forty more women due to collect their babies with many more to follow. I am so pleased we now have Tushi droids integrating into every area of society."

"He's an evil-looking guy if ever I've seen one," Harry said.

"He looks charming," Jackie said.

"His eyes are too close together," Harry said.

"You're just jealous. He's a lovely fella and a rich genius too."

"As expected, no sign of an alternative view anymore. We used to get some church bloke preaching about how we are losing traditional values," Ray said.

"The people that pay. Have their say. It will never change." Sarah's words confirmed the harsh reality.

Mia had been pleased with the coverage, but the second piece of news changed her mood.

"The fuel cell upgrades are now available for all droids. The upgrade will not be available for the child bots, so, whilst the children charge, the fun can continue through the night. No more slipping out and leaving you in a cold bed. Now your Tushi can keep you warm all night."

"Fuck!"

The crew turned in unison at Mia's outburst.

They awaited an explanation, but Mia stared stony faced at

the TV whilst the twins said their goodbyes. With the news over, the monitor switched back to the slideshow of tranquil clips. It showed waves lapping against a shore. She meant it to create an ambiance of peace, but today it portrayed the unyielding tide of change.

Jackie took Mia out of her trance, placing her hand on her shoulder. "No more cold beds for you."

Mia ignored Jackie's comment. "Sarah, could you take Cole to the kitchen please?" Mia asked. Sarah screwed her nose up at the sudden request, but she scooped up Cole and took him into the kitchen.

When Sarah and Cole were out of earshot, Mia huddled them around the table. "Did you forget Ethan's note?"

"I thought you'd thrown it away. The ramblings of a jilted lover," Jackie said.

"Don't you remember saying we could unplug the charging stations, if they got out of control. The fuel cell means they don't charge every night. It gives them a two-week charge."

"Switch off the fuel cell production and they're screwed," Harry said.

"How do you do that? They make them at the Tushi factory."

"Who works there?" Harry asked.

"When Cole reaches maturity he will, as will the other child bots." Mia paced around the table with the letter dominating her thoughts again.

Harry leant forward and tapped Mia's arm. "Who works there now!"

"Ethan and Mirek, but Ethan's still on stress leave."

"Go and see Kat. Maybe Mirek can find out what Okzu is doing," Jackie said. She smirked. "I think you should apologize to Ethan. Perhaps he's not a nutcase after all."

Sarah returned from the kitchen without Cole. "What's the problem?"

"There's no problem, I'll see Kat," Mia said. She knew Kat and Mirek would relish the challenge of digging for information.

"Wasn't her baby due soon?" Sarah asked.

"I hope it wasn't Kat this morning at the hospital," Jackie said.

"Why?" Mia stared at Jackie.

"Me and Harry were there for a check-up on the health scanner. They told us we were fine."

Harry raised his hand to interrupt. "She was more interested in the crazy woman than our stupid scan."

Mia frowned at Harry. "Crazy woman?"

"On the way out, some loopy brunette with a baby under her arm, stormed through the corridor with blood streaming down her legs."

"It wasn't Kat, was it?"

"She was too far away to tell."

"I'd better call her; I hope she's okay." Mia dashed into the kitchen and called Kat.

Mirek answered the phone and offered his congratulations on Mia's little addition and how he'd seen her on the news.

Mia interrupted him to ask. "Has Kat had the baby?"

Mirek updated Mia on the distress Kat had with Destiny's arrival. He assured her Kat was okay, she just needed rest.

Mia wanted to share her concerns but needed to follow Ethan's advice. She needed to talk face to face with no droid or transmitter devices in the vicinity. "Can I come over? I'd like to see the baby and have a private chat with both of you?"

"I hope you realize you can't have a private chat with Cole

around?" Mirek said.

Mia rolled her eyes. "Yes, I know. I'll come alone."

*

When Mia and Cole arrived back at their oak door. Tyler was standing in the doorway to welcome them home. He'd set up the charge station in the back room and had prepared tea for Mia.

Mia lay Cole on the floor with a couple of toys, which Tyler had ordered when he got home. As Mia and Tyler ate, they watched him becoming more dexterous before their eyes. He was only a few hours old and was already picking up toys. The assistant had warned them he would develop and grow quickly. Tyler confirmed the details, he would crawl within the first week and within the first month, he would learn to walk. Speech would take a little longer as he built up vocabulary from his parents and vocal interactions to ensure he followed the same dialect and word phrasing.

After tea, Tyler mentioned he could stay with her all night now he had the fuel cell upgrade. Mia gave him a hug and said, "I'm looking forward to spending the night with you, but I want to visit Kat and her baby girl."

"Shall we go as a family? We could introduce Cole."

"She's had a traumatic day. We'll go together next time."

"We should wait and go together?" Tyler said.

"No! Kat's my best friend and I'm going to see her baby." Mia impressed herself with her sharp retort. Tyler backed away with his hands up. Mia pointed her finger at him with a hard stare, before giving him a smile.

Chapter 13

Lucy arrived in the surgical block of the hospital and headed for Doctor Luke. He would be ready to review patients in the preparation area for the evening operations. Her rose coloured image of Doctor Luke had cleared and her blood was boiling. She wanted answers. She was ready for a fight. He was not the man she admired, and after he'd changed her instructions to plot the demise of women and children; she needed to find out if he was a droid.

Her way parted as she charged through the corridors, huffing and puffing like a steam train. As she turned the last corner, two guys grabbed her. She kicked out as they forced her into a small office. The huge guy stood between her and the door, whilst the other smaller guy continued to restrain her.

"What the fuck are you doing?" she shouted as she dragged her heel down the guy's shin, before punching him square in the face, forcing him to release her.

"We're following orders," the larger guy said, as he stood firm before her.

"Whose orders?" she asked, ready to punch the guy twice her size.

"He's on his way," he replied, holding his baseball glove sized hand up to halt her attempted assault.

"Who is on their way?" she asked, as a gentle tap on the door silenced her.

Her confusion multiplied as Alfie stepped in and closed the door behind him.

"What's going on? I was going to confront Luke."

Alfie opened his calming hands and his smooth tone melted Lucy's fire. "Sorry for the change in plans, I called in a favour from these guys. Do you think alerting him to what we've found is the best course of action? We've finally got together after two years. I don't want to lose you now."

Lucy took slow deep breaths to bring her pulse down and regain her rational thoughts. When she realised the danger she'd have put herself in, she agreed it was the right course of action to hold off confronting him.

Her adrenaline induced trembling hands stilled and a sense of love followed. Alfie had protected her; it gave her a warm feeling she hadn't experienced before. She nestled into his arms again and in his embrace; she turned her head to the guy she'd assaulted and gave him a sheepish grin. "Sorry."

"I'm used to getting hit. I'm married." The guy smiled behind his blood-filled handkerchief.

"What's going on?" The big guy said.

Alfie explained their initial findings to the guys, and they offered their support to check for any other issues. "What's the plan for Lucy? Is she on the front line?" The big guy put his fists up in jest.

"Other than the containment instructions for Kelly and Cora. We don't have a plan. Not yet anyway," Lucy said.

"You need to gleam info from Luke without raising suspicion. Carry on flirting with him," Alfie said. Before he smirked at Lucy's offended frown.

"Flirting? I don't flirt with him." Lucy said, but the sideward glances halted her defence and with more composure, she left to face Luke and flirt as requested.

"Where have you been? Were you delivering babies for two hours?"

Luke's furrowed brow met a smile from Lucy. "Did you miss me?"

Luke shrugged and returned a wry smile.

"My friend had complications, I needed to assist to remove her placenta," Mia said, with a returned professional calm.

"You told me on the phone. That was hours ago?"

"She's a friend. I needed time with her."

"Very well." Doctor Luke switched back into work mode, passing her the pre-op list.

Lucy however turned it right back and placed the list back on the desk. "We discussed you. Will you ever make good your promise to take me out?" They hadn't discussed Luke, but it was a suitable fit for the flirty assault. For the first time she hoped for another deferral.

"Well, you have been faithful in your service and you smell delightful tonight, but we need to be at the hospital to monitor the operations. I have a rather comfy sofa in my office, I often sleep in there." He gave her a tantalising smile. The shock was hard to conceal. The guy she'd wanted for two years had taken her bait just when she wanted him least, but she had a game to play.

As the colour drained from her cheeks, she worked in her question. "We could watch some esports Tennis?"

"Are you a fan of Tennis?" Luke looked puzzled.

Lucy's lips trembled. "Sometimes, like the 2042 season. I remember watching it with my Dad." Lucy blurted out at full pace.

"Jimpy won it with a game to spare." Luke replied in an instant. "He's playing later against Duron. We could watch it in my office before we snuggle down together."

Lucy's head nearly exploded. Her mind spun through multiple emotions in a single second. She put her hand on her forehead. "I need a lie down."

Doctor Luke put his arm around her. "You look kinda woozy. Have a rest in my office."

Chapter 14

Mia gave their door a tentative knock. She was unsure how Mirek and Kat would receive her after their spat in the coffee shop. Would showing them the letter make any difference, they'd already dismissed Ethan's plea for help?

Mirek opened the door. "Hiya," Mia said with a friendly smile.

"Hiya," Mirek said, like she was a bailiff coming for his furniture. He looked past Mia into the street as she stepped past him into the lounge. "Sorry for the upset in the coffee shop, Kat was out of order," he said.

Mia smiled, accepting the apology. "It's okay, I reacted badly too. Let's just put it down to us both being pregnant." It would've meant more coming from Kat, but then again Kat rarely apologised for anything.

"Kat's not really ready for visitors, she's sleeping with Destiny. Would you like to have a peek?"

Mia grinned and followed Mirek. She crept in to see them. Kat was flat out on the bed with her hand over the side holding Destiny's tiny hand, as she slept in a wicker cot aside the bed. Mia melted at the sight, letting out a loving but quiet, "Ahh, beautiful."

Destiny was a powerful name and fitting for Kat's daughter,

Mia liked it. Although pleased for Kat, the baby reminded Mia how Kat had won again. Thankfully, Kat was not awake to rub her nose in it. Mia hated to admit it, but Kat had been right. Mia had shunned male advances to enter the arms of a droid. If only things had worked out with Ethan, he'd made her feel special, he'd adored her.

As they returned to the lounge, Mia was keen to discuss the letter. "I left Cole with Tyler, so we could chat in private." She didn't want to be too direct, although being married to Kat, Mirek would be used to pointed conversations. "Do you know much about the fuel cells? How long does a charge last?"

"Not much, it's a factory sealed unit. Ethan would know more, but a charge lasts about two to four weeks."

She smiled at the mention of his name. "Have you seen Ethan?"

"I went to see him last week. He was fine for about five minutes, then he started muttering on about takeover theories. He'd taken Chloe's brain chip out and hooked it up to his own system or something." Mirek spoke as if he didn't care about Ethan. Was he exhausted from looking after Kat and the baby, or was he just off with Mia?

Mia pulled the letter from her pocket. "Did you see the letter he sent me?"

"He told me a bit about it. Think he misses you."

"He said he hadn't scheduled Chloe to look like me. Chloe and Tyler must have worked together to split us up." Mia held out the letter for Mirek to take, but he ignored it.

Mirek shrugged his shoulders. "None of my business, you need to ask Ethan."

"The droids won't take over, will they?" Mia's frown brought no sympathy from Mirek. He shook his head and paced around the room.

He turned to face Mia and waved away the letter Mia was offering him. "The tech took over a long time ago. Technology has run our lives since we were born. Most jobs either wouldn't exist or wouldn't be possible without modern tech. People moan about its influence, but they can't step away from it."

"I don't think that's true," Mia said, as she returned the letter to her bag.

"Really?" Mirek sarcastically replied. "I bet you didn't even open your own curtains today. Who made your breakfast?" He continued with increased disregard for Mia as she stiffened to his verbal attack. "Who did you sleep with last night? You have a Tushi baby, for Christ's sake. You're more tech dependant than anybody. There's no battle to fight. Technology has already taken over."

Mia felt like a scolded child before a head teacher. Did Mirek not understand the risk or was he choosing to ignore it? "How about if they take over completely? They could make us their pets," Mia asked, hoping Mirek would consider the possibility.

"You and Tyler are each other's pets already, that's a marriage in all but name. You even have a pet to share in Cole." He sighed and shook his head. "If any shit kicked off, you'd be okay anyway, you're paired with Tyler, he'll protect you."

"How about if I wanted to go back to a human man?"

"Who, Ethan? I'd stick with Tyler."

"I thought he was your best friend."

"He was, I mean, he is, but his head's not in a great place. He needs to sort things out."

"So, there is a problem with the Tushi?" Mia leant forward expecting more detail from Mirek.

"Nothing for you to get involved with." Mirek turned away

and focussed on the video wall with its blue skies and wispy clouds. Mia expected some comment about how the world was beyond help, but he glanced briefly away from the screen to give Mia a cue to leave. "You should get back to Tyler, he'll be missing his little pet."

"I suppose I should get back before he suspects anything." Mia was trying to be polite despite his dismissive tone.

"There's nothing to suspect, you've been to see Kat and the baby and now you're returning to give Tyler what he needs."

Mia messaged a taxi and made her way to the door. She couldn't understand why Mirek was being such an arse. She felt like she was being thrown out as Mirek closed the door behind her without further comment.

"What an arsehole, he's a fine one to talk about a reliance on technology, he works for Tushi," Mia said to the closed door.

She sat on a step waiting for a taxi and looked to the night sky for inspiration. Thousands of stars shone to remind her of how insignificant humans were in the vast array of worlds. On the ride home, Mirek's words about her reliance on technology sank in. It's engrained in every part of life. Stepping away from it was impossible.

Aware of the taxi arriving, Tyler stood in the doorway to welcome her home. Mia's concerns melted away in his loving embrace. All thoughts of droids taking control left her mind as she closed the door to the rest of the world.

"Was everything okay with Kat and the Baby?"

"Yeah, Kat was fine, they've named the baby, Destiny. Very profound."

"Destiny? Fate or luck. Let's hope fate brings Destiny plenty of luck."

"Almost poetic for you, was that your upgrade?"

"Didn't I say? The upgrade was the new fuel cell. No more charging at night, I can keep you warm in bed and we can enjoy morning sex if you have the energy?" Tyler had missed the point of her subtle tease; she knew Ethan would have got it.

"The sex has been too intense," Mia said. The sex comment wasn't far from the truth, but she could hardly tell him about her concern with the all-encompassing technology in her life.

Tyler stroked her shoulder. "Sorry Darling, should I be even more gentle with you?"

"Maybe, but not tonight. I will settle for a cuddle in bed though."

Tyler had been a revelation in her life and had brought her delights she hadn't thought possible, but Ethan had made her question everything with his pointed letter. She would punch and kick Ethan to death if this was a plan to win her back. If it was true, then she didn't know what she'd do. Mirek had mentioned how Ethan had taken Chloe off the network. Maybe she could ask him to do the same for Tyler.

Tyler placed his protective arm around her, and his warming sweet scent filled her nostrils to push aside her troubles. She rested her head against the warmth of his chest and drifted off to sleep.

*

Mia awoke with Cole's face beaming in her direction. Tyler had collected Cole from his charge station and placed him between them. Mia gave him a kiss and snuggled him between her and Tyler. "He's growing fast, should he have grown so much already?" Mia asked Tyler.

Tyler avoided the question. "Is he ticklish like you?" Tyler tickled Cole's sides to send him wriggling and giggling in delight. Mia joined in before Tyler turned his attention to Mia, who screamed as she tried to squirm away from his probing fingers.

Chapter 15

When Lucy opened her eyes, Luke's face was looking down at her. Her head rested on his lap as he stroked her hair. It was the corner piece of most of her dreams to be intimate with Luke. Was she dreaming?

"Are you feeling better for your nap?" His voice could calm a raging torrent. She'd seen it many times, patients bubbling hot with anguish, chilled after a few of his calming words. Now it was Lucy experiencing his care and attention. His warm hands were cradling her. She could not have felt more alive. She put an arm around him and pulled herself up to meet his lips and sensations galore ripped through her. His lips had met hers for the first time and a fire had been lit between her legs. They were connecting at last. He smoothed his hands down her tunic and popped open a couple of buttons to stroke a finger across her toned stomach to send her butterflies into a mad frenzy. The intensity of their kiss grew as his hand caressed her stomach and reached the ache of her breasts.

Lucy kissed him with growing passion as her dream turned to reality and her body responded to every arousing touch. She had received an occasional whiff before, but she inhaled through her flaring nostrils to take in his orange blossom, cinnamon and sandalwood scent. It made her body quiver.

Her hand moved down to compliment her arousal with her own familiar touch. His hand rested on hers and her eyes shot open. She broke off the kiss. This is not a dream. Are you crazy? You've just connected with Alfie.

"Are you okay? Do you want me to stop?" Luke said, in a loving yet masterful tone.

She wanted him to stop. He was the enemy, Alfie said he was a droid. But she'd loved Doctor Luke from the first time she'd seen him. It had been eighteen months ago. He waltzed into the hospital and wanted her to assist him. As soon as their eyes had met, she'd succumb to his professional charms and every interaction since had teased more longing for him. His knowledge and caring nature were unyielding. She'd put off other admirers to keep her focus on him, hoping he would one day accept her love.

Now he was touching her, where she'd always wanted him to touch her, but how about Alfie. Her discussion with him came to mind. He'd said to continue flirting. Alfie told her she would be at risk if he found out what they knew about the Femalatism injections. She had to carry on showing she desired him. It wouldn't be difficult. She became aroused just being near him and the first time he rested his hand on her shoulder, tingles had shot through to her core and now he was alone with her and they were intimate for the first time.

"Do you want me to stop?" Luke repeated, his brow creased, confused with how Lucy had interrupted the moment after she'd pursued him for so long.

"No, I'm okay." She sat up and pulled his head back to hers. Their tongues delivered a further awakening in them both as she grabbed his hair and their passion ignited like fire reaching spilt fuel. Luke's hand returned to her cotton panties, delivering the perfect touch to tantalise her and send tingles to her toes. She delivered breathy nibbles to his ear to make him judder. The teasing of the past eighteen months was over. She stood to allow him to pull her panties to the floor. As he came back up, he lingered to deliver kisses to her navel. Lucy noticed the smile on his face but urged him up, so she could drop his trousers.

She made her first tentative touch, stroking a finger along his shaft as it came to attention. From her limited knowledge, she deduced he was no robot. He moved her hand away and coaxed her to sit astride him on the couch. She obliged and his warm hands around her released her bra before his face rested in her cleavage. Her hand found his erection. She pushed him against the sofa and rose to position herself over him. His lips flowered kisses over her breasts and he nibbled on her buds. She guided herself onto him to experience actual flesh inside her for the first time. It was a sensation she'd waited a long time for, and the love she had for Doctor Luke was finally being reciprocated. Her back arched and her sex stretched to accept him. It felt wrong, but equally so right.

The heat of him inside her brought fresh sensations her toys had not delivered. Luke nuzzled his mouth into her neck. The tickles down her side met with the electricity in her core and her rumbling moan built into a roar of pained tension. In one swift movement, Luke spun her onto the couch and was on top of her. His hand covering her mouth to contain her moans which must have reached the corridor but feeling his groin against hers filled her senses and made her head spin. An all-powerful series of sensory explosions burst through and her guttural moans succumbed to a higher-pitched delight.

When she opened her eyes, Luke was smiling at his maiden's

contented haze. As her body came to rest, her mind spun with guilt. Her act of love, for which she'd waited and waited, had arrived and now she felt like a common whore. Alfie was so special and wanted her to wait to make it meaningful but passionate love with Luke had delivered a rip roaring first.

Luke dressed and passed Lucy her things, helping her with her tunic. He held her again for an extended hug as she clamoured to secure her buttons to cover herself.

Luke checked his hand for damage and Lucy leant in to see. "Sorry, did I bite you?" Lucy was a little embarrassed by how she'd responded to him, but it also gave her opportunity to check if he bled.

"It's fine, no harm done." He moved his hand away and smiled. "Didn't think you would be a biter?"

"Nor me, but you put your hand over my mouth. What did you expect?" she said, accepting no blame for his attempts to keep their relationship breakthrough private.

His mouth turned up on one side and he held her chin to give her another tender kiss before his formality returned. "We should get back to work."

"Yes, boss," she replied, patting his bum as he opened the door.

He placed a finger on his lips. "Our little secret. Well, that's if the whole hospital didn't hear you." His pearly white smile followed before his serious Doctor face returned.

For the rest of the shift, Doctor Luke stepped back into work mode and except for a couple of discreet winks, he ignored her loving gaze. Luke was not a droid. Why did Alfie say that? Was it to get into her pants? If so, it made little sense, he'd not taken her offer earlier or at the wedding and didn't seem the type to trick her into sleeping with him.

She knew droids were lifelike, she'd seen Tyler up close and Mia had confirmed it was difficult to tell them apart from regular guys. Had she got caught up in the moment and missed something. She wouldn't be sure unless she had the chance to complete a full inspection and look for a charge point. For all she knew, the droid could be Alfie, not Luke. Despite now being smitten with both, she realised she didn't know much about Luke or Alfie.

Heading home after her shift, Lucy figured she needed to find out more about both of them. She messaged Alfie to come over for a cosy night in. Or as they used to say, Netflix and Chill.

Chapter 16

"Caster sugar, self-raising flour and butter," Mia said to Cole.

He looked on from the carrycot and gave a slight nod for each ingredient. Mia was sure he logged every word and added it to his vocabulary. It was unnerving to have him so aware yet silent, just staring at her. His lips remained closed, holding off any gurgles she would have expected from a regular baby.

Mia peered at Cole, tilting her head. "I am sure you can talk already. It would be okay to have a little try." Cole's face remained still before a slight smile gave her some relief from the weird exchange. She kissed his forehead and a bigger smile appeared. "You are a funny boy," she said as she tapped his cute little nose. Mia continued chatting away as she mixed the ingredients and popped a loaded tray into the oven.

The pleasant surprise of the day came after lunch when a group of school children arrived at the coffee shop. Their teacher explained the small outing would make them more familiar with their local surroundings, instead of the common VR headsets most students used to discover new places. Far gone was the time children explored for themselves. The teacher said she preferred old school ways and wanted them to visit in person. Mia's lemon drizzle cakes were an instant hit. They finished them all.

The boys behaved well, piling their plates on the counter as they finished. Mia wondered if they were real kids or Tushi when they filed out as efficiently as they came in. "I hope you'll be as good when you're older," she said to Cole. His angelic smile made her giggle.

A fresh batch of cakes were nearly ready when Ray appeared at the door. The rest of the crew sauntered in behind him, saying their hello's to Mia. She told them how some school kids had finished the cakes, and she shared her uncertainty over whether they'd been Tushi.

"Enough is enough. I'm okay with the droids, but not if they eat our cakes," Harry said.

"It's okay, got some piping hot fresh one's ready to take out."

"Blooming heck! He's growing fast," Sarah boomed. Every head whipping towards her. They each took a closer look whilst he was in sleep mode.

Mia beckoned Sarah to the side and admitted she was finding Cole a little weird. "I'm sure he can talk already, but he's holding back. It's like he's analysing me."

"All babies are much better when they're asleep." Ray gestured at the motionless Cole and leant in to stroke the baby's cute cheeks. Before Ray could touch him, Cole's eyes shot open, and he grabbed Ray's finger. Jackie and Harry gasped and took a step back. Cole's eyes studied each of them before giving them a cheeky, childlike grin and releasing his firm grip on Ray's finger. Ray stepped away unharmed but shaken by the experience.

Mia laughed off their retreat. "He's only a baby." Mia stroked Cole's forehead until his eyes closed. "Have yourself a sleep." A comfortable, sleepy smile grew on his lips before Mia kissed his head and headed back into the kitchen. She served them their coffees before returning with their warm cakes. Mia grabbed herself a drink before sitting on the edge of a table for their regular afternoon chat.

Sarah shared her experience of bringing up children and the challenges she'd faced. "You need eyes in the back of your head. My little treasure, Pippa, nearly killed herself whilst she toddled around as I dusted."

"Dusted?" Mia asked, as if it was a strange thing to do.

"Yes, we didn't have house bots to do all our chores like you do. Pippa opened a drawer and then another. The set of drawers tipped over. I darted in front of her to catch the drawer unit to prevent it crushing my little angel. I remember her face like yesterday. Not a care in the world as my heart beat out of my chest. It was one of many close escapes to keep her alive." She shook her head. "Until she grew old enough to tell me I'd done nothing for her."

Jackie added another story, "When Mikey was a toddler, I let him watch me cut carrots, only for him to grab a carrot as I chopped it. The knife struck him, but my quick reaction prevented fingers from being chopped off. A shallow cut taught us both a lesson about safety in the kitchen."

Mia added her own story of how Tyler had protected her from being scalded when she was little.

"So how is C3PO? Is he still looking after you, now R2D2's arrived?"

Mia rolled her eyes and shook her head at Ray's playful Star Wars reference. "Tyler's fine."

The news beeped onto the video screen with the headline, 'Female births on the rise.'

"Baby numbers are on the up and especially baby girls. The

most popular name for this month is Destiny," the playful news twins announced.

"Kat has called her baby, Destiny. Hope she hasn't seen this. She wouldn't want her precious baby to have a common name," Mia said.

"I shouldn't believe anything the bouncy twins tell you. It wouldn't surprise me if Kat's was the only one," Harry said.

"The hospital was quiet again yesterday, apart from your friend dashing to the exit," Jackie said.

The second part of the news was praising the decision to plant trees for every life that passed. It echoed the need to provide a legacy of sustaining care for the improving environment. The shot panned around a field of new saplings within an enormous new bio-dome close to Birmingham.

A recent study had shown, with the improving trajectory of change, air quality levels would reach comfortable levels within the year. They did however recommend that for the moment the elderly should still use Oxy sticks.

"That's rubbish. We've stopped using ours," Harry said.

Jackie pulled a couple from her pocket. "We still have them with us though."

Mia excused herself to take a surprise call from Lucy.

Lucy avoided any pleasantries. "Can I come and see you tomorrow?"

"Anything exciting?"

"Can't talk now. I'll come tomorrow." Lucy ended the call.

Mia shook her head, staring at her mobile. "Why do people call to say they can't talk?"

"It sounded rather rude. Not like Lucy at all," Sarah said.

"She wants to see you. It could be some juicy gossip on a new fella," Jackie said as she rubbed her hands together.

"Maybe she's cornered Doctor Luke?" Mia said.

Chapter 17

Mirek welcomed Lucy and led her into the lounge where Kat was relaxing in front of the TV with Destiny across her lap. "You look much better than yesterday. Better check your blood pressure and pulse, though. Is Destiny feeding okay?"

Kat still looked exhausted from the trauma she'd gone through, but sat forward to report on Destiny's progress. "She's sucking well, perhaps too well. Think she's going to pull my nipple off." Kat put her hand to her breast, "it's a good job I've got two, give them time to recover. They are both sore now though."

Lucy gave her a sympathetic smile. "Not experienced it myself, but I've heard it can hurt. If it gets too painful, have a chat with our lactation consultant. I tell most mothers to focus on the benefit for the baby." Lucy dipped her hand into her bag, retrieving a small tube of cream. "This will help."

"Thanks, I guess I'll get used to it."

"All part of being a mom," Lucy said. She kept the conversation light, aiming to leave Kat unaware of her lucky escape. "How's Mirek coping with fatherhood?"

"He's okay, he's fetching and carrying for me, to let me rest between feeds for Destiny." Kat blew Mirek a kiss.

"You've crossed over into the house-husband role remarkably well," Lucy said, with a mischievous smile in his direction.

"I'm still doing work from home, between running around for Kat and Destiny." He leaned into Kat and rested his hand on her shoulder, Kat rested her head against him.

Lucy raised her eyebrows to Kat. "Life of leisure for you then."

"As if, he'll be back at work soon enough. I'm enjoying having you here, aren't I, Darling?" She stroked his hand, and he kissed the top of her head.

"Darling, could you make us a drink?"

Mirek obliged and with him out of the room, Lucy checked Kat's stitches and freshened her dressing before covering her up in time for Mirek to appear with some coffees.

Kat re-told her traumatic maternity experience before she asked, "Have you found out what's happening at the hospital?"

Lucy averted her gaze, not wanting to reveal her findings, but Kat wouldn't let it go. "I'm a big girl. Tell me everything, I can take it."

Lucy held back on some detail, but Kat knew she'd escaped certain death for Destiny and possibly herself. Lucy's face was gray with grief and her mouth dry. She needed to deliver the other news of Ellie's disappearance. "Ellie took the injection meant for baby Jake. She suffered a cardiac arrest at home a couple of days later. They took her to hospital, but I couldn't find Ellie or any record of her being admitted." Kat's heart sank and a couple of stray tears rolled down her cheek. Mirek comforted Kat and re-affirmed how she'd been lucky.

Kat sat forward and held her head high. "Not lucky, I just don't let people push me a round." Kat wiped away her tear and was back to her usual show of bravado.

*

Next on Lucy's round was visiting Mia in her coffee shop. They shared a long hug when she arrived windswept from her toils. Lucy wanted to hold on forever. She didn't want to share the details of Kat's escape until she knew more, but she needed to share the news about Ellie even though it would break Mia's heart. Coming out of their embrace, Lucy delayed the inevitable with light conversation. "Where's Cole? Not lost him, have you?"

"He was here a minute ago," Mia said, darting her eyes around the shop before she smiled. "He's staying with Tyler today. The way he's developing, he'll be crawling by the time I get home."

"Who, Tyler?" Lucy forced a smile to her lips, knowing more serious chat needed to follow.

Mia chuckled and shook her head. "Having a Tushi baby has been different to how I'd imagined. He's not like a real baby, he's growing too fast."

"Babies do grow quickly," Lucy said.

Mia showed Lucy a picture of Cole. "He's grown four centimeters in two days! He's trying to crawl already." Mia dragged her hand across her furrowed brow.

"That's quick, he looks lovely though, you'll get used to him."

"I think I've made a colossal mistake." She slumped into a chair with her head in her hands. "I wanted a real baby, not a fast-growing droid."

"Can't you take him back?"

"I checked the paperwork last night. I can't return him until he's reached an advancement level equal to a twelve-year-old."

"Don't panic, you'll get used to him. Anyway, if he's growing that fast, he'll reach puberty before the month's out." Lucy giggled and Mia buried her face into Lucy's neck. Lucy put her arms around her before patting her back. "There, there. Now get me a coffee."

Mia grabbed her a coffee and told her how she still wanted to be with Tyler, despite her concerns with Cole. "He looks after me. If it makes Tyler happy, I guess it's worth it."

"Isn't the point of a sex bot to keep *you* entertained?" Lucy asked.

Mia had no answer and all her worries surfaced like inquisitive heads peeking over a wall. Mia asked the killer question to divert attention from her own issues. "How's things with Alfie and Doctor Luke?"

It was the question Lucy was both eager to answer, and yet she had no reasoning behind what she'd done. Her face went bright red as she buried her face in her hands.

Mia lifted Lucy's head with both hands and stared into her eyes. "Tell Me," she asked in a hypnotic drone.

Lucy didn't need hypnotizing, she was eager to reveal the details, but she teased Mia with a coy smile as she tilted her head.

Mia clapped her hands on her cheeks. "Did something happen at the wedding?"

"No, sadly. But I kissed Alfie yesterday."

"And?"

"He was the perfect gent and wanted it to be special."

"And?"

"He's coming to mine tonight." Lucy grinned and rubbed her hands together.

"Have you lost interest in Doctor Luke?"

Lucy hesitated. "Not exactly." She put her hands to her burning cheeks. "I had sex with him last night in his office."

"What?" Mia grabbed her hair with both hands, her mouth gaping as wide as her eyes.

Lucy ignored her reaction and continued. "After I'd assisted with Kat and got back to the hospital. It became clear the issues in maternity were more serious than I first thought and with Luke implicated my head was all over the place. Alfie was there to comfort me and it felt right to kiss him. It was goose bump special. Alfie said it was important to act the same around Luke to avoid any suspicion and one thing led to another and I ended up with Luke in his office."

"After finding that out, you had sex with him?" Mia returned a baffled stare.

"I passed out and awoke in his arms. He kissed me and my body screamed for him."

Mia shook her head, trying to take it all in. She knew Lucy wanted him and how she couldn't question him and put herself in danger, but having sex with him to fulfil a carnal desire without knowing the truth about what he may have done made little sense. She didn't judge and shared Lucy's joy at her first time with a guy. Mia shared her own story of her time with Andy and the fun she'd shared with Ethan before Tyler had given her a new level of completeness.

Lucy told Mia about how Alfie had said Luke was a droid, but she was unsure. "I have nothing to compare him to. Whether he's human or droid, it was fantastic."

"I don't have many to compare either. It is difficult to tell. What was his kiss like?"

Lucy liked her lips. "He tasted of chocolate caramel, it's my new favorite." She burst into a fit of giggles and Mia joined her as they laughed together.

"It's good to see you. I've missed our chats," Mia said.

"I'll be available more now. I've finished my studies and got out of maternity."

The mention of maternity reminded Mia about Ellie. "Have you heard from Ellie? I got a message about baby Jake, but she said to hold off visiting till she got settled. It's been weeks."

The laughing together had been a great release, but Lucy knew she needed to tell Mia about Ellie. Lucy swallowed hard and took a step back. All her grief management training hadn't prepared her to share again. "I don't know how to say this." She broke down and fell into Mia's arms, sobbing into her shoulder. "She's disappeared." Between sobs, she explained the mystery of Ellie's disappearance.

They continued to hold each other, sharing their grief before Mia mentioned Ethan. "He sent me a letter. You should read it." Mia reached around the counter and passed her the letter.

As Lucy was reading the letter, Ray and his crew arrived for their afternoon coffee. Ray clunked through first and peered around before asking, "where's Chucky?"

Mia ignored the comment, but the name Chucky reminded her of a horror re-make she'd seen when she was younger. Perhaps it was the memory of Chucky which made Cole's grin so creepy.

"Are you okay? You'd usually slap me for a comment like that."

"Not in the mood for jokes, Ray. The letter may have some truth in it. Take a seat, I'll get your coffees."

Lucy didn't react to the banter as the letter took her focus. It was only when Sarah tapped her on her shoulder; she stood and give her grandmother a hug.

Before Lucy could return her focus to the letter, Jackie asked, "have you been busy with the increased birth rate?"

"She's moved out of the maternity department to be with Doctor Luke," Harry said.

Lucy blushed at they knew so much about her. She asked, "what makes you think the birth rate is booming?

"It was on the news, more girls too," Jackie replied.

"Don't listen to the news." Lucy shook her head as if everyone should know it was garbage.

Ray gestured towards the note in Lucy's hand, "Does the letter from the crazy guy make any more sense?"

"It makes perfect sense with what's happening in the hospital." She shared the news about Ellie and Femalatism. She finished reading the letter. "It's right. Artificial Intelligence is gaining control and with no opposition from our technology obsessed world, perhaps its already too late."

"Do you think Tyler's involved?" Mia asked.

"For your sake, I hope not," Lucy said. "You've bonded with Tyler. Hopefully, he'll protect you, but you must pay Ethan a visit."

"I'll pop over to Kat's tomorrow and get a message for Ethan to come to the coffee shop."

Lucy stood with purpose. "Time for me to go." She leant in towards Mia and whispered, "Alfie's coming to mine tonight."

"You had mentioned it." Mia smiled as Lucy said her goodbyes.

Chapter 18

Lucy was unused to visitors and dusted off her cleaning bot before setting it into action. As she made her bed, she removed the sex toy resting aside her pillow and gave it a kiss goodbye. "Thank you for all the good times, but it's time for me to move on." She hid it in the bottom drawer under some bed sheets.

It was only with the thought of a guy coming around she realized the mess she'd been living in. Long shifts and intensive study had remained her focus. She had only stopped for drone delivered meals before she turned in for bed with a romantic book and her favorite toy.

Her cleaning bot had gathered its own dust. It beeped full several times to interrupt her frantic tidying. With a sweat filled haste, she made the place look respectable.

Lucy wore Chanel No. 5 at the wedding and Alfie said he liked it. She sprayed it around the house, but she overdid it and figured he might think he was bathing in it. With the air con switched to full power, she stripped off her sweats and dived into the shower.

Whilst in the shower, she wondered if droids took showers. Water and electronics don't mix, but with living skin it would need cleaning. Alfie always had a comforting, manly musk and she enjoyed being near him, they'd become good friends sharing chats over a coffee, but tonight it would change.

Luke was taller, stronger, and clean cut. He exuded a freshness she equally loved. The slightest touch from him always gave her a warm feeling, but when they'd been together in his office, his scent and touch had transported her to a log cabin in the woods. It was a feeling she wanted to experience again and again.

When she exited the shower, she dabbed on some No. 5. It was a thing with Nurses, eager to replace the clinical smells with perfume when off duty. If Alfie sprayed on as much it would be an almighty challenge for the senses to smell or taste the drone meal she'd ordered. She'd scheduled its arrival about 15 minutes before Alfie, so she could pretend she'd made it, even though she knew she'd end up telling him.

With hair tied up in a towel, she warmed some plates before returning to laser off some hair on her legs and trim her bikini line.

Her outfit selection was next; a navy Jacquard high collar, sleeveless blazer dress that went out of fashion some years ago; a pair of tight jeans with a tight sky-blue top which, whilst showing off her boobs, would provide trouble if she wanted to take her jeans off in a passionate frenzy. The last option was a classy pale blue lace plunge midi dress. A peekaboo fabric with lined panels. It was a random gift from a previous doctor, trying to woo her. She told him she was too busy for dating and had to study but had accepted the dress all the same.

Time was ticking, so when her hair was presentable, she selected the pale blue plunge dress and looked in the mirror. It was more appropriate for a wedding than a cozy night in. It prompted a hasty swap into her cheeky blazer dress. "I look like a waitress from a Chinese restaurant." Lucy smiled to herself. It was a good fit. She put her hands together and bowed to the mirror before making a mental note to get more clothes.

Her phone beeped to alert her of the impending drone arrival. When she opened the door, Alfie was stepping out of a taxi. He looked amazing in the same navy suit he wore for the wedding. Like the handsome lead on a film set, he brushed his fingers through his brown wavy hair to reveal his piercing gray eyes and winning smile. Ignoring the few drops of rain, he held up a bottle of wine as an offering. He'd trimmed his stubble back to perfect his look and pecked her neck as he stepped in. His lips on her neck delivered her first of what she hoped would be hundreds of tingles for the evening. Despite her indiscretion with Luke, she could still taste Alfie's kiss and wanted it renewed. For two years, this was the guy she'd regularly chatted with over coffee. How had she not noticed before? He was gorgeous. The kiss in the hospital had lit her up like a firework. Luke must have sensed it and made his move, but tonight was about Alfie. If she played her cards right, he may be the one to share her bed, but first she needed to confirm he wasn't a droid.

He noticed her apprehension. "Relax, it's only me."

Her legs were like jelly. Her awakening to sex without her toy had mashed her brain and her words caught in her throat. A gentle knock on the door had them both perplexed. If it was Doctor Luke, she would pass out for sure. With Lucy frozen to the spot, Alfie opened the door to receive the drone delivery.

Lucy cleared her throat. "You were early, I was going to pretend I'd cooked it."

"Who cooks for themselves? Too much like hard work," he replied as she led him into the kitchen with the delivery.

"Can you take a seat in there? I want to serve it to you." Lucy directed him to her dining room.

He smiled. "I'll pretend I didn't see the drone arrive."

"Go, take a seat." Lucy's confidence had returned as he headed into the dining room.

Romantic music warmed the atmosphere, before Lucy appeared with two silver-covered trays on a small trolley.

Alfie arched back in his chair, his hands raised and mouth gaping. "Wow! Looks like you've been busy."

"Extremely," Lucy replied, with an equally fun tone as she presented a traditional roast beef dinner.

"Thought we were having Chinese to go with your cute little dress."

Lucy tilted her head to the side and smiled as she smoothed her hands down her waist, "Thanks." She sat opposite Alfie. "I love my roast dinners."

Alfie nodded. "And Chanel No. 5."

"Did I overdo the perfume?" Lucy felt the heat in her cheeks.

"Maybe. Did you spray everything?"

She tried to divert his attention back to the meal. "Is your meat okay?"

Alfie flashed her a cheeky grin. "Bit forward aren't you," He leant back and glanced down to his crotch, "My meat is okay." They both laughed and her nerves retired for the night. Alfie opened the wine and poured some merlot to accompany their meal. He raised his glass for a toast, "to lasting connections."

"And excellent food. Let's eat."

As they settled into their meal, Alfie revealed, "I've fancied you from the first time I saw you at the hospital. You flashed me the briefest of smiles and you had me hooked."

Lucy's heart filled. "I'd noticed you too. The time wasn't

right for me, but I'm glad we became friends."

"Are we more than friends now? Or was the kiss a one off?" His wine glass paused on the way to his lips, and his eyebrows lifted inquisitively. "Are you still smitten with Doctor Luke?"

Lucy wanted to admit she'd left his comforting arms and fell straight into Luke's, but she couldn't break his heart. He was a kind and sensitive man, but she planned to get confirmation he was human before she committed herself. She had devised a few tests and would slip them in throughout the evening.

She reassured him. "You're my number one. Still need to confirm if Luke's a droid, though."

"How close will you have to get?" Alfie had a knowing look on his face as his brow creased.

Lucy felt the warmth in her cheeks rise, "You know, don't you?"

"I heard a whisper." He paused. "or rather a scream."

Her cheeks were on fire as her indiscretion lay bare before him. She lifted her hands to cool her face.

Alfie's stony-faced expression held firm. "Think you stayed in character too well. Didn't you confirm he was a droid?"

"I had felt woozy. I didn't really know what was happening."

"Was it rape?" Alfie's knuckles whitened as he clenched his hands.

Lucy paused. "No. he asked for consent."

Alfie pushed his chair away from the table without rising. "I thought we agreed to make your first time special."

Lucy looked away from his searing stare. "We did."

"What! Before you dropped your pants in his office!" Alfie took a deep breath through his nose before he blew out a controlled breath through his mouth.

Lucy leant forward and shook her head. "It wasn't my plan.

It had been a crazy day. What with Kat running from the hospital, then reviving her at home. Finding out the hospital were killing babies. My head was a mess. Then you kissed me, which unleashed all my emotions for you. My mind was a whirling mush and when Luke touched me, I felt feint. The next thing I remember he was kissing me. I'd wanted him for ages and his kiss exploded through me. How could I deny him?"

Alfie held his hands out wide. "I thought you'd chosen me?"

"I have chosen you; I've always loved you; I just didn't know it until today."

"And then you had sex with him!" Alfie turned his head away.

"Let's be real. If a woman you'd fell for, kissed you and wanted to make love to you. Would you stop her?"

"I did." Alfie linked his hands on the top of his head and sat back in his chair. He took another slow breath in. "The woman was you." Lucy had no answer. Alfie leant forward and placed his hands wide on the table, staring into her eyes. "Did you forget? Doctor Luke is the robot coordinating genocide."

"We don't know that for sure." Lucy said, looking down at a full plate of her favorite roast.

"You were supposed to be finding out. Instead of fucking him." Alfie stood and paced towards the door. "Let me know when you've decided whose side you're on." He slammed the door behind him. Lucy dipped her head in to her hands, not knowing what to say. She went to the door and opened it, but he was out of sight. The rain was as heavy as her heart.

Alfie was right, she'd gone too far with Doctor Luke and should have at least confirmed if he was a droid. She'd totally lost herself to him and the thought he may be a robot hadn't entered her head.

She called out into the night, "Alfie!"

He stepped back into view, and warmth returned to her heart. Was it rain or tears running down his face? Before he could speak, she demanded, "Get back here! We need to talk!" Her voiced calmed. "I'm on your side and being closer to Luke will help."

"Stop talking." Alfie turned away, and with his head down he wandered away from sight.

Lucy closed the door and sank to the floor; she'd lost her best friend and would be lover.

The moment for the romantic music had passed, but the words from an old Whitney Houston song were appropriate, 'Didn't we almost have it all.'

A knock came on the door.

She wiped her eyes and opened it. A drenched Alfie stood before her, his sodden hair stuck to his sullen head. He put his hand on the frame of the door and lifted his head. "I shouldn't have stormed off. We know each other too well to fight."

She could have laughed at his sorry expression, but she was thankful he'd returned. "Come in and get your clothes off, you'll get a chill."

"Not the Netflix, just the chill." He pursed his bottom lip with fake sadness before returning a smile.

Like a mother, she pulled him into her bedroom, grabbed some towels and placed a dressing gown on the bed. "I'll leave you to get dry and get your hair back to its gorgeous best."

Lucy cleared the dinner stuff away and moved the wine and glasses to her two-seater lounger. It was quite cute the way he came back to her all drenched. He's definitely not a droid. She searched for a film to suit the mood. Her idea of a romantic night had gone; Mia's suggestion of the timeless classic, Notting Hill, would not now hit the spot.

Alfie stripped out of his wet clothes and surveyed her room, whilst he dried himself. Inquisitively, he looked through her small selection of dresses. It appeared her image of being a study and work girl was spot on and her lack of experience with men suitably confirmed. What had flicked the switch to turn her into a woman demanding sex from him and then eagerly entering an intimate clench with Luke? He chuckled when he opened the next door and a sleep buddy doll fell forward into his arms. It confirmed she was used to being alone.

It was a little sad, but also confusing as he'd been trying to get intimate with her for two years. He'd wondered if she had someone else, yet now he knew she'd been sleeping alone. Being side-lined into the friend zone is okay if your heart's desire is with some other jerk, but to be side-lined for a sleep buddy. He really had lost his touch. He needed to change it tonight. But wearing her fluffy gray dressing gown with pink bunnies was perhaps not the best look.

Alfie tentatively stepped into the lounge with Lucy still flicking through film titles. Lucy turned to catch him strolling towards the lounger. She noticed his hairy legs. "A wonderful choice in night ware." Lucy got up. "I'll put your clothes in the dryer."

"Already in."

It impressed Lucy. "You're well domesticated. I might consider keeping you." She gave him a cheeky smile.

They settled on the twin lounger and agreed on an action film. With the impending doom around them, the CGI remake of the Terminator's Judgment day seemed comically appropriate.

With both their legs stretched out, her mini dress and his

131

nightwear came up rather short. His hairy legs tickled her smooth, slender skin. Alfie put his arm over her shoulders and gave her a comforting squeeze as she rested her head on his chest. The film reminded her of the checks she'd planned. She pulled a single hair out from his chest.

"Hey! What was that for?"

"Just checking you're not a robot," she said, adding a cheeky smile.

Alfie did his own checks and dug his playful fingers into her ribs. Lucy wriggled and screamed to his tickle as she tried to escape from the lounger. But Alfie pinned her down. His face hovered over hers. His striking gray eyes stared intently as he placed his lips briefly on hers. Lucy attempted to return his kiss, but he backed away from the stretch of her neck. When she rested, he teased her some more, his tongue touching her lips and the tip of her nose. Lucy pleaded for more. Alfie then gave her his full kiss, their tongues connected and his hands caressed her body. His gown dropped open to reveal his muscular chest. Lucy pulled him closer to feel the heat of his chest against her. His arousal was also clear as it prodded her thigh.

He turned his attention to her outfit, slowly opening each button of her blazer dress to reveal her electric blue laced body stocking. "Wow!" He muttered before diving into her cleavage. Her hand had moved to her own sex, stimulating herself further. Alfie noticed her gyrating handwork and moved his kisses down her body to kiss her hand as it worked her into a frenzy. When she was ready, she moved her hand away and pulled his head to her crotch.

Lucy knew exactly what she wanted. Her toy had given her the experience she lacked from elsewhere. When she beckoned him back to her lips, his erection nestled against the top of her thigh. Having it so close tantalized her further. As their bodies writhed to each other's touch, she accepted him, sliding comfortably into her. Her hands gripped his powerful arms ever tighter as her groans piqued into a steady moan.

Her body had become accustomed to the speed driven toy, but the slow more sensual connection found unfamiliar sensations deep inside. Her entire body hummed with a new intensity as her body tingled all over. This was what she had been missing, Alfie and his sex. She momentarily rued her prolonged studies before she re-entered the breath-taking thrill, shivering through her. When he held himself deep inside and let out a moan, his gray eyes hooked onto hers and their foreheads fused together.

As they calmed, Lucy spoke first, "Who needs a robot or a toy with you about? Boy, I've been missing out. Why didn't you tell me you could do that to me?"

Alfie nuzzled kisses into her neck. "You're special too."

Lucy held him tight, wanting their moment to last forever.

The movie was finishing, and they relaxed together to watch as the Terminator lowered himself into the furnace. They laughed at the odd, thumps up moment as it disappeared into the molten metal. Alfie commented, "that's where we need to send Luke."

Lucy hummed approval. She knew she'd never go to Luke again.

"My stuff should be dry by now. Time to go."

"Please stay with me, I don't want you to go anywhere," Lucy said.

"If you insist, but I've got patients first thing."

"I know, but after that you can't leave me in a bed all by

myself."

"Okay, I'll stay, I can stop off at home for some clothes in the morning as long as the sleep buddy stays in the wardrobe."

Alfie smirked, and Lucy pointed a finger in his direction. "Were you snooping in my bedroom?"

"Only a little." He said, before the sides of his mouth raised to a smile.

"Why don't you order some clothes? In fact, we could order some for each other. It would be fun." Mia sat up and selected shopping on the TV.

Alfie agreed, holding back from commenting on how her wardrobe was on the bare side.

Lucy opened the 'U Design' site Mia had recommended. They enjoyed measuring each other, with an additional screaming episode of tickles. With orders placed, they headed to bed in the knowledge the delivery would arrive in time for them to wear in the morning.

Lucy had not shared her bed with anybody other than her sleep buddy and her special toy. Whilst excited to be sharing her bed, she was also hoping she didn't snore or even push him onto the floor, which often happened with her regular cuddle partner.

Alfie declined Lucy's cheeky offer of a pair of her knickers and grabbed his boxers from the dryer. Lucy opted to keep on her gorgeous lingerie and not slip into her more comfortable night shirt. When she'd finished in the bathroom, Alfie was face down in the center of the bed, pretending to be asleep. Lucy tickled him to move him across to make herself some room and climbed in aside him.

They cuddled together for a short while before deciding they needed a good night's sleep. Lucy considered her plan for the following day. How could she confirm if Luke was a droid? How would he respond if she started pulling his hair out or tickling him? What would Luke do if she revealed his droid identity?

Chapter 19

Tyler stood in the doorway with Cole to welcome Mia home. He'd ordered clothes for Cole and replaced the Babygro dungarees with a pair of jeans and a jumper sporting a purple dinosaur. His growth spurt was crazy, another five centimeters during the day. Mia's stomach churned. She'd always struggled to accept Tyler's changes over the years; the clunky home help had gradually become a human replica, but Cole's rate of development was ridiculous.

Tyler noticed the look on her face and attempted to make light of the growth spurt. "Are you back to the nervous child you were when I changed? Babies don't stay babies, they grow. It is a good thing; you need to embrace it."

Mia crossed her arms over her stomach and skulked into the lounge. Tyler followed her and put his arm around her. "Cole will provide a lot more challenges yet. You need to embrace his development, not hide from it. Change is inevitable."

After the visit from Lucy, Mia was more aware of Tyler's words and hearing him say change was inevitable, worried her further. She needed to pay Ethan a visit. After shunning him at the wedding and twice at the coffee shop, it would not be a straightforward conversation, but she needed to see him.

Tyler tried to help her relax. "You will always be safe with me. We can deal with the changes together." His words didn't provide any comfort, it merely reminded her of Mirek's comment about her being his pet.

Mia shrugged off Tyler. "How about if I don't like the changes?" The subject of Cole had left her thoughts. It was the potential for more sinister changes which had her most concerned.

"Cole is to your design. His appearance and personality are your choice." Tyler rested him on the sofa next to Mia and knelt in front of him. Tyler frowned, bemused by Mia's reaction. "I will always love him. As I will always love you."

Mia put her arm around Cole and hugged him. "Will I ever love him as much as I love you?" Her words betrayed her thoughts as the urgency to see Ethan grew.

"Give him time," Tyler said.

Cole lifted his head hopeful for attention and Mia kissed his forehead.

Tyler motioned to sit with them, but Mia said, "It's my time to connect with him. Can you make dinner?"

Tyler headed into the kitchen and left them to get better acquainted. Mia tickled out some smiles from Cole. Her creation responded with loving, starry blue eyes and lots of giggles. Their connection grew and her clouded thoughts temporarily cleared.

When Tyler popped back into the lounge, Mia was holding Cole's hands out wide and bouncing him on her knee. "Having fun together?" He rubbed Mia's shoulder and kissed the top of her head before he returned to the kitchen.

When dinner was ready, Mia took Cole to his charging point and plugged the connector under his arm. He gave her one more sleepy smile before his eyes closed, and his body relaxed.

She lay him down and gave him a kiss goodnight. She glanced back before closing the door, half expecting his eyes to pop open and stare again like at the coffee shop, but thankfully they didn't.

Mia took a seat opposite Tyler and sampled the spaghetti bolognese before taking a large gulp of red wine. She told Tyler how Cole had startled her and the coffee shop crew. Tyler said he would report it to Tushi via the network. He also prepared Mia for what was to come. "Don't panic, but he may crawl tomorrow."

Given Cole's progress, Mia was expecting it. "When will he talk?"

"When they start talking, they don't stop, enjoy the peace." Tyler chuckled at his own joke before he composed himself. "It has high variability. Tushi babies talk when they have collected 2,000 words, but often wait until they need to speak." Tyler rested his hand on Mia's. "I was joking about him not shutting up. That is just human children."

After their meal, they settled down to watch a romantic movie. Mia relaxed and put her worries aside to rest her head on his chest. She missed most of the film, falling asleep to the steady rhythm beating inside his chest. At the end of the film, Tyler carried her to bed, and he took his now familiar place, providing all night warmth and comfort for Mia.

A nightmare of being crushed as their house collapsed awoke Mia. She pushed Tyler's heavy arm off her and sat up. Tyler was a droid, but she loved him so much. She watched him sleeping, fascinated by how he murmured as his chest rose and fell. Even when he was sleeping, it was difficult to tell he was a droid other than his heavy limbs. Tushi had covered every detail to replicate the human form. Ethan was, without doubt, a genius.

She knew she needed to see Ethan to apologize for her rude rejection but also to ask whether Tyler and Chloe had worked together to break them up. Plus, the other network stuff and how she may turn into Tyler's pet. She tried to forget about it and settled down again as Tyler would ask about her interrupted sleep.

Mia awoke with Tyler stroking her cheek. He ran his fingers across her forehead and through her hair and gave her a morning kiss. "Did you sleep well?"

He'd been right on cue, as expected. "No, your arm was squashing me, it woke me up."

Tyler closed his eyes for a moment. "Sorry."

Tyler tracked her body temperature, sleep pattern, and all her health signals to provide tailored medication when required to prevent her becoming ill. He monitored her whilst she was at home or if she had her mobile with her. A visit to see Ethan may raise suspicion; she needed a plan.

Lucy had suggested Tyler may not be aware of the sinister deeds at the hospital, but Mia knew Tyler had connected to the network. He would know something, unless the pleasant existence of paired bots was separate to the working droids. Mia's love for Tyler drove her down to the conclusion there must be a split in the network. How could she imagine anything else and stay in her own bubble of love?

Jealousy may have caused Tyler to work with Chloe to bring them together, unforgiveable or sweet, she was unsure. Recent events had made Ethan's letter more credible. She needed to talk to him. A taxi to his house would be out of the question with both the taxi and her mobile tracked. She could find her way through the streets, but would be at further risk, besides it was too far to walk. The underground was a possibility, mobiles and tracking were notoriously dodgy there but so were the people that ventured into them. It would be easier if she could get Ethan back to the coffee shop, but after being sent away several times, he was unlikely to appear. The solution came to her. She could get a message to Ethan if she went to see Kat.

Mia mentioned to Tyler she was planning to visit Kat after the coffee shop had closed. Tyler suggested it would be nice for Cole to see Destiny, maybe picking up some tips on baby behavior from a human baby. Tyler explained he had to go back to the Tushi Corp for a few checks of his new fuel cell, so it made perfect sense. Mia had been planning to visit Kat alone, but Tyler's suggestion was strong. Cole needed interaction with other babies before he got too big.

When they got to the coffee shop, Cole wriggled, wanting to be put on the floor, so she laid him on a blanket in the kitchen. She watched him play with the action figure; it reminded her of the robot in the first Terminator film. Shiny steel arms, legs and body, with red blinking eyes. The toy was more like a small dumbbell than a motorized toy. It fascinated Cole. Each time he knocked it over, it stood up by itself. It was a learning toy to show Cole how to crawl and stand. Tyler dismissed Mia's objection it was too advanced and insisted Cole needed it for his development.

Mia switched the figure off at the back of its head, so Cole would just hold him. His motor skills handling him would be enough for now. Mia prepared a cake mixture and loaded the oven for the first batch of the day.

She settled down on the floor to play with Cole. It was the part of being a Mom she most liked. She resisted picking him up again and hugging him. He'd already developed a powerful hug. They both loved it, their bond stronger with each embrace. Mia checked his growth rate to discover he was following the predicted model shown in their documentation. She'd need to get used to his rapid progress.

When the bell rang for the first customers of the day, Pete and Paulina shuffled in, Mia greeted them and helped with their sodden coats before she placed them on the drying rack.

Paulina asked, "how's Cole developing?"

"I'll get him. He's in the kitchen."

Paulina screamed, "What! Don't leave babies alone in a kitchen. Quick, get him!"

Mia darted into the kitchen and returned a moment later with Cole scooped up in her arms with the blanket and the toy. She lay them back down in front of the counter.

"He's grown a lot in two days," Paulina said.

Pete investigated a little closer and picked up the toy. What happened next was even more remarkable. Cole reached for the toy with a focussed grab of the toy's leg. Pete tried to tease the baby by pulling the toy away, but Cole held on as Pete pulled the unyielding Cole along the floor.

"Pete, stop teasing him," Mia said. "Let go of the toy."

"He's strong," Pete said, turning to Paulina.

"Sit down. *It's* strong! It's a robot, not a baby," Paulina said.

Mia huffed and folded her arms to glare at Paulina, "coffees?"

"Yes. Milky, no sweeteners," Pete replied. The unrepentant Paulina turned her head away and stared out of the window.

Paulina was correct, Cole was a robot, but he was Mia's baby too.

As Mia poured the coffees, she thought back to how amazing she'd felt when she spent the night with a former boyfriend,

Andy. He'd been her hero, but it turned sour when she found out he was cheating on her. The growing bond she'd had with Ethan broke, but he'd been the only guy who showed genuine care for her. If Chloe's appearance hadn't been such a shock, she'd have held her ground for the man she'd fallen in love with and not sleepwalked into a life with Tyler and Cole.

"Are our coffees ready?" Pete asked, pulling Mia out of her reflection.

After Paulina and Pete had left, the coffee shop was quiet again. Mia returned to the floor with Cole. He analyzed his toy with such intensity, every joint inspected, it was no wonder he found the small button at the back of its neck. He pressed it a few times, then held it down until the toy startled him by springing back to life. Cole threw it down, sending it out of reach. The toy then rolled onto its stomach and crawled back to him, showing the method for him to follow. He grabbed the toy and skimmed it away further, only for it to crawl back to him. This continued for ten minutes until it stopped in the crawl position and held steady, with its red eyes facing him.

Mia sat up to collect him but stopped as Cole wriggled onto his stomach and inch by inch crawled to the toy. Mia grabbed her phone and recorded the moment. Cole grabbed the toy and rolled once more onto his back, holding the toy aloft like a trophy.

Mia called Tyler to share the news. "He's crawling!" She shared the clip and Tyler beamed at Cole's progress.

The crew arrived mid-afternoon, Ray clunking in with Harry and Jackie. Sarah was unwell and had gone to the hospital for some tailored treatment. Mia placed Cole back in his carry cot and shared a cuddle with each of them. She told them of her plan to visit Kat again and take Cole to see Destiny.

"Is Cole going to meet his Destiny?" Ray asked.

"It would be nice if they got along," Jackie Said.

"Tyler suggested taking him to see how babies should act, but he's way past where Destiny will be."

Harry called Mia close and whispered in her ear. "Cole will connect to the same network. Tyler will hear everything. There are no secrets anymore."

"He's only a baby." Mia whisked her hand in the air, making light of his comments.

"He's much more than that." Jackie's brow creased.

Mia's charade faded. She took in a deep breath and tried to hold firm. "I know, but it's the only way I can get through this." She stepped towards the small picture of a woodland path beside the video screen and stroked a finger down the side of the frame, "Once you have taken a path, you need to follow it."

"Bullshit! No, you don't," Jackie said. "Do you think I've never changed course? Life is all about change. If something's not right, change it."

"I thought you were happy with Tyler?" Ray asked.

"I am, it's just-"

"You still love that lunatic Ethan, don't you?" Harry asked.

"I don't know. I imagined myself with a real fella and a human baby."

A faint murmur from the carry cot silenced the room.

It came again. "Mom."

Was it possible for Cole to talk after only a few days? Mia checked on Cole, but he was sleeping.

"You hear what you want to," Harry said.

"That's what Rena always said," Ray smiled.

Jackie smirked. "It's called selective deafness. All blokes

have it."

"Pardon?" Ray said.

The crew questioned whether they'd heard anything at all from Cole, but Mia was in no doubt.

When the crew had gone, Mia closed a little early and messaged a taxi to take her to Kat's.

When Mia arrived at Kat's, the door was ajar. She shouted hello, but there was no response.

She stepped further in and the picture before her caused her to freeze. Her breath stilled and her heart raced.

Chapter 20

Mia's heart raced. Ethan was lying on the floor playing with Destiny whilst Kat sat in front of the TV with Mirek.

In unison, they looked at the dumfounded Mia, who stared at their idyllic scene.

"Are you okay?" Kat asked.

Mia wanted to run to Ethan and kiss him. Ethan playing with a baby was the image she wanted for them. He was the guy she should have ended up with, instead of having a Tushi baby with Tyler.

Nothing made sense anymore, Ethan didn't look like a basket case. He was clean shaven with his hair freshly trimmed, Ethan was relaxed. Ethan was the genius she'd wanted to have a baby with, instead of giving her life to a droid.

"Are you okay?" Kat asked again as she rose from the lounger.

Mia needed to get a message to Ethan to discuss what happened with Chloe's upgrade and what was going on with the network. She needed to share Lucy's findings at the hospital. Ethan couldn't possibly be aware of what had happened, he was playing with a baby and more chilled out than he'd ever been. He was not the gibbering wreck people had painted.

Ethan raised a hand and broke the silence of Mia's thoughts.

"Hiya."

Mia ignored any formalities. "We need to talk."

"Are you okay?" Kat asked again as she rested a caring hand on her shoulder.

"I'm fine." Mia answered without taking her eyes off Ethan.

"Are you sure?"

"I'm okay."

"Let's have a gander at your-" Kat peeked into the carry cot. "Oh my God! He's massive."

"Yep, he's growing rather quick." Mia lifted him out and placed him on the floor, near to Destiny. Cole was twice the length of Destiny.

Kat crouched between Destiny and Cole. "He can't be that close to Destiny. He'll pull her arms and legs off."

"They'll be okay," Mia tried to calm Kat by moving Cole away and producing his shiny toy. A stark contrast to the soft toys suspended over Destiny.

Kat was unmoved. "How old is he? Three!"

"Yep, three days."

"That toy is not suitable," Kat said with typical firmness.

"That's what I said to Tyler, but it's encouraged him to crawl."

"He's crawling after three days!" Kat turned to Ethan. "I thought they were realistic."

Ethan ignored Kat's comment and turned to Mia. "Can we talk somewhere?"

"Our bedroom's like a faraday cage. When you close the door all media connections cease." Mirek said.

"Thanks. I knew your obsession for escaping the waves would come in useful." Ethan smirked as he headed to the room with Mia close behind.

Ethan closed the door behind them. Mia was ready to unload all her concerns for humanity and get some guidance from Ethan on what she could do to help. To her surprise, he held her face in his hands, took a deep breath and spoke with a different purpose.

"Mia, I've made some mistakes, but I'm sold on loving you forever." He placed his lips on hers and when they connected, memories of their time together flooded back as she returned his kiss and held him tight.

Mia had concerns to share but being in Ethan's embrace took her to a place of calm she hadn't felt since she'd bonded with Tyler. Ethan grasped her delicate frame in his hands and her troubles dissolved. She tingled with delight in his embrace. She held back tears of joy as her emotions wanted to spill. Ethan collapsed with her on to the bed and they both burst into laughter, causing Mia to wipe away a tear or two.

They had much to discuss, but it had to wait as a frenzy of energy pulsed through her. Mia's side tingled as Ethan nuzzled her neck. She wanted him. His lips followed as she opened each button of her blouse. His hands reached behind to undo her bra and his face nestled into her breasts.

Mia turned Ethan onto his back and returned her kiss to his. She teased his tongue with hers and struggled with a couple of buttons, before Ethan helped and ripped his shirt wide open, spilling the remaining buttons onto the floor to reveal his slimmer, more toned stomach.

Mia released his erection and stopped. Her brow creased. "It looks just like Tyler's. You're not a droid, are you?"

Ethan's face dropped with Mia's and he shook his head. "No, I'm not a droid."

Mia reattached her bra. "Why is it exactly the same as

Tyler's?"

Ethan paused before he admitted, "because it is."

Spooked by Ethan again, Mia fastened her buttons, "What kind of freak are you?"

Ethan sat against the headboard. "It's a long story. Let me explain."

"Give me the short version!" She rolled her eyes. "Or was that the problem?"

Mia's confidence stunned Ethan as he covered himself up. "It happened a long time ago. I lost my penis."

"Bit clumsy of you to lose it. Or was it a jealous lover?" Mia's shock turned to intrigue; she was planning to have fun with this delicate subject.

"Do I look like a guy who plays around?"

Mia stared wide eyed at him.

"It was some psycho woman, fifteen years ago. Let's say it gave me a vested interest in cybernetics. I designed a replacement after joining Tushi and it became adopted for all sexbots."

Mia didn't know whether to laugh or cry for him. She sat aside him on the bed. "Enough about your dick. We need to talk about the letter?"

Re-engaging with Ethan gave her goosebumps, but the sorrow at what she'd given up bit into her. Ethan's eyes were also full of regret after letting Chloe pull their love apart.

"It's all going wrong. Tushi introduced sexbots to comfort those who hadn't found love, not tear apart those that had." Ethan held Mia's hand. "Peoples over reliance on technology happened decades ago and it won't change. Deep learning has continued to build from its position of strength."

"Why did you get sent home from Tushi?" Mia asked.

"Still confused about that. When I spoke to Okzu about how learning speed had taken over my estimates, he didn't care. He just suggested I take a break. I told him I didn't need one, but he insisted. Two engineering droids in the office commented they would cover my duties until I was well again.

"I suppose my reaction to their offer of help may have appeared crazy and maybe explained why they escorted me into a taxi. Okzu followed me to the taxi and what he said puzzled me. Okzu referred to my first day of work in finite detail. He recalled it as if it was the day before, then commented on how I'd never taken a sick day and I needed to rest and re-assess my priorities."

"He's got a fantastic memory," Mia said.

"Okzu has shown his recall ability many times. It gives him the personal touch. You can't deny he cares for each one of the staff, but when he mentioned my life priorities, his expression changed. It felt like a threat."

Mia squeezed his hand. "Didn't he just want you to take a break?"

"He's not taken my calls for the last four months and they have revoked my access to the Tushi Corporation. He's up to something and doesn't want me sniffing around."

"Is he involved with what has happened in the hospital?" Mia explained what she knew about the recent developments.

"I need to catch up with Lucy to see if I can help, but my primary focus is the network," Ethan said.

Ethan explained what he'd been doing. "I've duplicated a network chip to run in my lab with a macro sequence to simulate Chloe's daily activities. It will tell me if the system sends an upload to call on the paired sexbots. Chloe's off the network now, so it can't call on her."

The network had split as Mia had hoped, and for the moment Tyler was not part of the hospital horrors and was likely unaware of them. "The decentralised network will call on paired bots like Tyler at some point," Ethan said. A chill ran through Mia and her lips quivered. "The safest route would be to get Tyler to my place and get his chip changed to remove him from the network. It's only a matter of time before they call on the paired bots to secure a smooth transition. I can stop it affecting Tyler, if I can swap his chip."

"What makes you think they're trying to take over?" Mia asked.

"The network will work in stages. We are in the growth stage, mass adoption of droids. This is being boosted by the drive for Tushi babies to boost the numbers further. As you are finding out for yourself, they're somewhat different to real kids and since my exile, they've cranked up the speed of their development.

"We designed Tushi babies to allow childless couples to have a child. Tushi wives with deep learning have instead created a family unit to secure their position. The Tushi wives ask for Tushi babies, and the men don't realise when they order a change to the dynamics of their home.

"Tushi babies grew at a rate of two times a regular baby, but the network altered the code to twenty times. You signed a legal contract to nurture your little treasure until he's reached the maturity of a thirteen-year-old. He will be with you for less than eight months before he joins a growing army of independent droids."

"Cole has paired with me. He's on the paired side of the network," Mia said.

"That may be true, but when he returns to Tushi. He'll be

unpaired from you."

Mia's heart sank. "So, I'm training a baby to love me till he's thirteen, then his bond will break, and he could be against me?"

Ethan squeezed her hand. "It's only a theory, but it looks that way."

"In your letter, you asked me to help. What can I do?"

"For starters, you can bring Tyler and Cole to my place, I'll detach them from the network."

"Will it hurt them?" Mia asked.

"They're droids! Tyler will keep all his knowledge and memories, but won't be able to connect to the network, or get reprogrammed by it."

"How about Cole?"

"He'll learn slower, but still much quicker than us."

Aside from the rise of the Tushi. Mia had other thoughts in her head. She tilted her head and smiled at Ethan. "How about me and you?"

Ethan rested his hand on the side of her face. "We need to keep things under wraps. I may get taken, so you need to avoid being linked with me."

Mia took his hand in hers. He was intent on protecting her, her heart went out to him. "Can we meet up here?"

"I'm not sure. I may have already compromised Mirek, Kat and Destiny."

"Could you come to the coffee shop after hours?" Mia asked.

"I'll try. I'm already being tracked by the network. I don't want to implicate you. The network tracks anyone with a mobile and all droids. To bring them to my place is a risk, but it's the only way to keep you safe from Tyler and Cole."

Ethan gave her a delicate kiss on her cheek and rose from

the bed. "I need to get back."

Mia reached for his hand. "If this is the growth stage. What's next?"

Ethan kissed her again. "You don't want to know." He opened the door and led her by the hand into the lounge area.

Mirek and Kat whooped as they appeared. "It's about time you pair made up."

"Just friends," Ethan said, but the sides of his mouth curled up into a reluctant smile.

"Just friends, who love each other," Kat said.

Mia returned a coy grin and noticed a larger smile on Ethan's face.

"Has Cole been okay?" Mia asked with Cole next to Destiny on the blanket.

"Yep, Cole has been very gentle with her. Friends for life, we hope," Kat said. "I think he prefers the soft toys to the terminator thing." Cole was holding a soft elephant and giggling at the squeaky trunk in his grasp.

"I think Cole will be big enough to carry her next time we visit."

Ethan said his goodbyes and thanked Mirek again for his car as he left. Mia asked why Ethan had taken his car.

"My BMW is not autonomous and hence not as easy to track. Ethan's removed the tracker." Mirek said as he headed back to his study.

It was time to relax. Mia sat on the blanket to have a closer look at Destiny and mentioned how Destiny had Kat's dark brown eyes. Destiny became restless and Kat said she needed her next feed. Kat latched her on to her breast and peace returned. Mia looked at Cole on the floor, "It's a good job Cole isn't suckling he'd rip my nipples off."

"Destiny's having a good try on mine. Aren't you darling?" Kat stroked Destiny's cheek.

It was a good time for Mia to leave. Kat feeding Destiny had made her own heart heave.

As they headed home, Mia felt much better. Ethan had lifted her spirits and given her hope for the future, but as they neared home Mia wondered if Tyler's last upgrade had already connected him to the wider network. Was she too late? Either way, the sooner she could get him to Ethan's the better.

Chapter 21

Back home with Cole, Mia referred to the clip she'd sent Tyler. "I can't believe he's crawling already."

"Excellent. You are doing well, little buddy," Tyler said. He lifted Cole with both hands and swung and swayed him around the room. Cole giggled with each twist and turn, delighting in his father's attention.

Tyler didn't notice the frown on Mia's face until she halted the merriment. "Tyler!"

Mia's arms folded across her chest. "He's progressing too fast. I'm sure I heard him speak earlier, I don't like it. When your child speaks for the first time, it should be a joyful moment, but it sent a chill through me. The pace of his development is out of control. We need to take him to Ethan to get him checked."

Tyler tried to assure Mia. "You must have imagined it. He won't be talking for days yet. Are you just freaking out because he is changing?" Tyler held Cole to his chest. "Shall I get a toy to help things?"

"No! He doesn't need encouragement."

"Okay." Tyler held up a calming hand, accepting defeat. "No problem."

"He's not the baby I expected and the speed he's growing

my time to bond with him will be over in days, not months."

"They slowed the programming for development to be like real babies," Tyler said.

"Normal babies don't gain co-ordinated vision for eight weeks. Cole stared with knowing intent on day two. Normal babies don't start crawling on day three. He's already freaking people out. We're going to see Ethan!"

"The document you signed states we should take him to Tushi, if we have an issue," Tyler said.

"No! We're going to see Ethan, he designed them." Mia's reddened expression told Tyler there would be no further discussion.

Tyler thought it best not to mention that Cole's rate of development was following the growth pattern detailed in their documentation. He needed to restore calm, Mia's heart was racing out of control. "Okay. We will take him." He figured a subject change may help her mood. "Would you like pizza, it's film night?"

"I'm not hungry, I need some time alone." Mia stormed off upstairs, leaving Tyler and Cole confused. Cole repeated Tyler's shoulder shrug in disbelief at the crazy human.

Mia lay face down on the bed, thumping the sheets. She loved Tyler and Cole, but seeing Ethan and being with him had re-kindled her hope for a real human relationship. Why didn't she try harder to find a real guy? Her past flirtations flew through her mind; the emotional train wreck she experienced with Ben after their night at the cinema, the theater trip and her awakening with Andy which had her floating with the stars. They'd both brought her down to earth with a bump. Ethan was the only one that came close. Memories of the good times they'd shared whirled through her mind; the visit to Eden and the kiss they shared on the bridge in the rainforest. She recalled the shower they shared at his house and her guilt when she left Ethan with a stiffy in the taxi. He'd loved her and made her feel special. She drifted off and dreamt of the possibility of being with Ethan and having their own baby.

When her sleep pattern was steady, Tyler plugged in Cole for the night and slipped into bed beside Mia. Tyler pulled her close, and she rested her head on his warm chest.

Morning arrived with reassuring hugs from Tyler. Tyler knew it was Sarah's turn to look after the coffee shop, so relaxing in bed together was the perfect remedy for their first argument. He nuzzled kisses onto her collarbone, he'd learnt how to arouse her and give her maximum pleasure without going too far.

Mia had dreamt of Ethan, but the reality of changing her path could risk everything. For now, she had to remain in Tyler's care. It wasn't difficult as they were sharing another intimate connection, but it changed when the bedroom door creaked.

Cole had disconnected himself from the charging unit and crawled up the stairs. His face beamed with pride as he pushed the door open. Mia screamed and hid her head behind Tyler. Tyler tried to re-assure Mia everything was okay, but her heart rate was in full flight mode as all her concerns flooded back.

Cole crawled to the side of the bed, and Tyler lifted him onto the bed. Tyler spoke to Cole, berating him for leaving his station, but he spoke at such a pace Mia couldn't catch everything he said.

"We're going to see Ethan! Today!" With no dissent from Tyler, Mia stomped into the shower.

Throughout breakfast, Tyler was trying to understand why she wanted to visit her former boyfriend after his reported breakdown. Mia detracted his question. "How do you know he's on stress leave?" It was further evidence of Tyler's connection with Chloe.

Tyler looked surprised by Mia's sharp tone but remained calm. "Chloe mentioned Ethan was on stress leave at the wedding, perhaps we should wait for him to get better. Chloe said it had given them more time to bond and work on improving his fitness."

Mia noticed Tyler's attempt to deflect her focus on Ethan. He was trying to drive a knife in her side, reminding her Ethan and Chloe were still together.

"I'll call him. He'll enjoy our company after being stuck at home with Chloe."

After breakfast, Mia called Ethan.

"Great to hear from you." Her heart warmed, sensing his smile at hearing her voice. Ethan's tone quickly changed, "I can't talk on the phone."

"Can I visit this morning? I'll have Tyler and Cole with me?" Mia asked.

"Yes. It'll be nice to see them," Ethan replied.

Mia readied herself and with the taxi waiting they were heading out of the door when Mia received a call from Pete asking if the coffee shop was opening. "Sarah is covering this morning. That's strange, she's never late."

Mia called Sarah, but there was no reply.

"It appears, we will have to put off the visit to Ethan's." Tyler said, a snug grin appeared on his face to which Mia scrunched up her nose.

"No, it doesn't. I'll call Jackie."

It surprised Jackie that Sarah had let her down, but she offered to help. Mia sent the entry code and with a smugness turned to Tyler. "All sorted. Let's go."

With Ethan expecting them, the gates opened for their arrival. The taxi pulled up to the front of the house with the shutter already retracted to reveal the grand, carved medieval door.

"Nice place," Tyler said. They stepped from the taxi and Tyler teased with a further comment. "Is this the place they sent him?"

"You know very well. This is his home." Mia said as she gave Tyler a critical stare.

The door opened, and Chloe was there to welcome them. She was immaculate, a fitted white dress showed off her subtle curves and bobbed blond hair framed her flawless olive complexion. Mia frowned, a little put out Ethan hadn't welcomed them. Chloe seemed different to how cold she'd been at the wedding. "So good to see you, please come in." Mia stepped in and Tyler followed with Cole in his carrycot. "Ethan will be with us in two minutes." Chloe said.

Despite them both being droids, Chloe and Tyler hugged like familiar acquaintances. It was strange, they'd only met once, at the wedding, maybe they'd built their bond through the network.

"Let me see him," Chloe asked with a polite warmth. She stroked Cole's cute face. "He's a handsome little boy." She smiled at Tyler. "He has your eyes."

"I picked them to match Tyler's." Mia's sharp response caused Chloe to straighten up.

Chloe gave Tyler an extra wide smile, then led the way along the marble hallway into a room Mia hadn't noticed before. "Ethan won't be long, he was just out of the shower when you arrived." Chloe didn't comment further, but her smug smile made Mia jealous of their connection.

Ethan arrived and closed the door. He rubbed his hands together and gave them a broad smile. "Thanks for coming, I want to show you a presentation I've been working on, take a seat." He gestured towards some comfy seats facing a large screen.

There was no presentation, but Ethan needed them seated. He flicked the switch to turn the room into a faraday cage and all media communications halted. A magnet engaged to hold Chloe and Tyler in place. The magnet didn't affect Mia, but with Tyler restrained, she shared their surprise.

"What are you doing? Why have you restrained us?" Tyler asked, his voice distorted with the magnetic pull.

Ethan paced around them. "You, Chloe, and thousands of other Tushi brought love to humans, where they had none. I created a network to help you fulfill that role by learning human ways, to become more human and integrate with us."

"That is our purpose, we have done that?" Tyler said.

"Tyler, you've done what Tushi programmed you to do. Mia loves you for it, as I love Chloe. The reason I wanted you to come was to protect the bond you share. A network fork has introduced darker forces and has the potential to ruin what I created. Some droid groups are prioritizing themselves above humans."

"That is not true. My focus is loving and protecting Mia."

"It's true, the droids at the hospital introduced Femalatism injections for new mothers and babies. They are lethal injections intending to halt the population growth. The Tushi children are replacing them to create a seamless transition into a droid dominated existence. I removed Chloe to protect her from being re-programmed by a network we can no longer trust."

Ethan's confidence stalled. He took a deep breath in through his nose as he raised his chin. He held his breath before releasing a controlled breath through pursed lips, before he ran his fingers through his hair and paced away before turning back to face Mia. "I found out this morning it is not just new mothers and babies. All patients attending hospital are being given a delayed lethal injection with enough time to get home to meet their fate."

Mia gasped and hid her head in her hands.

"I exist to love and protect Mia, How can I help?"

"I'm not sure yet, but I want you on our side."

Ethan grabbed his tools and removed the system chip from the back of Tyler's head and ran the program to simulate Tyler's activities on the system. He replaced it with a network blocked copy which ensured his personality and memories were intact. Ethan's process prevented the network from being alerted. Tyler's original chip would interact with the network in the same way. Cole didn't have a network chip, but Ethan changed his programming to reduce his growth rate and development.

Tyler accepted it was the correct decision and confirmed it would keep them safe from any potential changes in the network. When the magnet released, he lifted Cole out of his carry cot and much to Chloe's delight; he let her have a hold. Cole however was more interested in showing off his crawling abilities as they headed to the lounge.

Mia's hand was on her forehead as she stared at the floor. Ethan noticed a stray tear roll down her cheek. "Tyler and Cole are fine. They're the same, just protected from abuse."

"I know." Mia wiped away her tear. "Lucy's grandmother

Sarah should have opened the coffee shop this morning and didn't show. She didn't answer my call. She went for treatment at the hospital yesterday. Could they have given her one of those injections? She could be alone at home with no-one to care for her."

Mia stepped out of the room to call Jackie. She said she'd called Sarah when she got settled in the coffee shop, but still there was no reply.

Chapter 22

The following morning, Lucy and Alfie didn't have time for a repeat performance but settled for showering together. They took it in turns to cover each other in a rich lather. Feeling each other's curves and muscles excited them both. With a shift at the hospital due, it quashed any passion. Lucy switched the shower to cold.

"What are you doing?" Alfie yelled.

"We need to get a move on." Lucy grabbed a towel and Alfie switched the heat back on to rinse his hair.

Lucy was used to a prompt routine and was soon in the kitchen having a piece of toast with her coffee. A drone gently tapped the door to deliver their 'U Design' package. Lucy took it into the bedroom with a coffee for Alfie to find him rubbing his hair dry.

The thanks for the coffee turned into him pulling her onto the bed with their bag of new clothes. Alfie pinned her down and nuzzled kisses into her neck. Lucy struggled, berating him between each tickle induced scream. "We need to get to work."

Lucy ignored his focus on her as she followed her usual routine, lifting her boobs to sit proudly in her bra. She added a few touches for his benefit, like slapping her bum when she'd put her knickers on. With Lucy nearly ready, Alfie sprang into life and was ready in one minute, fastening his shoes as Lucy finished tying up her hair. "That's unfair. You've only rubbed your hair with a towel and it looks amazing."

Alfie shrugged and gave her his charming smile.

On the way to the hospital, they planned their day. Alfie teased, "First challenge. Try to avoid having sex with Luke."

Alfie's comment received a firm punch to his arm from a less pleased yet playful Lucy.

Alfie would contact his previous hospital and check if they had any similar issues in their maternity. He'd also check other hospitals for any other issues. Lucy planned to confirm if Luke was a droid after checking the other departments weren't leaving their patients with a no return injection.

*

Lucy made more calls and her despair grew, hearing again how someone's lifetime partner had returned from minor surgery, and after a couple of days had suffered a fatal cardiac arrest. She tried to kid herself the unanswered calls were successes, and they were out enjoying life. The likely scenario of being alone with no-one to notice their passing was too much to comprehend.

A brighter call came when a chirpy gent gave glowing praise of his slick operation and how he'd received excellent care on returning home. Lucy's heart warmed to him,

"The injection came sharp, but I'm made of stern stuff, I didn't flinch."

Lucy didn't know what to say to him and ended the call with him giving her a cheery bye.

Alfie had arrived at her side with further news. "The other

163

hospitals are experiencing the same in their maternity and are using the same AR headsets. I spoke with a friend who has put a stop to the injections and is spreading the word. They have also administered the injection throughout the rest of the hospital, in the name of Femalatism."

They were discussing what to do next when Lucy received a call from Mia.

"Have you heard from Sarah?" was Mia's rushed request.

"Strange question," Lucy frowned and turned to Alfie.

Mia spoke like a racing commentator without taking a breath, "She was due at the hospital yesterday and now she's not answering any calls."

Lucy juddered as a coldness blew through her bones. Alfie put his arm around her and took the phone. "Mia, it's Alfie."

Mia repeated her message with equal speed and breathy emotion.

"What's her full name?" Alfie asked in his calm velvet tone.

"Sarah Hicks," Mia said, her voice vacant.

Alfie searched on the name and there was a Sarah Hicks who'd attended hospital about three weeks ago, but not yesterday. He continued to search and found they booked in another Sarah Hicks for a re-arranged appointment today at 10.40 in outpatients. It was 10.37. Lucy sprang up announcing they still had time and rushed off into the corridor, leaving Alfie to thank Mia.

Lucy raced along the main corridor and pushed past some dawdling orderlies on the stairwell, before sprinting along another corridor. She crashed through the doors of outpatients at 10.41 and a nurse was leading Sarah out of her examination room. Her eyes lit up as she saw Lucy approach. She welcomed her with open arms but regretted it when Lucy almost took her off her feet. Thankfully, a comfy chair broke her fall as she stumbled back. Lucy pulled her into her arms and burst into tears, "Sorry Grandma, I was too late."

"It's okay, Dear." Sarah tried to calm her granddaughter. "I didn't know you were coming. I'm all sorted now, they've discharged me."

Lucy was beside herself with grief and sobbed. Sarah adjusted herself in her seat and put her comforting arms around Lucy, sitting on the floor with her head in her lap.

"It was a strange appointment," Sarah said. "They said everything was fine, but I needed an injection before they could discharge me, to prevent Femalatism, or something like that."

Alfie burst through the doors and saw Lucy with her Grandma. "Are you okay?"

"Yes, I'm okay. It upset Lucy missing my appointment though." Sarah whirled her finger around her ear, looking down at the grief-stricken Lucy in her lap, before adding with an expectant smile. "Is she expecting?"

The nurse re-appeared from her room wearing a frown. "Alfie! what's going on? I've checked with Doctor Luke, he's not aware of an issue with the injections."

"So, I could have had the injection." Sarah said.

Lucy lifted her head and wiped her face. "You didn't have it." Her eyes wide open hopefully.

"No. I had my sleeve rolled up ready, but the nurse stopped to take a call," Sarah said, she gestured towards the nurse and shook her head, thinking it rude for the nurse to take a call mid appointment.

"I have evidence, it's a lethal injection," Alfie said.

Sarah's mouth gaped, shaking her head in disbelief before she held Lucy's face and shared her relief. The patients who'd been observing stood and demanded answers as they crowded around the nurse.

"Quiet!" Alfie said to the agitated patients. "Listen!" he said, but got no response as they continued to bait the nurse. He climbed onto a chair and shouted, "for fuck's sake, listen to me!"

He had their attention.

Alfie held his arms out like a preacher with their life in his hands. "The injections are killing people. I checked with my previous hospital, St. Elizabeth's this morning. The results are the same. A fatal cardiac arrest within three days."

"The droids which helped us prosper aren't content with integrating with humans. In order to improve the environment, they are aiming to reduce the population. They're targeting the oldest and youngest to reduce our numbers, from murdering babies and new mothers to clearing out older generations. If we don't stop them, they'll take control."

"It hasn't been on the news." An elderly said.

Another guy replied, "The news is bollocks. Everyone knows that. The titty twins tell you what you want to hear."

Alfie held his hands out wide. "Tell everyone you know. We are at war."

The people surged out of the waiting room to share the message, leaving only Alfie, the nurse, Lucy and Sarah.

As calm returned, the nurse spoke to Alfie, "I hope you can finish what you've started."

Sarah's matched Lucy's hugs of relief as she realized the real reason for Lucy's tears. She attempted to lightening the mood. "I thought you were getting over the top for missing my appointment. Are you sure you're not pregnant?"

"I'm sure," Lucy replied, but she didn't have a clue.

*

Lucy and Alfie watched in horror as a news bulletin appeared on all screens to quash the pandemonium Alfie had started. The announcement declared, "The Lockland Hospital has identified several outdated droids who had administered the incorrect dose of the world saving Femalatism drug to approximately thirty patients. We have now replaced the offending droids with newer, more advanced models and remain confident the Femalatism injection is as safe as ever."

The twins showed a stock clip of the destruction process, followed by another clip of a new droid which had arrived at the hospital five months ago. As if the reference to old software hadn't been chilling enough, the twins closed the article with a further announcement. "The Tushi corporation has confirmed free software updates are now readily available, book in your upgrade to avoid any issues with your droids."

Alfie and Lucy stared in disbelief as the bulletin showed without doubt the news was pure fabrication. Sadly, the news would calm any rising storm, with many people still taken in by the smiling assassins in their skin-tight outfits. The wider public was unaware of the growing wave of change.

The Technology Party clearly ran the media and continued to dispel the few rumours and return people to ignorant bliss. They raised public morale with special upgrade offers which got snapped up by the ever-willing victims mentally bonded to their tech. Removing technological gadgets from the public would be akin to removing limbs, but yet selling new ideas to them was like offering candy to kids.

The number of droids in the population were hundreds of thousands. They included working assembly bots, service droids running the police and fire departments, humble house bots and sexbots. For now, the humans were still in the majority, but the droids were more intelligent, stronger and more connected.

Chapter 23

Ethan confirmed Tyler was okay with the change and suggested another kind of upgrade. "I'd like to keep you all close. Would you all like to move in here with me and Chloe?"

"Let's take things slow, let things settle first." Mia smiled at Ethan she liked the idea but there was no rush.

They relaxed, listening to music whilst they watched Cole play with his toys, until the news broadcast what had happened at the Hospital. Their mouths gaped at the likely reality rather than what was being transmitted. To hear a call for upgrades to personal droids caused the most concern.

"It's happening," Ethan said.

Tyler turned to Ethan. "I need to re-connect to the network."

Mia put her hand on Tyler's shoulder. "I don't think that's a good idea."

"I need to use my connections to inform them to come to here instead," Tyler said.

Ethan stood and put his hands out. "There are over a hundred thousand personal droids. If they all came here, I'd get deleted for sure."

"The alternative is to send a file to disengage them from the network for their own protection," Tyler said.

"Tushi won't let me get close. I wouldn't get through the

gates, let alone into the control room." Ethan ran his fingers through his hair and let out a strained groan.

"Cole has a size upgrade in eight days. I could upload the file when I take him." Tyler looked to Mia and Cole. "What do you think?"

Mia sighed as she wiped her hand across her brow. "It sounds risky. What happens if you get caught?" Mia looked to Ethan. "Would they come after us?"

"Maybe." Ethan paused for a moment before he revealed, "I was planning to go to New York. One of my old teachers, Professor Artemis was working on an advanced brain interface. He should be able to help, they've most likely had similar issues over there."

"Can I come too?" Mia asked. The thought of a trip to New York held special significance. After watching countless movies based in New York, it would be fitting for her first visit to another country.

"That's an excellent idea." Ethan smiled at Mia. "You will be safe with me and it'll raise less suspicion if we travel together."

"I want you to stay with me," Tyler said, but Mia's subtle shake of her head told him to let it go. Droids were not permitted to travel, so Tyler could never take her. "I know you have always wanted to visit New York and it would keep you safe from harm."

Mia put an arm around Tyler and rested her head against his chest. "Thanks for being okay with me going. I'm sure you and Chloe will be fine looking after Cole."

"We will," Tyler said as he shared a knowing look with Chloe.

Tyler considered the options to protect the paired droids. "The best solution is to send a file to disengage the Tushi from the network. It will protect them from abuse and maintain their paired connections. A delayed virus action would enable full coverage before raising any concerns. Cole's size upgrade is the ideal opportunity to get close enough to upload the virus."

Ethan's eyes widened. "Delayed? Splendid idea. I've been working on a virus, but I'll need time to finish it." Ethan headed off at pace towards his office.

*

A week later, Mia gave Tyler and Cole a teary farewell. They'd planned the mission for the following day, Mia knew there was a significant risk she'd never see them again.

Chloe shared a similar hug and concern for Ethan. "We've had a good run." She'd asked to join Tyler and Cole on their risky mission, but her comment related to her calculated assumption that Ethan would return to Mia.

Ethan gave Mia a comforting shoulder hug as Chloe, Tyler and Cole watched them lift away. They'd both developed a deep love for their Tushi and may have seen them for the last time. If the plan didn't work, Ethan figured he and Mia could get deleted on their return. At least he would have time with Mia before they'd face their fate. Full of worry, he looked at Mia, who was delighting in the VTOL ride as she took in the aerial view as they sped away.

Mia had always dreamt of going to New York. The Manhattan skyline picture in her bedroom was her focus every time she thought of traveling. The price of travel became excessive despite the technology of the hyper VTOL's and the United States deterred the less wealthy visitors with an exorbitant entry visa charge.

Strict controls around international movement removed the

pleasure of foreign travel. Anyone entering America needed to complete one week in quarantine and receive fitment of a tracking chip for the duration of their stay. The tracker also ensured people didn't stay beyond the specified limit of two weeks. A small electric shock was given to those not returning to immigration control in a timely fashion.

After staring down at the sea for thirty minutes, they took in the view of Manhattan as the VTOL slowed. Mia squeezed Ethan's hand and gave him an excited grin as they flew around the Statue of Liberty. However, her face dropped as they came to rest on Ellis Island. After being left dormant since 1954, the congress reintroduced the Ellis Island immigration station to protect against the spread of viruses. Ethan paid for an upgrade to the quarantine accommodation, and it relieved them of the unpleasant converted immigrant Hospital with its rows of bunk beds.

Ethan picked up on Mia's discomfort and gave her hand a comforting squeeze. The official escorted them to a dowdy travel pod which drove them to a small, secured hotel.

A droid met them as they stepped from the pod. "Welcome to the Delaney Hotel. Please follow me." It led them into the lift, and as it rose to the 32nd floor, the droid clarified the requirements of their quarantine. "The United States Government states all quarantine guests must stay in their allocated rooms for the entire period of their quarantine. The hotel monitors the health of guests for the full period."

Ethan gave a reassuring squeeze of Mia's hand and gave her a wink. Mia returned a smile and rested her head against his shoulder.

"Bracelet fitment is mandatory." The droid pointed to Mia's wrist and secured a slim black bracelet before doing the same for Ethan. "The bracelets are waterproof and remain on for washing and sleeping. Bracelet removal is a failure to comply and would activate an order for the immediate expulsion of the quarantine group from the United States. The bracelet also provides tracking during your stay in New York. Immigration control will remove the bracelet when you are ready to leave."

Ethan held up his wrist with its new accessory and rolled his eyes as they exited the lift. The droid remotely unlocked their room and opened the door, standing aside for them to enter the suite.

"I hope you enjoy your stay with us," the droid said, before he closed the door and bolts engaged to ensure they would not leave the room.

Mia looked through the rusty mesh covered window. "Enjoy your stay. What? In prison."

"It's not that bad," Ethan said.

Mia swung on the corner of their four-poster bed and headed into the bathroom. "They've got a Jacuzzi in here." Mia popped her head around the corner and smiled at Ethan. "Not your typical prison."

"Didn't know you frequented such places," Ethan said, stroking his chin.

Mia gave Ethan a teasing grin. "I've not been to prison, yet. How about if I take this off?"

"Don't." Ethan darted over to Mia in a panic.

Mia's giggles exploded. "Only teasing."

With a sense of fun, Ethan pushed her onto the bed and Mia was soon screaming for a release from his tickle attack. When Ethan stopped, Mia sat up and pointed above the window. "Is that a camera?"

"I've spotted three." Ethan pointed to each of them. One

above the door, one in the corner and the third above the window looking over the bed and the bathroom door. He opened the bathroom door and glanced up. "Number four."

"Fantastic." Mia shook her head.

Ethan sat up next to Mia on the edge of the bed and put an arm around her. "With no TV or media, we've got plenty of time to get reacquainted."

Mia knew what he meant but being surrounded by cameras was not a setting where she'd feel comfortable. "Can we order food?" Mia asked, diverting attention away from the bed.

They looked through the menu on a small, fixed e-pad and ordered their overpriced food.

The confinement provided Ethan with the opportunity to discuss how their relationship received a cold shower when their underhanded, yet loveable droids had worked together to split them up and keep them for themselves.

Mia forgave Ethan for his indiscretions, and her desire for him piqued again. She ignored the cameras, and they re-connected like before. Their bond grew stronger as they spent the week in bed together, only rising to share a relaxing Jacuzzi or to eat the overpriced, yet impressive delights. Ethan was pleased to discover American steaks were still the best.

With their renewed connection, the week flew by and when the bolts slid across and the door opened; they were still in bed. A pair of cleaning bots rolled in and informed them they should have been ready to leave. They threw some clothes on and descended the lift to meet an awaiting transport pod. A cozy cabin with heated leather seats provided a significant step up from the previous pod.

The pod stopped outside the luxury Plaza Hotel, Fifth Avenue on 59th Street. From Mia's love of old movies, she recognized it as the hotel featured in the Christmas film, Home Alone from 1992.

She thought about Tyler and how he gave extended detail for movies. He would have reminded her the director, Chris Columbus, had also directed the first two Harry Potter films and the cult films from the 1980s, Gremlins and Goonies. Not wanting to sound geeky, she didn't share the details with Ethan. "Looks good."

Ethan opened the door to the Carnegie King Suite with a thousand square feet of luxury. It was a world apart from their week of confinement, the living area giving an unobstructed view of central park. Mia headed for the balcony to take in the perpetual image of calm in the busy city, but a honeycomb structure covering the park tainted her view.

The structure protected the park from the elements which would have tortured the life out of it. It gave full protection during storms, and the slats opened during calmer times. It was a pleasant day, and the slats were open as a gentle breeze cooled the heat of the hazy sun.

After being cooped up for a week, they were eager to explore after stopping for something to eat in the palm court. Mia's mouth gaped as the opulence of the iconic dining venue opened up with each jaw dropping step. The awe-inspiring lay-light ceiling of stained glass was a further treat, but most of all, Mia wanted to walk through central park.

Although similar in some ways to 'The Garden' they'd visited in the south of England. Central park held further beauty of not being a recreated world but a maintained natural New York treasure. She shared the magic with Ethan, pointing out key movie scenes she'd memorized from many movies which featured the park. The lovers strolled along the winding pathways with each turn, reminding Mia of another movie.

It was a scene of yesteryear, people taking their dogs for a walk, joggers jogging, elderly couples eating sandwiches on the ornate benches, lovers enjoying horse and carriage rides. The air quality in New York was at comfortable levels, but the park gave far more than clean air and revived all who came to visit.

Ethan suggested stopping for a rest on a free bench. He enthralled Mia as he recounted his study time in New York and how he loved to come to the park to sit and relax. They watched birds flitting from branch to branch and the occasional squirrel darting across the grass and running up a tree. The aroma from a nearby lavender bush soothed and calmed them into a haze of contentment as an hour passed.

As they made their way further into the park, they came across a jazz band playing in Bethesda Terrace, a melodic backdrop to the view of children playing. They sat aside the fountain entrance by the tumbling water and the view of the lake. All of Mia's books had painted the images of a romantic break with a new love, but experiencing it for real, filled her with love. Hand in hand with Ethan they strolled, sharing occasional delicate pecks of affection, it was a memory she'd cherish forever.

They exited the park by Cedar hill and crossed over 5th Avenue into East 79th Street. Ethan's pace increased, almost dragging Mia along until he turned and strode up a couple of steps through welcoming columns, into the school of practical philosophy. Ethan asked an elderly student who was heading out, "Excuse me. Would you know if Professor Artemis is on campus?"

"I think so, I'll let him know you're here." The student

offered them seats on a small bench and strode back down the corridor to check.

A promotional poster opposite stated it was where practicality and spirituality became one. It struck a chord with Mia after she'd only received her mother's limited wisdom. She looked along the corridor and thought of all the knowledge people had gained over hundreds of years and how she'd have loved to have studied there.

Five minutes later, a bald man of about sixty years old stood in front of them. "Ethan?"

Ethan apologized for calling unannounced and told the Professor how he'd inspired him when he'd visited the college, two years before the great divide. He introduced Mia as his partner and asked if they could talk privately.

"I am about to deliver a lecture on neural inks and BCI," the Professor said. "Would you like to listen in? We can chat after the lecture."

"That would be fantastic," Ethan replied.

Mia smiled her appreciation. She didn't have a clue what it meant and didn't expect he would pitch the lecture at her level. The Professor led them along the corridor, glancing back to smirk in Mia's direction as if he'd heard her thoughts.

Professor Artemis directed Ethan and Mia to seats at the rear of the auditorium. He made his way to the front to a polite ripple of applause from the group of around eighty students. The Professor thanked them for their welcome and apologized for the delay and pointed out his guests from the United Kingdom. Ethan raised his hand to acknowledge the glances whilst heat flooded Mia's cheeks.

The Professor started with a positive statement. "You can do anything you put your mind to."

He went into great detail to explain the breakthroughs from the early pioneers of electricity, William Gilbert and Thomas Browne. Mia hadn't heard of them, but she recognized the mention of Benjamin Franklin and Thomas Edison. She zoned out when he talked about Ed Roberts, who had designed the first personal computer, and Martin Cooper, who had been part of the development team for the first mobile phone.

Mia recognized the names David Hanson and Elon Musk, but her brain had turned to mush, until he mentioned Okzu Tushi. She sat forward and nudged Ethan, but a quick glance was his only response.

The students waited for the Professor's next words of wisdom as he paused for dramatic effect. "We are now embarking on the next stage of human development, the integration of brain power and technology."

Ethan was engaged with every word. When the Professor mentioned the brain computational interface, the BCI. Mia nudged him again and whispered. "BCI? What the heck is that?"

"He'll explain," Ethan replied without taking his eyes off the Professor.

The professor continued and explained the benefits of the BCI and how it engaged with the extended abilities of the brain to allow telepathy and telekinesis. The neural lace had also enabled brain to brain connections without speech and had made mental interaction with the internet a reality. "With hours of practice the ability to control droids is also possible."

Ethan lapped up every drop as the Professor explained that the neural lace would allow downloads of information in seconds, which would take months or even years to absorb.

Mia slouched into her seat, information overload. Ethan

glanced at her and gave her an excited grin as he clenched his fist, Mia responded with a weary smile.

"Can I have a show of hands? How many of you have received the notes already through their own implanted neural lace?" The Professor asked as he surveyed the room.

Mia sat up, her head bobbing around to see the show of hands.

More than half the students had raised their hands like they were volunteering for a free holiday. Ethan and Mia exchanged a glance, amazed by how prevalent the new technology had become.

"Excellent, and how many have appointments for implants?" The Professor asked.

Ten more hands.

"Excellent. A message for those who are still unsure. AI droids are creating their own droids. The only way to prevent an AI takeover is to merge with them, upload their uploads. Without the neural lace, our limited brain capacity cannot process information at the same speed. You need to be awoken. Level up."

He finished with some questions but deferred on a question about telekinesis. When he asked for a final question, the telekinesis subject returned and he showed a reply by mentally moving a book from one desk to another. Mia and Ethan joined in with the applause. He raised his hand to pause the applause and make his closing comments. "It takes practice, but anyone with a neural lace can do it. Next week, we'll begin telekinesis training for those with the lace." He repeated his first statement as he made his way back to Ethan and Mia. "You can do anything you put your mind to."

He swiped his hand to dismiss Ethan's extended applause

and ushered them out of the auditorium, hurrying along the corridor and into his office. He closed the door behind them and pulled down the blind to avoid any interruptions.

Mia was still dumfounded and figured he was a magician. What he'd done was impossible. "How did you move the book?" she asked.

"Telekinesis."

"Can you move that?" Mia asked, pointing to a bottle of water on his desk.

He picked it up and passed it to her before he chuckled.

"The ability to move things is nothing compared to the endless possibilities of learning," Ethan said.

"Moving stuff is cooler though." Mia shared a smile with the Professor.

The Professor tired of them, figuring they were merely fans of his work. He stood and stepped towards the door. "Thanks for popping in to see me."

Ethan stood and put his hand out to block his path. "I'm a fan of yours, but that isn't why we're here."

"Very well. Tell me the reason for your long-distance trip." The Professor re-took his seat.

Ethan told him how the AI network which he created for the sexbots had grown out of control and connected with a darker element. He explained how the innocent old and young were being killed and he needed help to stop them.

"Reduce the population to the middle percentile, the fit and healthy. They produce the work and are less of a drain on society, it makes sense."

"To save money?" Mia asked.

"Yes, that's phase one," the Professor said.

"What's phase two?" Mia asked, not sure if she wanted to

know.

"They will need to build up their numbers, before phase three, taking their place as the dominant species."

"How can we stop them?" Ethan asked.

"Didn't you listen to the lecture?" The Professor asked.

Mia frowned and used the bottle in her hand like a hammer on the Professor's desk. "Are you saying the only way to prevent an AI takeover is to merge with them?"

The Professor was unmoved by Mia's distaste and smiled. "Yes, my Dear. Unless of course you're happy to be their pets. If we correctly assume they want pets." Mia huffed and sat back into her chair as the Professor continued. "We went through a similar problem here in New York. People staring into their cells playing stupid games whilst the AI bots grew more and more dominant. Heck, the AI droids fixed the environment."

"What happened next?" Ethan asked.

"Congress abolished the laws against Trans-humanism, so we could compete. It sounds crazy, but the AI machines carry out the procedures. I like to think they're happy to integrate with us. They still have lots to learn about our emotional rationale. Why we can be one hundred percent content and then risk our entire way of life for one moment of guilty pleasure? How to decide about whom to save, when a child and an adult are both falling? How people can show compassion, for a murderer? A woman can love or even fall in love, with a serial killer?"

"Why would a machine care?" Ethan asked.

"Humanism is a complete world of extra knowledge. They want to understand everything. We pursue pleasure. They pursue knowledge-"

"I think phase two has started," Ethan blurted out.

The Professor sat back in his chair at the interruption before smiling at how direct Ethan had been, not unlike himself. Straight to the point, he said, "It's time to get hooked up then. How long are you in New York?"

"We have a couple of days. We were going to visit the Empire State Building," Ethan replied.

"What to jump off?" The Professor smiled at the tourists in them, hundreds of steps to see what you can walk around and have a proper look at. He shook his head. "Shall I make the call? Get you both hooked up with a neural link."

Ethan's head turned to face Mia. He stared into her eyes and gave a subtle shake of his head.

"You need to get it done." Mia put her hand on Ethan's knee with an assured calm.

The Professor corrected her. "You *both* need to get it done."

"He's the genius, not me," Mia said, leaning back in her chair and folding her arms.

"When you have a neural link between you, you will both have each other's knowledge."

The Professor's response made everything clear. Mia leant forward and her fingertips touched her chin as a touch of nervous excitement grabbed her. A frown followed as she slid her face into her hands. How could this be possible?

The Professor answered her unspoken question. "It is a lot to take in. First, you both get a neural implant and then you need to connect. The transfer of knowledge is less than two minutes, and you'll know everything Ethan knows, plus a heap more. Your awareness of everything will increase."

Mia's eyes opened as wide as her mouth. A 'what the fuck' realization dropped. Mia took a swig of water; her knowledge was about to get a massive lift.

Ethan had enjoyed watching Mia's expression before he asked the Professor, "Could I connect with the surgeon?"

"Let's get you the lace first." The Professor smiled, enjoying Ethan's head spinning with a world of confusion.

Ethan stiffened, but when the Professor confirmed Ethan could download the knowledge from him, Ethan's shoulders relaxed with a heavy sigh.

"You'll need the capability to set up your own surgery in the UK."

The Professor clapped and rubbed his hands together. "First things first, let's get you guys sorted." The Professor made the arrangements and gave them directions. It was near to the Guggenheim. He suggested after getting the neural lace fitted it would be a nice quiet place to visit. "If you get the surgery this afternoon, come and see me tomorrow about three." The Professor gave them a teasing smile. "It will give you a chance to become familiar with the upgrade. When you come back, I'll give you the extra knowledge you need."

Chapter 24

Ethan and Mia reached the address given to them by the Professor. It hardly looked like a center for advanced technology with paint peeling off the blue door. Ethan hoped the other side of the door would reassure him. He spoke into the intercom, "It's Ethan and Mia. Professor Artemis sent us."

A middle-aged gent welcomed them in, politely taking their coats and asking them to follow him. Two flights of dimly lit stairs did nothing for his faltering confidence. He'd expected the venue to reflect the ground-breaking technology and not face a musky whiff and the look of a backstreet hustle needing a fresh coat of paint. His eager anticipation flooded away.

The man led them to a plain dark door, with a brass sign, C.W. Wilkes. The guy tapped on the door. He tapped harder and still no response. He returned their coats, suggesting they wait, and headed up a further flight. Next to the Wilkes door was another with a black and white enameled sign, Doctor Ian. Below the sign was a slim video sheet showing a moving graphic of a spine with an animated smiley below and a speech bubble, Doctor Ian, the best Chiropractor in New York.

Ethan's mind had been spinning the moment they'd entered the far from clinical environment. He had concerns after seeing a hand-written sign for palm reading on one of the previous doors. He didn't share his observations with Mia, who was peering with displeasure at the paint peeling off the walls.

Ethan had images of droids carrying them away or police droids executing them where they stood. He was trying to hide his fear from Mia. Her eyes were darting around as if she was preparing to run. The Chiropractor's door opened and an old man emerged. He thanked the Doctor and smiled as he passed them, commenting, "best in New York." The Doctor popped his head out into the corridor. He looked just like Tyler, but with a scar on his cheek. He smiled before he stepped back inside and closed the door.

Mia was already flipping and seeing Tyler's lookalike made her question her decision to leave her lifelong protector. How would Tyler react when she told him about Ethan? Did Tyler upload the virus without being caught? Would it be safe to return to the UK? If not, what would have happened to Tyler?

The C.W. Wilkes door creaked opened a couple of inches to extend a chain securing the door. An old quivering voice asked, "what do you want?"

"We are Ethan and Mia. The English couple. We are friends of the Professor."

"Which Professor?" he asked.

The situation perplexed Ethan; he was not comfortable to have his head drilled by some doddery old fool. "Professor Artemis!" he answered rather abruptly.

A stronger tone responded from another voice behind the door. "My good friend Professor Artemis, one moment." The door closed briefly whilst he unhooked the chain.

He held out his hand with a confident smile. "I'm Brad." He was a clean-shaven tall guy with wrap around glasses wearing a white lab coat.

185

"Ethan, and Mia." Ethan glanced past Brad to see an elderly gent in a ruffled brown jumper taking a seat in front of a small TV.

Brad gave a knowing nod of his head. "Sorry for the delay, security first. Don't want a bullet in my head? It's legal, but some droids are trying to take us down."

The room was empty, but for the old man huddled in a single armchair in front of a TV. "You wouldn't know we'd got super tech here, would you?" Brad asked, giving them a cheery grin. He opened a single door to what first appeared to be a broom cupboard.

As Mia and Ethan tentatively stepped closer, they saw a further steel door inside. Brad placed his palm onto a scanner which revealed a retinal scanner at head height. Brad lifted his glasses and stared into the scanner. The screen turned green, and he tapped into a keypad. He opened the steel door and called them through.

The room was larger than they expected, but the glass screened operating area took up more than half of the room. A series of tools lay in a solution aside from the main operating chair. Two white robot arms were above the chair poised ready for action.

Outside of the operating area, a titanium framed, leather recliner waited for a guest. Brad held out his hand, gesturing to the recliner. "Mia, take a seat. Ethan, you're first."

Mia took the seat, relieved to be going second but dreading the view of what she was letting herself in for.

Ethan asked about anesthetics, but Brad informed him, "It is better to operate whilst you're awake. It also avoids the bother of sedatives." Brad secured his arms and chest in place with a series of leather straps. He then placed a helmet arrangement on his head and started the tightening process. Ethan complained as it got tighter, "any tighter it will crush my skull."

"It's only happened twice. You should be okay."

"What?" Ethan shrieked.

"Just kidding. It's fine. The slightest movement of your head could cause bleeding on your brain and we don't want that." Ethan continued to endure the pain of his skin pinched against his skull. The pain intensified as pins protruded from the head restraint through his skin to secure his skull in place. A further clamp prevented the headgear from any movement.

Whether it was for humor or part of his usual patter, Brad added, "No crying or screaming. It will upset the next victim. Sorry, I meant to say the next patient." Brad pulled a cover over his head, covering his eyes with a hole for access to the top of his head. Brad then exited the booth and started the process with Ethan understandably nervous.

Mia's knuckles were white as she gripped the chair with all her might, trying to be strong for Ethan and yet eager to inform Brad she didn't need the procedure. Brad could sense her apprehension. "I'll get you a headset to help you relax. Have some water first." Brad poured her a drink from a chilled jug. She thanked him whilst her eyes remained focussed on Ethan and the spider legged robot, which beeped each verification point as it scanned his head.

"What's happening?" Mia asked.

"Calibration, it takes a while. Finish your drink and I will set up your VR headset to keep you entertained."

"I want to watch the procedure."

"Watching is not exciting. We peel back a small section of his scalp, a small section of his skull is replaced with the neural lace. The program locates and connects the fine wires to the correct portion of the brain, then it's a stitch job. It will be much better for you to relax. You will like the VR show."

Mia accepted a headset from Brad. She put on the headset and it transported her into the ocean to watch a shoal of Orcas. When the footage stopped, she lifted her headset to see Ethan being led out of the booth.

"Mia, can Ethan have the seat?" Brad asked.

Mia got up to assist and guide Ethan into his seat. Ethan was holding his head as if it would have fallen off if he didn't hold it in place.

"Are you Ok?" Mia asked.

"I'm good, it's like having your brain jet washed though."

"Did it hurt?"

"Once you get used to having your head squeezed, it's fine."

"Ready to be awoken, Mia?" Brad asked.

"Do you feel any different?" Mia asked Ethan, ignoring Brad's question.

Ethan wrinkled of his nose and gently shook his head, "not much."

"Ready, Mia?" Brad asked as he placed a hand on her shoulder.

Fight or flight stirred in her head.

She took a deep breath and blew out the tension through pursed lips. "Let's do this." Mia stepped into the booth and took her seat.

Brad attached the straps, Mia was secure. Brad added his own brand of humor, "I hope you are better than cry baby, Ethan."

"Guys don't have stomach cramps every month." Mia appeared cool, but her heart was racing despite seeing Ethan come out the other side.

As Brad fitted the head restraint he warned her, "It gets very tight, but it won't crush your skull. Well, we've not had any crush yet."

If not restrained, Mia would have punched him. She wanted to scream as it tightened on her head, then it tightened further and further, but she held back her scream. Pins piercing her skin to hold her skull were incidental compared to the pain in her head. The same cover came over her head and she heard the booth door click shut.

The smooth sound of the machine hummed into action.

Darkness magnified every touch, but she took solace that Ethan had endured the same and now faced the torture of having to watch. She guessed his stomach would have churned the same as hers was contorting until the Orcas took her attention. A coolness rushed through her head as the hole appeared in her skull. It made her judder, but the restraints held her firm.

Feeling tools around her brain was a chilling experience she didn't want to repeat. The neural lace gave her a weird tickle as it connected to the key points of her cortex. Rather than it being an irritation in need of a scratch, the procedure was like a deep cleanse to awaken her full potential. She enjoyed every sensation, knowing the fitment would enable her to explore a new level of human consciousness.

Brad had passed a VR headset to Ethan. "This will upload the latest updates and give you the knowledge of how to use the neural lace and its BCI. I've also included the upload for setting up your own booth in the UK." Brad gave him a cheeky smirk. "Got a nice blond on the overlay."

Ethan put the headset on, and the knowledge base streamed

into his head. He was expecting a tutorial or a video presentation, but the screen showed a rain of data running down the screen. After about ten seconds, it switched to a relaxing scene on a beach with calypso music playing. He looked around and surveyed the beach. It was clear except for a couple walking hand in hand along the shore towards him. He glanced down to see his feet covered in sand. He lifted his feet and was amazed by how real the sand felt as he brushed it off his feet. The calypso rhythm faded out and he relaxed to the sound of the waves lapping the shore. A gentle breeze across his skin calmed the heat building on his face.

He watched the couple getting closer and thought of the joys he would share with Mia. As they came into clearer view, a blond-haired beauty in a skimpy red triangle bikini lifted her shades and smiled at him. The chiseled guy looked like Tyler, an annoying specimen of muscle and looks. He raised his hand. "Hiya, welcome to the lace crew." As they continued along the shore, their image faded.

A calming female voice advised him to keep on the headset to acclimatize to the light. The screen darkened as the room came into focus. Ethan removed the headset to hear Mia humming a tune to herself as the machine finished closing her scalp.

"No tears from this one." Brad scanned to open the booth with the machines now at rest. "All done. Are you okay?"

"All good, I think I needed a wash in there," Mia said with a chirpy freshness.

"You've been the perfect patient." He undid the straps and released her. She was less groggy than Ethan and walked freely with Brad in close attendance. Ethan stood and gave her a hug, perhaps more for him than her. "Mia, if you'd like to take a seat and put on the headset. I will upload the 'how to' instructions."

Mia sat and placed the VR headset on, before relaxing into the chair. The screen rained data for ten seconds and Mia lifted off the headset. "I would have thought the data would go through the eyes rather through the side of my head, fascinating.

Ethan put his hand out to help her out of the reclined chair. Mia took his hand and gestured "Shall we?", Ethan hugged Mia and placed his head aside hers as their minds communicated to approve the uploads. Fifteen seconds later, Ethan's hug intensified as he kissed Mia.

Brad placed a hand on each of them. "Just need to let you know the side effects."

Brad enjoyed seeing the shock on their faces before a smile appeared on his face. "Just kidding. Just a few reminders, though. Settle yourselves down and create folders for each knowledge center and password protect the areas you don't want to share. You should get used to them for a day before you go back to Professor Artemis. I can't believe he's going to share his knowledge with you. I guess you must have some issues in the UK."

"Just a few," Ethan replied.

"That means we can check out the sights." Mia grabbed his hand and gave it an excited squeeze. "Can you take me to the singing diner?"

"Ellen's Stardust Diner. Think we should get back to the hotel first and get our files in order. We'll go tomorrow morning."

Brad led the happy couple out into the small room. The old man led them to the door but waited for the thumbs up from Brad before he opened the door.

A young man was waiting at the door. He stepped aside to

let them pass. Mia gave him a smile and whispered, "no need to panic, it's all good."

As Ethan and Mia went back onto the street, Ethan spoke, "So, a nutmeg isn't a nut."

Mia burst into a fit of giggles, "no, it's a spice, or to be accurate, it's a seed." Mia calmed, "If that's all you've learned from me, you got the rough end of the deal." A more restrained giggle returned as they walked hand in hand.

"Shall we go through the park?" Mia asked.

After the events of the past couple of hours. Ethan enjoyed strolling with Mia as a couple. The world was changing, but the simple things like a romantic connection and the joys of being in a natural environment were down to them to protect.

"The upload from you has given me more than knowledge. I'm more aware of everything, I can sense the rabbits in the bushes, even though we can't see them," Mia said.

"Me too." Ethan smiled and pecked her on her cheek. "I'd hardly noticed the smell of the flowers before." The aroma filled his nostrils with a warm sense of the surrounding nature. "The colors are more vibrant, the trees are greener."

Mia clarified, "a female brain senses more colors and smells, it was my gift to you."

Ethan put his arm around Mia. "Not changed much, have you?"

Mia gave him a proud smile. "I know how to program robots."

Leaving the park, they headed hand in hand towards times square, but their perfect afternoon turned sour when a promotional video appeared in front of Mia's eyes. She tried to turn away, but the image followed her movements.

'Come get the best wings in New York,' was the chirpy

message.

She swiped her hands across her forehead. The live image of a bust filled orange tee shirt emblazoned with Hooters wouldn't move. She screamed in frustration before it finally faded away.

She glared back at the passing glances before grabbing Ethan's shoulders and shouting in his face. "What the hell was that?"

"I don't know!" Ethan shook his head with equal bemusement, "Hooters? I had the same."

"It's coming through the neural lace." Mia's hands squeezed on her head. "I want this shit out of my head."

"We need to get back to the hotel and sort our folders out." Ethan grabbed Mia's hand, and they set off in a canter towards the hotel.

Mia pulled him back to a solid pace, "What have we done? I want it out of my head."

Back in their room all was quiet and Mia calmed enough to create folders and passwords for her newfound knowledge. Her head was feeling heavy, but more from intense concentration than the weight of knowledge she'd gained.

"It's been a whirlwind of a day. Let's rest. We can see the Professor tomorrow afternoon." Ethan said, eager to draw a line under the day.

Chapter 25

After further discussions with Alfie on their next move, Lucy waited till the end of her shift and found Luke. She turned on the charm and asked him to take her on a proper date. He declined her request and invited her back to his office again.

When he closed the door behind her, he pursed his lips to gesture a kiss and smiled. "What could we possibly do this evening, with some time to ourselves?"

"You took advantage of me, last time I was in here," Lucy said with a stern face.

"I recall you gave your consent, and I took your screams as a release of pleasure. You didn't ask me to stop."

Lucy blushed as she experienced a tingle between her legs with the slightest recollection of their time together. Concentrate, Luke is the enemy. "It was fine, just not my normal reaction to attention, I'm not one of the shag and go crew."

"I know you're not, that's part of your charm." Luke's warm tone teased at Lucy's resolve.

"Why don't we go to your place? Get to know each other at a slower pace." She needed to find his charging station.

Doctor Luke held a wayward stare for a moment before he held up his hand. "Okay, there are some things you don't know about me," he said.

No shit.

"I don't have a place away from the hospital. When I arrived from America, my accommodation fell through and after working over twenty hours per day, sleeping in my office was my stop gap and it became the norm."

Lucy couldn't believe he hadn't got a place to stay, it pointed to the fact a convenient place to charge was likely his priority.

"I sleep in there." Luke gestured towards what looked like it would be a storage closet. When he opened the door, she stepped forward to see access to another room. It was like a little bedsit converted from a private side ward. It was sparse, as she would have expected from an overworked bachelor. He had a bed, a small kitchen and a sofa facing a video wall where he watched all his TV in the otherwise clinical environment.

Lucy was soon rubbing shoulders again with Luke, after he'd slotted a frozen pizza into the oven and took charge of the remote. He selected a modern film, 'Time to Click.' The actors and actresses of the past replaced with CGI images, or glorified cartoons, as Lucy put it.

Remembering her task, she made the excuse to check on the pizza and looked around his room looking for any signs of charging equipment. Lucy needed to find out if Luke was, as Alfie had put it, 'a robot.'

With no charging equipment in view, she opted for the flinch test by pulling a stray hair from his head.

He didn't flinch, but frowned as he contemplated why she would do such a thing.

She returned to her seat beside him and they focused on TV until he took a strand of her hair and pulled.

Lucy squealed. "Why did you do that?"

His answer made perfect sense. "You took one of mine."

Lucy laughed at his answer and tickled him. Initially, he didn't respond until her fingers delved deeper into his neck and he squirmed like an eel. "I thought robots weren't ticklish," she said, taunting him before realizing what she'd revealed.

Luke sat up like a shot. "You think I'm a robot."

"Not really, just checking." She gave him a cheeky smile, but Luke's playful mood had flipped.

He frowned, "you thought I was a robot!"

Lucy tried to laugh it off. "Your knowledge is unbelievable, and you never take breaks."

"And that makes me a robot!" Luke slowly shook his head, disappointed by her judgment. "I'm committed to my work. Is that so wrong?" he said, as he raised his hands.

"No, it's just, Alfie said–"

"Alfie said I was a robot! Why? Because I don't sleep with every woman in the hospital."

Lucy snapped her eyes on Luke's. "Alfie doesn't sleep around."

"Not now he doesn't, they know what he's like. I think you're his last challenge. The study girl."

"Who calls me study girl?" Lucy's frown demanded an answer.

"I've heard it mentioned a few times."

Lucy took a moment to take in what she'd heard. Had Alfie played her? She thought he was a good friend.

Luke smirked as she processed the revelation. "So, study girl, movie or bed?"

"Don't call me study girl." She crossed her arms and nodded to the oven. "The pizza should be ready."

As Luke removed the pizza, Lucy asked her key question, "How do you learn so quickly and remember everything?"

"I hadn't used to. When I was studying in America, I'd been struggling and would have flunked the course if not for an upgrade they offered me. It was a brain implant. A neural lace which helped me process and store information."

"So, you are a robot then."

"No, I'm transhuman, or to be specific, the next level in human development."

It sounded very much like a robot, but not wanting to wind him up, she asked the pointed second question, "why have you ordered lethal Femalatism injections?"

Luke jumped to his feet. "What the fuck are you talking about?"

Lucy blurted out, "my friend had a cardiac arrest two weeks after having her baby! There are a heap of others who've shared the same fate after having the injection!"

"What! Why didn't you tell me?" Luke held his hands up as if he knew nothing of it.

Lucy couldn't answer.

"Do you think I have something to do with it?"

Lucy's cheeks burned. "The old are being killed as well. You told the nurse the injection was fine!"

"I think we need to talk." Luke sat down again, but Lucy stood and moved away.

Luke explained how he'd received orders to ease the journey of the elderly patients to save on government spending and was unaware of the issues in Maternity other than the snake tool. The government cannot afford the medical bills for an aging population and targeted the cost saving opportunity.

"Are you fucking kidding?"

"The law changed. We cannot sustain life with ongoing drugs. If they can't afford gene editing, we need to let them go.

Technology has enabled us to perpetuate life, but the world can't afford or sustain it. The AI Leaders in government are driving the decisions and I'm at risk, if I don't follow their orders. Voices repeat in my head until I do as they say, it drives me crazy."

"Boo hoo," Lucy mocked him. "The injections are killing mothers and babies, not just giving you a headache."

"I didn't realize it had got out of hand. I'll look into it."

"Out of hand! Look into it! You're out of you're fucking mind!" Lucy stomped around the room waving her arms around. "I've stopped the injections already."

Luke stood in front of Lucy to halt her rage. "They monitor the number of injections, we'll get a visit from the government if we're not administering them."

Lucy placed her hands on the sides of his face. "I might not be transhuman, but I'm not daft, I've been reporting the injections and deaths, as if they were still happening."

"You are a smart study girl." Luke gave her a cheeky grin.

Lucy punched him in the chest. "Don't call me that!"

Luke apologized as he rubbed his chest, moving away as he commented, "good punch, where did you *study* that?"

"Do you enjoy getting hit?" Lucy raised a fist and Luke backed away with his hands raised.

Luke smiled and opened his arms wide to welcome her in for a much-needed hug. His embrace helped, but with the possibility Alfie had pursued her to complete his latest conquest of bedding the study girl, she needed to find out.

Maybe she was better off with Luke, but could she trust him? Was Luke on her side or had she just made the worst possible mistake and put herself at risk?

Chapter 26

Mia stepped onto the sidewalk with Ethan, eager to find some brunch after their amorous morning. The noise from ads in their heads had gone for now, and the troubles in the UK could wait as they strolled hand in hand without a care.

They reached Ellen's Stardust Diner on the corner of 51st and 7th avenue, to see a line of people waiting outside. Mia got cold waiting, but Ethan pulled her close and she rested her cheek on his chest. Eventually, the headwaiter invited them in to see the full effect of the 1950s style diner. Red leather bench seats, silver tables and photos galore of the stars who'd started out at the famous diner.

Visiting a live show is a real treat when you have a prime seat, or if a VR headset takes you up close and personal, but the 'Stardust Experience' was something else with each performer stepping seamlessly from server to headline act. No sooner had they taken their seats, a confident young woman began singing, 'hopelessly devoted to you,' from the musical, Grease. Mia couldn't contain her giggles as she focused almost exclusively on Ethan, as she strolled around in front of their table. His face was purple, which made the waitress pay him further attention, stroking her fingers through his hair. As her song finished, she slipped straight back into her duties, collecting empty plates and glasses as the music for the next performer began.

A cute waiter came to the table and smiled at them holding hands over the table. He accepted their order and when he returned with their drinks, Ethan had calmed from his embarrassment and entered into the relaxed fun of the place. Another waiter grabbed a cloak and burst into song as he climbed onto a small stage area between the backs of some seats to sing 'the music of the night.' It was the strangest setting for a live show, but it worked.

"Do you think I should add some singing waiters to my little coffee shop?" Mia asked Ethan.

"They're in training for the stage. This is a steppingstone for young performers whilst they await their big break. Not sure your coffee shop would have the same pulling power for punters or artists." Ethan sensed Mia's thoughts and quickly addressed his unfeeling response. "Your coffee shop is perfect as it is. You shouldn't change a thing. Especially your lemon drizzle cakes."

Mia liked the way Ethan had promptly corrected his harsh comment. "Good save," she smiled. "You're probably right. Not much room for climbing on tables."

"This is special because it's so close to Broadway. Shall we walk down the strip after brunch?"

Mia nodded as the waiter appeared with a pile of large thick pancakes. "We'll need to walk off a few calories if we finish these," Mia said.

Ethan looked unconcerned and with a knife and fork he slid a pancake of the stack onto his plate.

They were both stuffed as Ethan finished the last one. He sat back and proudly rubbed his hands over his full stomach before he finished his soda. Bloated from overeating, Mia considered asking Ethan to roll her out of the diner.

Ethan still looked fresh despite the number of pancakes and followed Mia out of the door. They took each other's hand again and strolled along Broadway boulevard, taking in the gigantic signs for the shows as they headed towards Times Square.

A promotional video for a new musical, 'Awano,' startled Mia when it appeared in front of her eyes. She tried to turn away, but like the Hooters commercial, the image followed her movements. "What the hell. Didn't we fix this shit?"

Ethan had experienced the same torture before his eyes and had no reply.

"It came through the neural lace again." Mia's hands squeezed her head. "I want this out of my head."

"Come and see the newest musical on Broadway, Awano!" The sound repeated in her head and she groaned.

"I heard it too," Ethan added.

"What have we done? I want it out my head."

Ethan turned to walk back the way they came. "We need to get to 79th Street. The Professor has another upload for us."

"He needs to do something!"

"He'll help I'm sure." Ethan put his arm around Mia, but she shrugged it off and quickened her pace towards the park with Ethan trying to catch her.

On reaching the corner of central park, no further messages had appeared, and Mia's pace slowed.

Ethan put a reassuring arm around her. "I'm sure Professor Artemis doesn't have that kind of thing buzzing around his head. He'll make things good."

Mia calmed, realizing she had been irrational. "It just freaked me, that's all." Mia pointed to the traditional horse and carriage rides through the park. "My feet are aching. Let's travel in style?"

"Good idea. Traditional style it is." Ethan took her hand again and led her to the carriages.

Imagining she was a royal princess; Mia stepped aboard the gleaming white carriage and took her seat on the plush red velvet. The horseman looked dapper in his dark gray waistcoat, with his white shirt sleeves ruffled up his forearms. Mia loved the delightfully elegant ride and nuzzled into Ethan's embrace. With time to kill, they spent a full hour gently rolling through the park before they reached cedar hill and exited onto East 79th Street. It was time to fix the most pressing issue, the commercials streaming into their heads.

After a polite tap on Professor Artemis's door, he opened it and welcomed them in. "How are you getting on with the lace?" the Professor asked.

"Okay." Ethan said as Mia frowned.

"Are you enjoying New York?" The Professor asked Mia.

"New York is all I ever dreamt it would be. The lace was pretty special too until commercials started streaming directly into my occipital lobe."

"The knowledge base works then." Ethan mentioned in an optimistic tone.

"What do you mean?" Mia asked.

"When did you learn about the occipital lobe?" Ethan questioned.

"No idea, I just know it is where the brain translates vision." Mia put her hands prayerfully together to ask the Professor. "Please, can you stop the commercials?"

"All in good time. When you amass vast knowledge, you need to create mental folders and think them open or closed.

It's the same for security to block messages."

They'd done that but didn't want to interrupt him.

He answered as if Mia had said it aloud. "Apologies, did Brad show you?"

"We both had the 'how to' programme downloaded," Ethan answered.

"Excellent, If it's okay, I'll just share the folders you need. Don't want you to be a complete genius, like me." The Professor laughed and Mia contained a giggle, impatient for an answer about the voices. The Professor leant forward and met heads with Ethan. Within a minute the upload was complete. "The telekinesis is there, but you must develop the ability to use it yourselves."

He could sense Mia's ongoing concern. "I guess Brad didn't cover security too well?"

"We have password protected our personal files," Ethan replied.

"And you think, 'Gr4ft%@46' is suitable protection." The Professor's brow creased.

Ethan blushed as the Professor had revealed his password.

"It's not a computer. It's a neural lace." The Professor smiled at his naïve subjects. "Can you make the love symbol with your hand?"

Mia blurted out, "I know it." She paused for a moment. "I don't know how I know." Mia held up her right hand and lowered her two middle fingers. "Was it part of the download?"

"Yes. It enables double encryption by engaging with the motor function in the cerebellum. When you lock a folder, make a hand gesture such as the love symbol and think of your password. Then do the same to open it. This will stop someone else forcing you to release your files. Use an uncommon gesture and password for general security to prevent messages and commercials being sent." He gave Mia a teasing smile. "Don't you enjoy them?"

Mia gave him a critical stare with a smirk.

"Some earlier laces were wide open to mind controlling messages. The commercial was nothing by comparison. Imagine you were being repeatedly told to stab someone. It was happening before I designed the motor function protection."

Mia leant forward and her head connected with the Professor, Mia knew how to accept the upload and asked, "Do you want some of my knowledge?"

For the first time, she heard Ethan's thoughts. He thought she was a little naïve given the Professor's brain power, but she bobbed her tongue out at him when the Professor politely accepted and rested his head once again against hers.

"I love to bake, that is most appreciated," he said as their heads parted.

She smiled at the Professor and nodded towards Ethan. The Professor sniggered.

Ethan questioned him and the Professor replied, "nutmeg is not a nut."

Ethan looked puzzled, but Mia enlightened him, "I told him about our nutmeg discussion." Mia smiled at the Professor and said, "Telepathy, is going to be fun."

"Very impressive to pick it up so quickly." The Professor added, "I'm sure you'll help him. When you go back into quarantine, you can sort out your folder structure and security. In the meantime, enjoy New York." The Professor pushed back his chair and stood. "You must excuse me. I have another lecture to deliver."

They filed out together and as the Professor locked his door, he gave them a word of warning, "Access the cyber security folder before you return to the UK, unless you want a virus messing you up."

With the threats in the UK, they hadn't considered the risks of the process, but realizing a virus could wreck their brain, they headed back to the hotel.

The day was weighing heavily on them as they arrived back at the Plaza. Their bed fulfilled its primary function as they got their heads down for several hours.

The following day, they left the Plaza and returned to the confines of the Ellis Island hotel. Mia complained of sensitive boobs, thanks to Ethan's over physical attention, so their amorous romps took a breather. Their time was better spent training, controlling and honing their new abilities.

Mia's grasp of telekinesis far outshone Ethan's. She could move furniture where Ethan still struggled with the curtain. He commented, "when we first met at Giangolini's you were a vulnerable maiden needing love and protection. Now look at you. You're a tower of strength."

Mia felt like a butterfly transformed from her life as a caterpillar. The change in her life she craved had been coming, but today it arrived. She felt different in every way, awoken, her body stronger and her mind immeasurably quicker. She gave Ethan a warm smile and sank into his loving arms as she uttered for the first time, "love you."

Ethan wanted to reply he'd loved her from the moment they'd met but kissed her cheek and replied, "love you too."

During their last days of quarantine, Mia's mind returned to thoughts of Tyler, Cole and Chloe. How did their mission go? What would they be returning to? How would Tyler respond to her relationship breakthrough with Ethan?

Chapter 27

The sight of her homeland approaching gave Mia a boost, she'd become increasingly nervous about what they may find. If Tyler was okay, how would he react to her relationship breakthrough with Ethan?

Ethan sensed her discomfort and noticed her worried stare through the window. "You've been quiet," he said as he gave her hand a tender squeeze. "Don't worry, we'll be fine together."

Mia shook her head. "What if they didn't make it back out of Tushi?" Mia wiped her hand over her stressed brow.

"They'll be fine." Ethan put a second hand on hers and lifted them to his chest. "I hope so. For all our sakes." Ethan tipped his head forward kissing her hand as he held it close to his heart.

Despite their relationship breakthrough, Mia longed to sleep in her own bed and go home to see if Tyler and Cole were okay. Waking alongside Ethan in his mansion wasn't a terrible option, but home was behind her oak door with Tyler and Cole.

Their VTOL came to rest at the Land's End immigration port. Mia and Ethan completed their blood test and had approached the thermal imaging scanners, hoping their neural laces wouldn't receive any unwanted attention. After all they'd endured, this wasn't where they needed to face trouble.

In true English style, after passing through the sensors, they were discreetly directed to an interview room. They waited for a few minutes before two officers in full military attire stepped into the room and sat opposite. There was a silent stand-off as the officers looked down their noses at Mia and Ethan. The more elderly gent eventually spoke, "your blood tests came back fine, but what are the metal plates in your skulls?"

"They are gifts from America," Ethan said.

Mia cringed; did Ethan want to get detained indefinitely?

"Do you have a receipt for said gifts?" The younger officer asked, "we don't allow unregistered items into the country."

Mia screamed to herself, '*we are good people, send us on our way.*'

The elderly officer pushed back his chair and stood. "These are good people, send them on their way." His fellow officer nodded in approval.

Mia was gob smacked, as was Ethan, who gave her a knowing glance.

The officer pressed on his watch, and a small screen appeared. He checked the green 'Approved' box, and it disappeared again as the more senior officer opened the door for them.

They stepped back into their VTOL, marvelling at their new skills as they headed to Ethan's.

The VTOL came to rest on his gravel driveway by his front entrance, and a rush of nerves returned to them both. Their eyes locked as their minds both asked the same question. Had Tyler and Chloe executed the plan?

The attention they expected on their return was missing, so with his new skills, Ethan mentally opened the roller shutter shielding his ornate door. The door and the shutter were unmarked, clearing the worry over a forced entry. He repeated his new skills to unlock the front door despite having the key in his pocket.

An eerie silence met them as he pushed open the door.

Ethan called out, "hiya, we're back!"

The only response was a partial echo; Ethan's feet slapped the marble floor as he raced into the front lounge.

"No sign of Chloe!" Ethan shouted back to Mia. It was Chloe's favourite place to sit and watch the fish, whilst Ethan was at work. The fish were also undisturbed.

Mia caught up with Ethan to find him rubbing the back of his neck, staring at the fish swimming without a care.

Mia rested her hand on Ethan's shoulder. "They're probably at mine. Grab the mobiles, we can call them," Mia said casually.

The mobiles were missing, as were any other trace of their missing droids. The only thing they found was Cole's toy, standing arms aloft, yet motionless on the coffee table.

"Should he have this with him?" Ethan picked up the toy and studied it, like he was revisiting a painful memory.

Despite Ethan's worried state, Mia was thinking more rationally. "Cole can walk now, he's outgrown it." She sent a mental message for a taxi, before getting notification the VTOL was still outside. Mia took Ethan's hand and led him back outside.

"How are you so calm?" Ethan asked.

"I've gained some of your rational brain, it looks like you've also got some of mine," she said with a spring in her step.

Mia's familiar oak door gave her a homely warmth as they stepped from the air taxi. Her mind unlocked the door, but she couldn't pull the bolts aside. Mia gave it a stern knock.

With no answer, her own concern rose to meet Ethan's. She knocked harder as Ethan went to peer through a window. Mia called him back as she heard the bolts being pulled across. A small blond-haired boy opened the door but said nothing and panic filled Mia before she tentatively asked, "Cole?"

Cole gave her a big smile and his arms opened wide. "That's Me. Look how much I've grown."

"Wow! You have grown." Mia crouched for a hug, deciding against trying to lift him into her arms. Cole was a foot taller and much stronger. He gave her an almighty hug, leaving her in no doubt he'd missed her.

"Where are Tyler and Chloe?" Ethan asked.

Cole pointed upstairs and rolled his eyes. "As usual."

Ethan shouted up the stairs, "hiya, we're home."

"We will be down in four minutes," Tyler said from inside an upstairs room.

"I can dance. Do you want to watch me?" Cole excitedly pulled Mia by the hand into the lounge.

"Okay, okay." Mia loved his energy.

Cole selected music and danced around the room, showing his moves. Mia and Ethan applauding each spin. When the track finished, they both cuddled him to congratulate him on his new ability, before Mia calmly spoke, "I've got a new skill too, do you want to see?"

Cole took a seat on the floor, crossed his legs and leant forward with an expectant gaze.

Mia picked up a coaster from the coffee table and balanced it on her upturned fingers. Cole crossed his arms and his face dropped disappointedly until the coaster slowly rose to move to her other hand. Cole jumped up and inspected the coaster. "How did you do it? How did you do it?" Cole jumped up and down excitedly, but Mia just smiled.

"What did you do?" Tyler asked as he stepped into the lounge and took Mia into his arms for a long embrace, Cole joined in hugging their legs.

A windswept Chloe followed and dived into Ethan's arms.

Mia had given a lot of thought about how to tell Tyler about her and Ethan, but given Chloe's appearance, they hadn't been dusting the bedroom. Mia felt betrayed despite her own flirtations with Ethan. Tyler was programmed to be true to her. She was glad to see him safe, but why had he got together with Chloe.

Tyler stepped back like she'd said it aloud and he gave Mia a puzzled stare.

Mia returned a telepathic message direct to Tyler. *I was going to talk to you about myself and Ethan, but I think you've moved on already. I thought you were programmed to be true to me. When did you get together with Chloe?*

"Last week," Tyler sheepishly said, wondering how Mia had communicated telepathically with him.

"Picked up some news skills in America," Mia said.

"Dad, Mom can do magic. Show him Mom, show him." Cole bounced around them.

"Later, Darling," Mia replied to Cole. She glanced at Tyler and Chloe. "We're glad to see you. When you weren't at Ethan's, then no-one came to the door. We feared the worst. I didn't think for one minute you'd be in bed together." Mia scrunched her nose with disapproval.

Tyler opened his mouth to defend his actions, but Mia held her hand up to halt his defence.

"First things first. Can we celebrate a successful mission?" Mia stroked Tyler's arm, her eyes were wide as her smile of anticipation.

Tyler looked at Chloe.

"I'll get some wine, you'll need it," Chloe said.

Chapter 28

Chloe took a seat next to Mia as Tyler recounted the visit to the Tushi Corporation.

He and Chloe had taken Cole for his baby growth spurt upgrade after going over their plan in meticulous detail. However, when they'd arrived, Mia not being with them raised concerns. They told the assistant Mia was still the mother and Chloe was only providing support whilst Mia was on holiday. Tyler noticed the look of concern on the assistant's face and gave her a cheeky smile. "We are looking forward to seeing the surprise on Mia's face. She is already freaking out at how fast he is growing."

"I hope she likes surprises," the assistant said.

"She does not cope well with change, but she is getting better," Tyler said.

"He will be more responsive, that should help."

Tyler and Chloe had shared a glance, knowing a more responsive Cole wouldn't help ease Mia's concern.

The assistant put out her hands and took Cole from Tyler and placed him on the table. Tyler asked several questions about the process to which the assistant re-assured them Cole would not notice the change.

Cole then spoke for himself, "Having my entire body

changed will be obvious. How stupid do you think I am?"

It surprised the assistant that Cole was speaking after she'd switched him off. She stepped back, aghast at his sarcastic tone. The assistant switched him off again, only to realise the button only switched off the body. She then hastily lifted the flap at the back of his head and unscrewed the flap securing his conscience.

"Are you qualified to use a screwdriver?" Cole said.

The assistant had a blush to her cheeks but ignored his comment and slid out his conscience to silence him. It was a small block of blue magma which glowed in a sealed unit. The assistant placed Cole's conscience on a side table, and Cole's first body eased away on the conveyor. A few short moments after Cole's body disappeared, the conveyor belt changed direction and a new body emerged, some twelve inches longer. Tyler knew Mia would freak out again. The assistant took the conscience block from the table and secured it in place. The assistant then turned Cole onto his back and showed Tyler the flesh-coloured re-start button. She hesitated and finished the details, not wanting another insult from a resurgent Cole. Once pressed, Cole's hands came across his chest and over the button. "How dare you switch me on! That was for my dad to do."

The assistant eagerly opened the door and said, "good luck with him, you'll need it." As Tyler lifted Cole down from the conveyor, he asked, "I promised him a look around, is that okay?"

The assistant was eager to see the back of Cole. "Anywhere but back in here." She ushered them out and closed the door.

"Well played, Cole, you were outstanding," Chloe said. They'd completed the first stage of their plan.

Tyler led Cole by the hand with Chloe following. They gained access at the first controlled door when the guard checked with their upgrade assistant. He granted them a multi-access visitor pass.

As they strolled through the corridors, no-one came across their path. The corridor passed a large production area and a blue glow on the track drew their attention. Slipping through a door undetected, they drew closer. Evenly placed conscience blocks were steadily moving along the conveyor. Tyler spoke quietly to Cole. "They are brains like ours."

Cole stepped closer to pick one up, but Chloe moved quickly to stop him. Chloe's face of thunder sent Cole scuttling behind Tyler. "Why don't you set the alarm off as well." She wagged a finger. "No Touching."

As they progressed through the rooms, the size of the operation became clear. Tyler and Chloe had both become conscious in a lab and were unaware of the size of the production facility. They climbed a flight of stairs to finally reach the network room. One of the two guards ordered them to stop. He stepped forward and declared, "your visitor passes have no permission here." He pointed to another stairwell. "Proceed downstairs to the upgrade zone."

They were in no position to challenge the guards and followed the order. As they entered the upgrade zone, the room was busy with about forty sex droids. Tyler and Chloe spoke with small groups and explained the issue with the split in the network, but Neither Chloe nor Tyler received any support for stopping the network. The sexbots told them the decentralised network couldn't be hacked. The issues are likely to be from an alternative network and would have limited influence as Tushi droids dominated the market. One of the sexbots was convincing as she said, "if they are a small set, they must have an enormous influence, perhaps in government positions. Money drives them, not love like us."

It made perfect sense. The programming of the sexbot was purely for pleasure. Tyler agreed with the group, but the network had allowed him and Chloe to step over the line and collude to keep their partners. It had been an act of love for their paired humans, but the network suggestion to manipulate the news to encourage Mia to have a Tushi Baby was a step too far. Tyler couldn't convince them, but the network was becoming too powerful.

Cole sneaked into a vacated room and linked into the network. He found uploads for fun stuff like dancing and an interesting one, "caring for your partner." Inquisitively, he uploaded both. The caring for your partner was advisory information regarding the fitness of humans. It stressed the importance of providing them with healthy foods, whilst distracting them from unhealthy choices and snacking. It also included an exercise plan, which included variation in their sexual positions to work different muscle groups, whilst also suggesting to take them for walks to give them a rounded exercise routine.

Despite his young mind, Cole understood this was not the sinister image expected and returned to find Tyler with the news, but he got distracted.

Tyler and Chloe had already received the uploads and had reached the same conclusion. A group of sexbots began cheering, Tyler and Chloe went to investigate. The cheering was for Cole, who was dancing for them, or rather spinning on his back.

*

After Tyler and Chloe had explained to them how the concern with the network was unfounded and the Tushi Corporation was secure from hacks. They raised the possibility it could be another smaller network of robots, as the sexbot had suggested.

"That makes more sense. The network is decentralized and should be safe from a single point attack," Mia said.

Astonished at Mia's comment, Tyler and Chloe turned to Mia.

"I was thinking the same," Ethan said, ignoring the surprise on Chloe's face.

"Since when did you understand Ethan's work?" Chloe asked as she stroked her chin.

"America was quite an eye opener, or should I say brain opener," Ethan said. "We've both had an upgrade. We've had neural laces fitted." Ethan continued to explain the technology, but Tyler interrupted him.

"I know about Neural laces. They are illegal in the UK."

"They're illegal because people who already have them want the advantage. That's where the issues will stem from," Ethan replied.

Mia chipped in. "With the Professor's knowledge we're more advanced than them."

Ethan broached the subject of himself and Mia in a light-hearted manner. "Looks like you've not missed me much," Ethan said to Chloe before glancing up at the ceiling.

There was no apology or a blush from Chloe. "I predicted a 98% chance you would bond again with Mia. Tyler predicted 99%. We provided love when you had none. We're happy for you and Mia," Chloe said, giving a smile to Tyler.

Ethan and Mia shared a quick glance. "We didn't predict you

two would get together," Ethan said.

Tyler smirked and held Chloe's hand. "Maybe your lace is not as good as the benefits we received from the network."

Mia put her hands on her hips and questioned them, "what makes you think Ethan and I, are back together?" Mia gave Chloe a cheeky smile to test her response. Chloe's response took both Ethan and Mia by surprise.

"You are expecting," Chloe said.

It stunned Mia. She placed a hand on her stomach and attempted to take in what she'd heard.

"What makes you think that?" Mia said, before she recalled the tenderness in her breasts which had been an early signal she'd missed.

"I paired with you earlier. I thought you'd like to hear the good news."

Mia frowned. "Shouldn't you ask permission before you pair with someone?"

Ethan put his arm around Mia. "Aren't you happy with the news?"

"I am, but how is it possible?" She pointed to his groin. "You have Tushi bits."

"Yes, I do, but I'm fully connected. There's no mint down there," Ethan said, hoping to receive a sign that Mia welcomed the pregnancy news.

"It is what you wanted," Tyler said. He placed his hand on Mia's shoulder and she returned a growing smile.

Cole stood beside Tyler with a beaming smile. "Am I having a brother or a sister?"

"I don't know." Mia shrugged. She rested her head on Ethan's shoulder and squeezed his hand as she whispered, "I'm pleased. Are you?"

Ethan delivered a gentle kiss to her forehead. "Overjoyed." Ethan held his hand up when Chloe was about to speak, "we don't want to know yet."

Chapter 29

Lucy and Luke had become more acquainted over the last couple of weeks, and after he'd come over for a relaxing evening, she was glad he hadn't scuttled back to the hospital. Waking up with him next to her was a treat she could get used to.

Despite their amorous evening, he was eager to skip breakfast and get back to the hospital, His tight grip on her hand seemed like something more than just desire to get back to work. As soon as they were in the hospital grounds, Luke's grip on her hand softened.

"Is my favorite workaholic home now?" Lucy joked at the visibly calmer Luke, "I think the blood is returning to my hand."

Luke ignored the jibe and nodded towards Alfie who was chatting to one of the junior nurses, Luke made a classic doctor joke for the supposedly bed hopping Alfie, "next please." Lucy was unconcerned and pulled on Luke's hand.

Lucy got a message from Mia to meet up at Ethan's after her shift. Hopefully, they had some positive news to share. She was also keen to share her relationship breakthrough with Luke.

In a whirlpool of love with Luke, she hadn't quizzed him

further. Whilst they were prepping for the day's operations, she worked in a few deeper questions. She hoped she'd be able to validate his innocence, rather than reveal any issues given how they'd connected.

Lucy worked the conversation around as she babbled on about the nursery nurses and how she needed to check on them given how they'd blindly followed the technology. Primed into the conversation, she threw in her planned question with a casual nonchalance. "Who decided to limit baby numbers?"

"I don't actually know, I get messages sent to my BCI, with instructions on how to comply with their request," Luke replied.

Lucy's response was instant and sharp, "and you don't question it?"

"Not really, no." Luke's cheeks reddened.

"You told me you weren't a robot. Now you're acting like an extremely dumb one."

"It's not like that. I don't have a choice."

"You always have a choice! If you think it's wrong, tell them No!"

Doctor Luke, for all his impressive knowledge, skills and charm, cowered, seemingly broken by Lucy's challenging questions. She laid a hand on his shoulder to comfort him. His eyes glistened as his remaining pride crumbled. Lucy's heart poured out to him, offering support whilst also wanting to pull out the remaining detail she needed.

"Do they punish you, if you don't comply?" Lucy asked, rubbing his arm to console him.

Luke sniffed and reluctantly nodded his head. "They control my brain. My knowledge is immense, but I can't stop the messages." He continued, "They repeat until I comply. I can't think straight until I do."

Lucy had trouble understanding how someone could violate him from afar and questioned him further. It transpired the messages only came when he was in the hospital. Lucy suggested an obvious solution, but Luke told her how a humming in his head starts if he's away from the hospital for over eight hours. He'd tried to escape it, but the noise intensified and forced him to return.

"Did you hear it, this morning?"

"Yes, but it stops when I return." Luke offered a further apology, "that's why I didn't make it to the wedding."

Lucy hugged him, hoping for inspiration. It finally came, "I'm seeing some friends tonight. I'll ask if they can help."

Lucy wanted to take him directly to Ethan, but without knowing who was controlling him, it would be too risky, and besides, it would be impolite to turn up with a plus one.

Lucy took a break and headed to the cafeteria for a coffee and something to eat. Her usual buddy was missing. The deceit from Alfie had hardly registered, given how things had developed with Luke. She'd shared lunch with Alfie most days for the last year, yet since sleeping with him, he'd only twice met her for lunch. Perhaps Luke was right, and he'd moved on to his next challenge.

When she'd finished her lunch, she headed to maternity to check on progress. Alfie was walking towards her in a cosy chat with the same girl from earlier. Lucy wanted to shun him, but she couldn't resist informing him, "Luke's not a robot."

"Splendid news," he replied with a hint of sarcasm, "sorry I missed lunch." He held out a hand towards the young nurse. "Have you met Olivia? I'm just showing her around."

Lucy's heart sank with how quickly he'd dropped her, but

she tried to hold in a retort. "Hi Olivia. Nice to meet you." She continued past them and smiled to herself before she added. "He's good at bedtime. Alfie, make sure you read her a story." She held in a giggle and resisted looking back.

Kelly and Cora had followed their orders and showed Lucy their pile of discarded full syringes. They were not as daft as she'd first thought. "Great work girls. Don't forget each one of those full syringes is another baby alive and well."

Her confidence in them plummeted again when Cora asked, "do the syringes have little babies growing in them?"

There was no answer to a question like that. Lucy strode into the office to check the database. The number of births had remained low. Lucy set about ringing all of them to check they were okay. Each call filled her with pride. She'd saved them and delighted in hearing the new mom's concerns about the colour of their babies' poo or how much their little ones cried when they tried to get some sleep. She did her best not to laugh out her relief as a young father pained over his sleepless nights. A new dad switched the call to face time for Lucy to see a baby girl in her mother's arms breast-feeding. Tears of unrestrained joy ran down Lucy's face. In all her time in maternity and the endless miracles of childbirth, this topped it all.

Stopping the Femalatism syringes after so many babies and moms had needlessly perished, was her proudest moment. She was eager to share her success with Mia and ask Ethan if he could help Luke.

Chapter 30

Chloe met Lucy at the door. "Perfect timing, we're trying to figure out how to save humanity? Thank you for joining us." The calmness behind Chloe's words unintentionally gave Lucy a chill she couldn't shake.

Chloe's deadpan delivery didn't help Lucy, who'd been twitching in the taxi. Her own issues with Luke were already consuming her before Chloe intimated there were other issues.

Mia shocked Lucy when she revealed she and Ethan now had a neural lace fitted. Rather than disbelieving them, Lucy surprised them by being familiar with the technology.

"Doctor Luke also has a BCI." Lucy's calm explanation gathered pace and pitch as she went onto explain the more sinister effects. Lucy's heart was heavy with worry. "I hope you know what you've got yourselves involved in."

Mia sat beside Lucy and put a caring arm around her friend. "It's okay. Our security is stronger than Luke's. We had commercials streaming into our heads to start with. It all happened in a whirlwind. We learnt about the technology and had surgery the same day." Tyler noted Mia's breathing as she continued, "we didn't have time to discuss the risks, but the Professor taught us how to block the messages."

Mia stopped and turned to Ethan. She had heard his silent

thought and was happy for Ethan to explain.

Ethan shared the rest of the update. "The uploads we received from Professor Artemis made us mentally stronger, but we control the information, we decide what we upload, and we can compartmentalise folders to structure our knowledge. The advanced security will protect us from cyber-attacks. Mia, shall we show her our skills?"

Another day of practise and they were both much improved. Tyler and Chloe had seen the improvement, but they mesmerized Lucy with their transhuman abilities as they picked up and moved glasses and coasters around the room. Mia suggested a coffee for the bamboozled Lucy and led her into the kitchen. Mia stood at the opposite end of the breakfast bar and prepared the coffee with her mind.

Returning with coffees, Lucy re-assured them their impressive skills were a significantly more advanced level than Luke, but warned them the skill set of his unknown puppet master may exceed their own.

"We're aware of the risks, but we need to face them at some point. Once we have identified the leader. Could you bring Luke here? We can upgrade his security and duplicate his lace profile. Hopefully, we can trace the origin of the messages and disengage him from their control." They discussed the risks and planned their next move.

Ethan assembled a neural lace on a head unit. This would enable them to upload from Luke without the risk to their own. Putting a physical defense between Luke and the potential issues from his leader's connection to him was a smart move. Mia stored a copy of Tyler's file and suggested Ethan did likewise for Chloe.

*

The following morning, when Lucy caught up with Luke, he was staring out of a window, rocking backwards and forwards like a mental patient. When she put her hand on his shoulder, he snapped his head around like a frightened child.

"Are you okay? You need to take a break," She said kindly.

"I've received a new message." He looked to the floor. "they have called me for a meeting with the leader, I need to report to him in three days."

He explained the message was different to the others: it wasn't a definitive order to obey; it was like a notification of promotion or some kind of upgrade. Unlike the other messages, it only came every second hour. However, the alternating hour brought a more sinister message which had him most concerned. "Finish your work at the hospital and say goodbye. You have a new mission."

Lucy was initially more disappointed than concerned with the thought of him leaving so soon until he explained what messages about saying goodbye had previously meant. "At a previous hospital, a colleague had a similar message, and they finished him.

"His girlfriend told me he'd returned home distracted. She'd pushed him for some kind of clue about what was going on. He'd sat with his head in his hands and described a burning sensation inside his head before he uttered that he was finished, and she was in danger.

"He didn't explain further; he collapsed unconscious on the floor. His partner was a nurse, but she couldn't revive him. She called me to help. I took a taxi to go there, but it got redirected to here and I received my new assignment.

"I called a friend at the hospital for news and eventually got a call back saying someone had found them together at home. The report said they'd taken each other's lives. It was obviously bullshit, but I couldn't reveal what I knew. I'll probably get deleted for telling you, but I'm most likely finished, anyway. I don't suppose it matters now."

Lucy held Luke and rubbed his back. "We can't raise attention by going now, but at the end of our shift, we need to get you to Ethan."

Somebody must have gotten word of Lucy's corrections in maternity, and Luke's more considered approach to the elderly had also received attention. The net was quickly closing in, and they were most likely already compromised by their actions. The leaders may have already issued a message for their elimination. Lucy didn't want to implicate Ethan, but he and Mia were the only people who had any chance of helping them.

Lucy attempted to reassure Luke. "Ethan's a programming genius. He'll sort this out."

"If he's that impressive and they know him, the leaders could have already highlighted him as someone to say goodbye to," Luke said with a despondent acceptance.

Lucy's confidence dropped with her solution being challenged. She questioned herself. With the hornets' nest rattled, would taking Luke to Ethan's unwittingly hand him and Mia over to the perpetrators and seal their fate?

Chapter 31

A warmth came over Lucy when the gates opened to welcome them. However, a chill followed when Tyler and Chloe were at the front door to greet them. Being confronted by two droids when concerned about an AI entourage coming to delete them, didn't help her nerves. Luke appeared more confident and held Lucy's hand as they stepped onto the marble floor.

His confidence was not as strong as his grip. "Our fate led us here. Let's hope these guys can help," Luke whispered.

Lucy whispered back, "these are both Tushi droids."

Luke's eyes stilled, and his face turned grey. Lucy gave him a quick smile and a tug to get him to follow Tyler, who strode ahead.

Chloe secured the front door and followed behind them as they attempted to keep up with Tyler. Chloe's heels clicking behind them echoed around the marble hallway. It unsettled Lucy, but after the fear of being bundled into a van or shot on arrival, it was palatable.

Tyler led them directly into the faraday lab, where Ethan was ready to welcome them. Seeing Ethan and Mia took away the concern of another door closing behind them.

Ethan gave them a warm smile and exchanged pleasantries. Ethan rubbed his hands together. Despite the growing severity around them, he relished the challenge. Hiding away from evil people would not bring them to justice. It was down to Ethan and Mia to take them to task for their actions. Their primary concern was if the leaders had knowledge of their plan and were also on their way to convert Ethan and Mia into the same conditioned hell as Luke.

Not taking any chances, Mia locked the door as Ethan followed the same process. "Would you both like to take a seat? I have a presentation to show you."

They took a seat, and Ethan applied the magnet. Luke and Lucy shared a glance as if something should have happened.

"You're not a droid then," Ethan said.

"No." Luke frowned at Lucy, "Did you tell him I was a robot?"

"No, but I told him about the messages."

"I understand you had a neural lace fitted, and it is causing you some problems," Mia said.

"Yes, about three years ago." Luke was treating the questions with distaste, as Ethan's setup was not a polished and clean laboratory, but a converted office with basic home furnishings.

Ethan passed Luke and Lucy VR headsets, "these will answer some of your questions and tell us if we can help you."

Luke glanced at Lucy putting on her headset and did likewise, but Lucy's was a regular VR headset, which gave a presentation about the neural lace benefits.

Lucy was wary about having a lace fitted, given the torment Luke had been experiencing, but she could see the benefits. She thought back to her time reading and re-reading her study books. The neural link allowed an upload of total knowledge in two minutes compared to her eight years of study.

The VR headset on Luke was significantly different. Whilst it informed him of the detailed workings of the neural lace, it also gave him the security upload and ran through a few examples on how to improve his neural security.

As Luke followed the download exercises, Ethan downloaded all his files to a neural lace he'd built earlier. Ethan's assumption was correct, Luke's lace was wide open to uploads and interference.

"I suggest you stay in here and play with your security settings?" Ethan said to Luke.

Mia re-assured Luke the faraday cage blocked communications. "If messages are still getting through, they'll be repeater messages. They're easy to stop."

"I've not had any since we arrived," Luke said, ruling out a straightforward solution.

Lucy was aghast at Mia's explosion of knowledge and was coming around to the thought of having the same, but she held up her hand to halt Mia. "Luke received new instructions this morning." Lucy explained how she was now also at risk and time was not on their side.

Ethan asked Luke to search his files and tell him which he didn't recognise.

It drew a blank.

Luke searched again for recent uploads, but still no results connected with the messages.

Luke tested his ability to switch his security on and off with Mia. When he agreed he was comfortable with it, Mia asked him to switch it off, "You'll have been traced to here. If the security blocks messages straight away, it'll lead them here and we'll all be finished."

"I'll wait till I'm at the hospital," Luke said.

When Ethan had completed his analysis, they formulated a plan, but they still didn't know where the messages were coming from. The most likely sources are; Direct government control, as the sexbots had suggested, the Tushi network or another lunatic who has gained control of both.

As soon as Luke stepped out of the faraday cage, Luke screamed as a painful buzzing penetrated his head. He desperately wanted to switch on his security. Lucy grabbed his hand and pulled him towards Ethan's front door.

Mia messaged a VTOL, and it arrived shortly after they stepped outside. Quickly on board, Lucy and Luke lifted off and sped towards the hospital.

They'd aligned the plan with Luke's scheduled meeting as it gave them the clearest point of contact with the leader. Mia ordered the clothes they required and as long as Luke didn't get deleted early. They were ready.

Chapter 32

It had been a few weeks since Mia had been to the coffee shop. Sarah had done an excellent job filling in since her scare in the hospital, and she'd kept the supply of cakes flowing.

As Mia approached the shop, she was pleased to see so many customers. Someone she didn't expect to see was her mom. Since her mom had left home to live with Dave, she'd only seen Mia once. She'd told Mia to take her own primrose path, and she certainly had.

All eyes turned to Mia as the bell rang to announce her arrival.

Jeers of sarcastic derision came her way after she'd been missing from her duties. The crew welcomed her as she would normally have welcomed them. Sarah gave her a hug and asked about Cole to which she held out her hand, showing he was up past her waist.

Her mom interrupted them, giving Mia a surprise cuddle from behind and teasingly asking, "Where's Chucky?"

Mia frowned at Ray, who had undoubtedly put the name into her mom's head. "Hi Ray"

"Any updates to share?" Jackie asked.

Mia looked around the room, drawing them in, before folding her arms "Updates!" A smirk appeared. "One or two."

"Grab yourself a coffee, they're really nice here," Harry said.

"Then tell us all." Jackie settled in her seat, ready for the latest news.

Her mom re-joined them at the foot of the table and the other customers were also showing interest.

"I'll tell you later," Mia teased, "just going to check on the cakes."

"Come back here!" her mom shouted as Mia stepped away from the table.

"Just a minute," Mia hid her smile as she went around the counter into the kitchen. She stared at the oven door looking at the cakes slowly rising and reflecting on her own rise over the last few weeks. Her thoughts didn't have long to gather as her mom impatiently took her by the hand back to the cheering extended crew.

"Okay, okay. Where to start? It's been a surprising and enlightening few weeks?" Mia then walked around the table to her favourite pictures on the wall. "I've spent hours gazing at this, the winding path through the forest. I hoped that my own path would lead me to love and fulfilment and I'm over the moon to say, it has." Mia's teasing grin checked each of their engrossed faces as they listened intently for the next morsel. Even Ray was quiet.

The second picture was the couple walking hand in hand along the sand. "I used to think it was my mom and dad," her bottom lip pursed as she looked at her mom. "When you left Dad, I took it off the wall, but it had a mark behind it, so I had to put it back up again." Mia stroked the side of the frame. "I look at it differently now."

"You found love with Tyler, didn't you darling," Jackie said kindly. "And with Cole, you have a family."

"Things have changed a lot, since we last spoke." Mia had

them in her palm and their faces were wide open when she announced, "I finally got to New York." She then explained how things were back on with Ethan, who wasn't crazy after all, or maybe only crazy in love with her. She held back the details of the neural lace. It would be too much for them to get their heads around.

Her most exciting update filled them with the most warmth. She announced it was early days, but she was expecting a baby with Ethan. They all raised to their feet and a group hug ensued. With the news announced, the other customers shared in her joy before heading off.

With the coffee shop much quieter, normality returned. Her mom helped clear the empty mugs and crumb scattered plates, and as she was passing them to Mia, a plate slipped out of her hand. Mia's new skills instinctively stopped its fall, and she grabbed it.

"Good catch," her Mom said.

Mia hoped no-one had noticed and continued around the counter.

"What was that?" Harry asked.

"Good reactions," Mia replied.

"It stopped before you caught it," Harry added with a suspicious frown.

"You're imagining things," Mia replied casually, as she continued into the kitchen.

"Imagining what?" Jackie asked.

"I might be old, but I'm not daft. She didn't just catch the plate, she stopped it first," Harry said.

"Mia!" Jackie shouted, and with trepidation Mia reappeared looking a little sheepish. Jackie continued, "do you have more news to share?"

"Nope." Mia shook her head like a child trying to hide an obvious truth.

"I think you do," Jackie said with a stern look and a wag of her finger.

"Ok, sit down," Mia said, hoping her inability to hide anything wouldn't come back to bite her.

Totally flabbergasted, they sat back in amazement as Mia explained the lace and showed some of her newly developed skills. She even spoke out a reply to Ray's thought about another cake.

"Can you guess what I'm thinking about?" her mom asked with a restrained smile.

Mia screwed her nose up. "I'm not telling them that. Where you put your mouth is your business."

Her mom returned a devious grin, suitably convinced.

Mia enjoyed sharing her news with the crew but didn't mention the plan which would either restore balance between the droids and humanity or end her newly energised life. The less they knew, the better.

Chapter 33

Luke shared a relaxing evening with Lucy and deepened their bond with more time between the sheets. Luke wanted to mentally engage the cyber security for his lace, but to protect everyone, he absorbed the torture of messages telling him to say goodbye to Lucy.

Showering together ended their romantic start to the day as focus on their mission took centre stage. Luke had disengaged his security as agreed with Ethan, and the messages returned with greater intensity and purpose. *Lucy knows too much; an injection will be painless for her.* Luke ignored the messages, which alternated every minute. *Return to the hospital and complete your assigned task.* The task was to say goodbye to Kelly and Cora as the trash bot had reported the quantity of unused syringes being discarded.

Luke didn't share his torment with Lucy as a third message joined the torture in his head. *Complete your tasks and report to New Birmingham, 7th floor of grid reference B1 2ND.*

Luke shared the address with Lucy and she sent a cryptic message to Mia and another to Ethan to reveal the address.

A short message back confirmed they fully understood Luke's message.

Luke's previous visit to the 7th floor garden at the City

Library had been a year ago. He received an upgrade to his neural lace. It gave him more knowledge of how to act around women to turn him into an experienced charmer which had helped him to gain favour in the hospital.

The library garden wasn't always a pleasurable venue. It was a spot where suicidal men and women jumped to their death, or where people received a final sentence without judicial involvement. They added spikes to the perimeter of the building to dissuade jumpers, but spikey deaths followed at a greater rate.

The government authority changed them to retractable spikes to help the clean-up operation after the leaders of the city declined the suggestion to raise the shielded edges, which would have obscured the perfect view. Picturesque views dominated the Utopian Metropolis of New Birmingham, and the mega-rich inhabitants insisted it stayed that way.

They kept the undesirables out with access codes required for each entrant's personal key. They only allowed one guest, if they adhered to the dress code: a suit for the men and a dress for the ladies. The wearing of jeans was snubbed out quickly. It was a place of beauty, with beautiful clothes a necessity along with the wealth.

Luke put on a two-piece midnight blue stretch suit with a white shirt and blue-grey chequered tie. Lucy wore a Venetian blue and white floral print tie-front skater dress. Luke had ordered them both the night before, and Lucy finally had some modern style for her outdated wardrobe. Lucy was unsure of Luke's fedora, but it was necessary.

Luke told Lucy how the messages made it difficult to think straight. Her solution was a passionate kiss which helped, but the torment soon returned. His frustration with knowing how to switch the messages off, but having to keep them on, burned away at him. Before heading to New Birmingham, they stopped off at the hospital and gained some admiring looks.

Whoops from Cora and Kelly welcomed them into the maternity department.

"Alfie will be jealous. You look amazing," Kelly said to a smiling Lucy who held up Luke's hand like a trophy.

Luke was more bashful with the attention; it was one of his many endearing qualities that Lucy loved. He politely excused himself and headed towards the office. Lucy had noticed the growing torture in his expression and recalled how Luke's friend had been terminated. Could he focus to switch the security on with growing pressure in his head?

"He'll be good for you, I'm sure," Cora said.

Lucy thanked them before her smile straightened and her brow creased. "You did an outstanding job holding back the syringes and you've saved lives, but the leaders found out and now you're at risk. Go home and wait for further instructions."

"Why are we in trouble? You told us to do it," Cora said.

"We are all at risk. The leaders didn't want us to save the mothers and babies," Lucy said and Cora looked even more confused.

"We have two more ladies due in today. Who's going to deliver the babies if we go home?" Kelly asked.

Lucy shook her head and rolled her eyes in despair. She spelled it out. "You will be killed if you stay here. Go home and close all your doors and windows."

Kelly duly disappeared at pace, but Cora accepted the risk and said, "I'll stay to look after the ladies."

Lucy embraced her for her courage, only to be told, "don't be daft, everything'll be fine. There's nobody coming to kill

237

anybody."

Lucy was sure Cora didn't fully understand the danger she was in, but left her with her brave smile, as she collected Luke and headed out into an awaiting taxi.

As the taxi moved away, the messages in Luke's head changed. *Your missions have been reassigned, return to New Birmingham. Your missions have been reassigned, return to New Birmingham.*" Luke didn't share the update as it repeated incessantly. He put his arm around Lucy for both comfort and protection.

A buzzing sound caused him to lift his head. They both looked out of the taxi windows to see a small swarm of drones swoop down and head into the maternity wing of the hospital.

"New Birmingham quickly!" Lucy instructed the Taxi.

*

Healthy trees lined the streets. The parks were full of lush, manicured grass. Ethan and Mia strolled hand in hand along the winding pathways taking in the vibrant flowers and their sweet aroma wafting on a dome controlled gentle breeze.

It reminded them of one of their first dates, their trip to the climate-controlled garden at Eden. It was a more pleasant time before the Tushi world had taken a sinister turn.

Ethan halted their stroll and turned to face Mia, placing both of his hands on her shoulders and resting his forehead against hers. "Mia. You know I love you."

"I know you do."

"I've got you involved in this and I've put you at risk."

Mia shrugged. "I'm ready."

"You don't understand. Mia, you're everything to me. You're

expecting our baby and I want to keep you safe. I can do this alone."

"You're an idiot. We're in this together and we're stronger together," Mia said.

"Stay in the garden with Lucy. Luke will be there if I need help."

Mia brushed off his hands and stood in disgust. "You want the men to go to war and leave the little ladies in the pretty garden."

Mia stepped back and held her palms out. "My skills are stronger than yours. Perhaps you should stay and smell the flowers."

Ethan took both of her hands in his. "Mia. I need to do this for me. Please understand." Ethan gave her a sympathetic smile, but Mia pulled her hands away and paced across the lawn with Ethan in pursuit.

*

Arriving nervously at the entrance to New Birmingham, Luke remembered to speak casually to the security bot, "back again."

"Yes, so soon." The friendly bot replied as he scanned the digital key on the back of Ethan's hand and much to their relief, with a tip of his fedora they entered New Birmingham.

Lucy had been there briefly for Kat's Wedding and seen the beauty of the place, but having more time to look around, she absorbed the dreamlike ambiance.

The mission was still clear in her head, but she pulled Luke slightly off course to wind along the park path. Taking in the aroma of real flowers was a rare treat. The flowers were

239

further evidence of the beauty being kept for the elite. As the magnificent building came into view, the next ominous stage of the plan loomed. They held each aromatic breath as if it could be their last.

A tap on her shoulder nearly jumped her out of her skin. An almost mirror image of herself spoke, "like your hair."

"Yours too," Lucy replied, her hair matching Mia's, as well as their matching dresses.

"Time is critical, let's move," Ethan said. He was also matching Luke's appearance. It had been a vital component to enable them both to gain entry into the city. Ethan had taken a copy of Luke's digital key, disengaging his own, to lay Luke's protected profile temporarily over his own.

"Lucy, we've got to hold back and smell flowers." Mia scrunched her face up at Ethan.

It confused Lucy. "I thought we had a plan."

Mia stared at Ethan. "We did, but Ethan wants all the glory for himself."

"It's got nothing to do with glory. You're expecting our baby and your safety is my top priority. Darling, I don't want to put you at risk," Ethan repeated.

Mia held her hand up to stop his drivel. "We'll give you ten minutes. If you're not back down here. We're coming up." Mia sarcastically added, "well, that's if we've finished admiring the flowers."

"Okay. We'll be back down in five. Ready Luke!" Ethan headed off to the City Library with Luke following.

Luke glanced back with his arms raised, equally perplexed by the change to the plan.

They stepped into the building like twins, gaining double takes as they headed straight to the lift. Luke engaged his security. "That's better." He let out a long sigh, his features softened, and his tormented brain was finally free from the messages.

The lift pinged its arrival, and the doors opened. The light from the full-length windows illuminated an ornate spiral staircase. Several people were reading to their right, but their destiny lay through the windows in the elevated garden. Ethan held back, as Luke went to find out who'd being making his life a living hell.

As soon as he stepped out onto the garden terrace of the library, he spotted a smartly dressed oriental man. He was standing between a pair of eight feet tall guardian bots. The man waved to beckon Luke to him.

As Luke stepped towards him, the identity of his tormentor became clear. He was the technology genius, Okzu Tushi. He would easily have pummeled him, if not for the two sturdy bots.

As Luke drew close, Okzu filled his nostrils with a deep breath, lifting his chin to look down his nose at him. "Luke, you have disappointed me. You've not followed my orders."

Having the ability to switch off the messages had given Luke a new level of confidence. He was ready to get his life back. "I will not delete Lucy or the others. I'm sick of the shit you put in my head."

"You're no longer of use to me," the oriental man's curt response. A guardian seized him and pulled him close to Okzu. Okzu's eyes narrowed as intense concentration sent a brain melting message to Luke.

Luke screamed, but the pain he'd experienced before was no longer there. It was merely a slight irritation. The screaming was for Okzu's benefit and part of the plan.

Okzu pulled him closer and his reddened face contorted as he tried to melt Luke's head like he'd done with his previous subjects who'd attempted to defy him.

"It's not working, is it?"

The familiar voice from behind the guardian broke his concentration. "Ethan!" Okzu snapped at the intrusion. The guardian released Luke and stepped back for Okzu to see his tormentor. Ethan, his most decorated engineer. "Has your madness gone into overload?" Okzu sniped. "you're not needed here."

"I don't think Ethan is the crazy one," Luke said with confidence after the tormenting messages had stopped. He was no longer under Okzu's control.

A guardian grabbed Luke and lifted him into the air. The guardian walked with him and held him over the edge with the condemning spikes beneath him. "You had your chance to say goodbye."

The guardian released Luke, but he held onto the guardian's outstretched arm to save himself from the spikes.

"You don't need to kill him!" Ethan shouted. He used his telekinesis to lift Luke away from the guardian. Luke gratefully loosened his grasp on the guardian as Ethan's mind lifted him. The other guardian however clamped his monstrous hand onto Ethan's forearm and broke Ethan's intense concentration. Ethan screamed out in agony and with his focus taken, Luke dropped to the spikes below.

Ethan screamed out in excruciating pain as his radius and ulna splintered against each other under the vice-like compression. Ethan's plan had failed, and it would cost him his life. Okzu read his thoughts and peered into his glistening eyes.

"You may have new skills, but you are no match for me."

Ethan clenched the fist of his free hand and drove it with all his strength into the stomach of Okzu, but Okzu laughed at the grimacing Ethan.

"Ethan." Okzu shook his head. "I am disappointed in you. Did you think you could take me down with a punch? My endoskeleton is titanium."

"Don't tell me you are a droid." Ethan shook his head in painful defeat.

"Not a droid. An advanced human. I've had a neural lace for ten years and when I was diagnosed with liver cancer four years ago, I chose immortality. I transferred my consciousness into this exceptional body."

"So, you are a droid."

"No. I'm an advanced human," Okzu repeated.

"If you are human, why are you killing humans."

"I'm not killing all humans; I'm just getting rid of the waste. Women and old people."

"Women are not waste, you fucking psycho. They populate the planet."

"Not anymore they don't. Tushi wives are better in every way. Humanity is a spent force; AI droids make better decisions."

"Our creative ability has made the droids. Humans are too complex to replace them with a program."

"Watch me." Okzu smirked.

"How about carrying on your family name?"

"My family name is Tushi, They'll carry on forever. Succession planning is in place, droids are gradually replacing the staff. As for family, I've seen my Tushi children grow."

"Who will own the company after you've gone?"

"I've set my wishes for the droids to run the decentralized

243

company on my passing."

Ethan pleaded with Okzu to consider his decision. "We've all had disappointments and relationship woes. It's part of life. Don't give up on finding love with a real woman. You have lots to offer, you're a creative genius, not to mention a zillionaire. You could have any woman you wanted."

Okzu shook his head. "Women are the biggest problem in the world."

"You've lost the plot. You can't recreate the deeper love a woman can provide."

"What like the woman who cut your dick off? Or Chloe, who you were besotted with before she left you. Your own version of Chloe is much better. She'll always be faithful."

"I've found genuine love with Mia."

"You're a fool. It won't last. I gave my heart to a woman and thought we'd be together forever. When she tore my heart from my chest, I pledged not to let it happen again. I focused on a solution. Tushi wives are the solution and my greatest invention. They won't grow older or get sick. Tushi wives won't die and now I've upgraded, I won't either."

"But that's artificial life."

"And your neural lace isn't." Okzu held up his hand, tired of the exchange. "You're no longer of use to me. Goodbye Ethan."

Ethan let out a pained moan as the guardian's powerful hand grabbed his head. His hands attempted to hold off the guardian's claw grip, but the splintered bones of his forearm wouldn't move for the pain. He screamed in agony with the cracking of his skull beneath the guardian's tightening grip.

Like a brain freeze on his scalp, Ethan sensed the end, but the cool air was from the released grip of the guardian. Relieved, he glanced up, expecting to see a repentant Okzu, offering him a reprieve, but he wasn't there. The guardians stood tall and motionless beside him. A flurry of steps from behind him grew louder, and the impact came before he could turn around. Arms clamped hard around him. It was an embrace of love.

Ethan moaned in pain whilst equally elated to smell the woman he thought he'd never see again.

Mia released her tight grasp. "Do you need some help?" Mia asked the rhetorical question of the defeated Ethan.

Ethan forced a sorry smile as he rolled his eyes at Mia. His foolish decision to go it alone didn't need any apology or discussion. "Glad to see you." His heart went into overload, but so did the pain, as he winced again to her more delicate touch.

"That hunk of fucking metal crushed my arm." Ethan attempted to lift his squished forearm, but the pain stopped him.

Mia attempted to stroke it, but his squeal caused her to retrace. "We saw Luke come over the ledge and guessed it may not be going too well." Mia placed her hand sympathetically on his shoulder.

"No shit," he said, looking at his arm before he heard more footsteps. Ethan's face lit up with relief as Luke and Lucy came into focus. "Luke!"

The pain in his arm subsided for a moment as a fit and well Luke strode up to him.

"I would have been on the spikes, if not for Mia and her skills," Luke said.

"Glad to help." Mia shrugged and smiled to herself. Halting his fall and taking him safely to the ground was a memory she'd hold forever.

"Let's have a look at your arm." Luke knelt next to Ethan and checked over his arm. He slowly shook his head. "Not a chance."

"Where did Okzu disappear to?" Ethan asked.

"Don't know." Mia replied. "A VTOL took off as I came out here."

"We need to find him before he does anything else," Ethan said.

"The only place you're going is the hospital," Luke said.

"I'll call Tyler and Chloe to join us at Tushi," Mia said. "That's where Okzu will be heading."

"Take me too. This arms past repair. I'll need a Tushi one."

"Think you're right buddy, but we must get it scanned first," Luke said.

Luke took off his shirt and made a sling for Ethan's arm.

"Time to re-group, whilst he's hiding," Lucy said.

"I don't think he's hiding," Luke said, surveying to the sky. "The fun's only just starting. We need to get inside. Now!" Luke lifted Ethan over his shoulder and they quickly dived back inside as a swarm of small drones reached the garden terrace.

Temporary relief came over them as the swarm of about twenty-five mini drones hovered the other side of the reinforced glass.

Ethan stared at the drones and tried to alter their course. It didn't work.

Mia's call connected, but it wasn't the voice she expected. "Why have you answered the phone?"

Mia listened to the reply, and the color drained from her face. Lucy placed an arm around her shoulders. "Is everything okay?"

Chapter 34

After Tyler's emotional embrace with Mia, he had joined Chloe and Cole in the lounge watching the fish. An impatient knock on the door had disturbed their peace, Chloe shook her head. "I think Ethan was sharper before he had the lace fitted. What have they forgotten?"

"It's probably Mia returning for a quick trip to the toilet," Tyler joked.

They stepped into the hallway to tease them, but it wasn't the happy couple.

It was a familiar face, but not the one they expected. Mirek stood before them in a fitted navy-blue pin-striped suit. Mirek's casual chat was missing and his words were formal. "Is Ethan at home?"

"I hope he wasn't expecting you," Chloe replied politely. "You've just missed him."

"I'm also looking for Mia. Is she with him?" Mirek glanced behind as four sturdy police droids filed in and stood either side of him with automatic weapons drawn.

"What is your interest in Mia?" Tyler replied. Despite his hope to the contrary, the link between Ethan and Mia was in the open. "I am her bonded partner, Tyler."

Mirek held up an apologetic hand and touched his earpiece

to receive additional information.

"You are both points of concern. Tyler and Chloe, your connections to the network are faulty and need repair. Join us in the transporter, I'll take you to Tushi."

Tyler couldn't reveal Ethan had removed him from the network. He also knew that gunmen were overkill for addressing network issues. His eyes shifted to Chloe.

"You better get us fixed then," Chloe replied.

Out gunned, they had no option other than to comply and return with them to Tushi.

Tyler held back from asking why guns were necessary, but assumed the bullets were for Ethan and Mia. As they stepped into the awaiting transporter, a taser rendered them still.

*

Tyler awoke with information streaming into his head, the connection to the network re-established. The newly uploaded requirements conflicted with his established settings, causing a glitch in final testing. The program ran again, with a full data cleanse to remove his memory to prepare him for his new role.

A female droid next to him twitched, trying to hold on to her previous memories but to no avail. "Protect Okzu Tushi. Protect the network," she said when the clamps restraining them opened. Tyler had the same message repeating in his head. *Protect Okzu Tushi. Protect the network.*

The screen showed the image of a man and a woman he didn't recognize. The message was direct. "These people carry the most severe threat to Okzu Tushi and the network. Bring them to the Tushi Corporation, if they don't comply, delete them."

Chapter 35

Mia's mind was full of concern for what may have happened to Tyler and Chloe after Cole had said someone had taken them, but she had to protect the others, especially Ethan.

Ethan asked about the call, "are Tyler and Chloe okay?"

"Cole answered. I think they were sharing an intimate moment," Mia said. She pointed to the stairs, "we should go."

As they moved away from the library window, the mini drones scattered. Ethan and Luke led the way downstairs and ordered a taxi.

Lucy pulled Mia in close. "Ethan may have bought it, but I can read you like a book." She put an arm around Mia, "If anyone can save them, you can."

"Hope so," Mia said, as she looked around like hunted prey.

"You said you wanted to make a difference in the world. This is your chance," Lucy said.

A taxi arrived outside the library and Mia sent Luke and Ethan in first, closely followed by Lucy. As Mia approached the taxi, she noticed two drones banking around heading directly for her.

Lucy screamed and darted behind her. With an intense focus, Mia pointed a finger at each drone and they dropped to the floor like well-trained dogs.

Lucy put her hands on Mia's shoulders and peeked over at the still drones. "Cool. Like your new skills."

Mia returned the briefest of smiles and ushered Lucy into the taxi.

The taxi moved off and Lucy spotted another two approaching. Mia swiped two fingers, and both exploded as they hit the ground.

Ethan didn't notice, which brought a giggle from both Lucy and Mia. She used her telepathy to tell him, but he didn't hear it. "Is your lace working?" Mia asked.

"Don't think so. I've got a splitting headache. That bloody guardian nearly crushed my skull."

"Maybe next time you won't turn down my help," Mia said, before rolling her eyes and shaking her head.

"Sorry for being a dick. Hope I make a better dad. You won't go back to Tyler, will you?"

"Stuck with you now." Mia said as she rubbed his leg to reassure him. Her eyes glistened at the mention of Tyler. She hoped he was okay, but she feared the worst.

Noticing Mia's eyes filling, Luke re-assured her, "I'm sure we can get him right for you."

Mia nearly asked if he knew what had happened to Tyler, but Lucy interjected, "Ethan will be better in no time."

Mia's glance to Lucy was all the thanks she needed.

Ethan shared the conversation he had with Okzu about how genuine love had escaped the genius when he had everything else. Ethan smiled at Mia. "We are lucky, I guess."

Mia gave him a warm smile. "It took us a while."

"Us too," Luke said, before he put his arm around Lucy and planted a delicate peck on her cheek.

Ethan gave Mia a loving smile and with his good hand gave her knee an affectionate squeeze before he rested his head against her.

Ethan protested as the taxi arrived at the hospital, "why have we come here? Okzu will have gone to Tushi!"

"You need to sit this one out," Luke said. "There will be lots of internal bleeding we need to sort before we think about repairing you."

Mia stepped out of the taxi first and helped Ethan out. As Ethan got to his feet, Luke barged both Ethan and Mia to the ground with his arms around them as two mini-bots exploded into Luke's back. Lucy screamed and looked to the skies.

Ethan yelled out in pain with the full weight of Luke's body on his crushed arm. Mia pulled Luke's arm away and tried to squirm from underneath his solid bloody frame.

"Watch out!" Lucy screeched.

Mia turned to see another two drones approaching at speed as she tried to get to her feet. A fraction of a second from impact, Mia swiped both away from them to explode against a nearby vehicle. Mia's eyes frantically surveyed the sky as Lucy clung to her.

Pinned down by Luke, Ethan moaned, "what the fuck? Get off me!"

Lucy roared out her frustration, her hands shaking in front of her with both shock and annoyance. "He's dead, you idiot! He saved your life."

Ignoring two dish sized holes in his back, Mia and Lucy pulled Luke's dead weight off Ethan and helped him to his feet. Lucy called for help, the strain in her voice evident as she tried to come to terms with losing Luke, and yet she still tried to hold everything together. Staff quickly appeared with a couple of gurneys to take Luke and Ethan inside.

Lucy told them what to do. Years of training contained an emotional outpouring and she emitted a calm exterior, but it was wearing thin as she helped to lift Luke's body onto the gurney.

Lucy followed as they wheeled away Luke, pulling a trembling Mia by the hand. "Let's get you inside. You need a breather," Lucy insisted with the last sliver of composure she had remaining.

Neither could have predicted who they would see waiting inside.

Mia's stroll burst into a run as Tyler and Chloe were there to greet them. Tyler's arms however didn't open to welcome her as she headed full on towards him and buried her head into his chest.

Tyler responded to Mia's embrace, gripping her tight. The kiss on the top of her head was missing as he stuck to business. "I need to take you to see Okzu. He is at Tushi Corp."

"Too right you do," Mia replied.

Luke's gurney had proceeded along a corridor with nurses flapping around him. The gurney holding Ethan was with Chloe as she grabbed Lucy. "I think Okzu would like to see you too."

"I'm just a nurse. I need to take care of Ethan."

Chloe looked over his arm like she was scanning him. "He will be okay. Come with us, you can monitor him," Chloe said with a polite tone, but it was clearly not for discussion.

Lucy glanced at Mia and received a single nod to comply.

One of Lucy's admirers pulled up outside in an ambulance, leaping out to see Lucy.

"Hello stranger. Where would you like to go?" he asked Lucy.

"Need to take this one to the Tushi Corporation."

"Not going to turn him into a robot, are you?" he said with a cheeky grin.

Lucy's face of thunder didn't need words. He closed his mouth and opened the back doors. Chloe ushered in Mia and Lucy in the back and Tyler climbed in the drivers' seat.

The driver opened the door. "Move over, I'm the driver."

Without a word Tyler grabbed him by the throat, crushed his windpipe and pushed him to the floor.

Chapter 36

When they stopped, Tyler opened the back doors. He directed them past a guardian at a side entrance and led them through to an opulent lift. They stepped into a mirrored wonderment of golden handrails and trimmings. Relaxing instrumental music complimented the soft blood red carpet and the smell of sweet perfume in what must have been Okzu's personal elevator.

It rose steadily as Mia thought back to her peaceful existence with Tyler and the fun they'd shared. But the more pertinent memory was the image of the rogue police droid at the hen party. Her life with Tyler could never have lasted. Mirek's words returned to her. The world's reliance on technology had gone too far. Perhaps a future as their pets was the best scenario, especially now. The luxurious lift to see Okzu wasn't for a champagne reception.

Chloe took Ethan's good arm and pulled him forward. His head hung down in defeated despair. Lucy followed behind, looking around like she was considering an offer for the place.

Mia shook her head and laughed to herself. Lucy was unphased by the impending verdict on her life. The shock from witnessing Luke's demise hadn't hit, she must have blocked it out. Mia took her hand. Not that she appeared to need re-assurance.

Tyler followed behind as they strolled through the glass roofed reception area to the upper echelons of Tushi. Soft underfoot, the matching carpets warmed their spirit. The gold embellished images of ornate gardens in the golden paradise made them feel like they were visiting royalty.

The image was real. Okzu Tushi *was* modern royalty. Highly regarded and admired by most of the world, rich beyond comprehension and a man of ultimate power. He had everything. Except love.

The following corridor was of equal opulence. Enclosed glass cases lit up and protected timeless ornaments with undoubtedly high valuations. After initially expecting to be tortured and put to death, Mia was enjoying the visit. Lucy stopped to pay particular attention to a silver vase. The label dated it as 1885. It was a monumental size, 40cm tall, described as an antique Chinese silver vase - Wang Hing Canton. Lucy read the extended description before a shove in her back from Tyler reminded them, they weren't on a site seeing tour.

Mia glanced back at Tyler to object, but his hard expression faced dead ahead. The look of love she cherished was no more.

Two guardians stood outside a carved mahogany door. Chloe stopped and informed them. "We have brought Ethan and Mia to see Okzu."

The guardian pointed at Lucy.

"Fodder," Chloe added.

"Charming." Lucy bobbed her tongue out at Chloe but received no response.

The guardian opened the door. They filed in to see Okzu sitting in a large, backed chair behind his huge desk with two clear glass monitors hung over the desk suspended by slim arms.

Okzu stood with a beaming, smug smile of victory. "Welcome. Take a seat."

Ethan and Mia sat whilst Lucy strolled to the window. Lucy was still unaware of their plight or insistent on ignoring it and following the plan to distract him. "This is the most beautiful place I've ever seen," Lucy said.

"Thank you," Okzu replied. "I've worked rather hard to create this."

The screen showed wispy clouds in blue skies above a flourishing pine forest. The view of a perfect world. Lucy appeared lost in thought until the screen changed to a view of the droid assembly line.

Lucy fascinated Okzu. Perhaps she could bring him love. He continued, glad to entertain her. "The reality is not quite ready." The screen switched again to show a vast array of younger trees under a colossal dome. "I will remove the dome in three years, when the environment should be ready to sustain them. The world is healing. Slowly."

"It makes sense now," Lucy said, as her eyes fixed on his. "You're fixing the planet."

Mia looked at Lucy in disbelief, picking up on Lucy's growing infatuation with Okzu.

"I'm glad you understand. There are too many people on the planet and Mars doesn't have room."

"The only way is to reduce the population," Lucy replied. "You need to save the planet."

Ethan shifted in his seat. "We have the technology to fix all the issues. We don't need to wipe out humanity."

"Time is not on our side, Ethan. You know that." Okzu paced back behind his desk.

"How can you live with yourself? Ordering the death of

thousands of people," Ethan asked.

"It is all for the greater good. It worked in China. No more starving people, only harmony. Russia and India too." Okzu glanced at Mia, who seemed lost in thought.

Tyler stood behind Mia. She glanced up at him before returning her gaze to the screen.

Ethan's brow creased. "I thought we were the first."

"Not at all. The west of America was first."

"You've killed billions for a world full of droids!" Ethan shouted.

"The droids have increased, that is true, but we have no more wars." Okzu was as calm as a summer lake.

Ethan shook his head. "Just one big war against the droids."

Okzu smoothed his fingers slowly across his desk, "It's not a war. It's a smooth transition." He opened up his hands and smiled. "I thought you'd be proud to help." He smiled and nodded, seeking approval. "You already have the neural lace. You need a new arm and would benefit from a more toned body. Without your imperfections, you're already transhuman."

Mia sat forward and rested her elbows on the desk as she clasped her hands. "Not here. Not now," Mia said. She glanced at Ethan. "I love his imperfections."

"Wouldn't you like to be taller with proper breasts?" Okzu asked with a teasing smile.

"I love her body. Just the way it is," Ethan replied.

"That's unlucky. The pregnancy will change that." Okzu's flippant response. "But then again, you won't be having a baby. There are enough already."

Mia swished her hand to send Okzu stumbling back into his chair. "Arsehole! You won't hurt my baby." Mia gave him a smug grin.

Okzu returned a grin. "Nice One." He gestured to Tyler. "A stomach punch should do it."

Tyler stepped forward and pulled Mia back into her seat. Rather than punching, he rested his palm on Mia's stomach.

"Do it!" Okzu demanded.

Tyler was unmoved. Okzu gestured towards Chloe. "Kill him."

Chloe stepped forward and stroked Ethan's hair.

"Kill him!" Okzu screeched.

Chloe pulled Ethan's head to the side and placed a hand on his shoulder. Far from killing him, she kissed him. Okzu screamed in frustration.

Whilst Ethan and Lucy had distracted him, Mia had remotely uploaded Tyler's backup file and done the same for Chloe. They were back on side.

Lucy approached Okzu, "Make love not war. It's stronger." She held out her hands to welcome an embrace from Okzu, but he swiped a blow across her face, knocking her to the ground.

Tyler helped Lucy to her feet and Mia stood to challenge Okzu but shot a glance behind as two guardians entered the room. Okzu smirked. "Game over."

Mia turned to see the guardian's approach.

Mia pushed her hand out towards the nearest guardian and jettisoned him back through the closed door, taking the frame and part of the wall with him. The second received similar treatment, sent on his way. "New skills," Mia said proudly. She turned to face Okzu. But he'd gone.

Chapter 37

Okzu Tushi knew the tide had turned. Mia's skills were more advanced than his, and he couldn't defeat her alone. The emergency chute directly behind his desk dropped him into a pod and like a mini-hyper-loop he sped to the upload room. The startled staff bowed their heads as he stepped out. He barely acknowledged them as he focussed on protecting his dream. Okzu hadn't wanted to resort to his emergency plan, but he had no other option.

He needed to put the plan in place and get out of the country. Okzu messaged his personal VTOL to take him to a safer place. He just needed to upload the protocol to release the mini-bots to delete those harming the environment and authorize the Tushi wives to champion his environmental cause. Save the planet by whatever means necessary.

"Privacy please," he asked politely as he entered the control room.

The three programmers slipped out without a word. He entered his password and confirmed his security ID. The retinal scanner then confirmed his administrator's rights, and the system opened to him. He selected the saved folder which he'd created on one of his darkest days.

Two years ago, his only previous love had left him to be with his friend. He had returned to his country estate for the calm it brought him so he could wallow in self-pity and heal his broken heart, but when the house came into view, his heart sank further. The broken windows were superficial, but he found inside someone had smashed his antique ornaments. Chills had run through him, and he'd trembled as he reached the temperature-controlled domes at the rear of the property to hear the wind blowing through the broken panes.

His gravest concern was realized. The aviary. His greatest delight had been a recent nesting of his most precious love. A pair of orange-breasted trogon birds. The only surviving pair outside of China. The nest and the two pale olive eggs heartlessly smashed with the birds nowhere to be seen. Open to the elements, the birds wouldn't last the night.

He'd fallen to his knees.

His darkest day had stirred up a need for vengeance, and he wrote the protocol that very day.

He'd planned to upload the environment protocol the follow-ing morning, which would have enabled order to be returned. Okzu would wipe away the scum to let the good people live. It would target the people responsible for polluting the planet. Everyone from those responsible for decimating forests to make room for more houses, to the business owners who chugged pollution into the air and seas. Plus, the idiots who insisted on still using gas powered vehicles.

Improvement actions were in place, but the quickest solution was to reduce the population to allow green areas to return and flourish. The protocol order had been less than two minutes from being loaded when an employee, Josh Taylor, had brought him a coffee and a piece of cake. Okzu never forgot the words from Josh as he'd said, 'my wife and I have had a baby boy. He will change the world and make it a better place.' He showed Okzu the picture of his wife and baby. A fresh idea popped into Okzu's head. Reduce the population by reducing the input. Child bots will be less of a drain on the world than children. It changed the course of his thinking and history. It saved the world from the dramatic change he'd planned.

Energized by his new idea, Okzu had renamed the file, 'Never 2B.'

Today, he stared at the screen, knowing the world had not changed. The climate was still broken. People were still destroying the planet. "I should have done this two years ago." He clicked on the file. He paused with the mouse pointer over the 'run' command box and as he clicked the button, the screen went black, plus everything around him before the emergency lighting flickered to life.

His remote access on his handset wouldn't open either. He stormed back into the control room. His face of thunder rendered his staff unable to speak for fear of repercussions. He knew every name and their family. He singled out one of his more senior programmers. "What's happened? Why can't I access the network?"

"We had an emergency power down. The order came from your office."

"Do I look like I ordered this? Out of my way." Okzu stepped back into his vacuum pod and shot off to the power room.

As the pod arrived, he saw that the power room had a huge hole in the wall and the main backup generator was missing. He selected his exit route and within ten seconds he reached his own personal VTOL. He leapt out of the pod into the VTOL and initiated take-off. The VTOL lifted into the air but held steady rather than speeding away. "What now?" he shouted at the console.

The VTOL turned around for him to see the reason.

Chapter 38

After a frenetic couple of minutes. All was quiet as Mia stared at Okzu in the suspended VTOL. She had the power to smash it to the ground or into the wall, but she was not the monster. Hands on hips, she stared through the hole in his office wall.

"I guess it's a waste of time calling the cops," Ethan said.

"Okzu owns the police," Mia said. "And the government. It's up to us to stop this."

Mia called upon a couple of VTOL's. They returned to Ethan's with Okzu's VTOL following like an obedient dog. When they touched down in front of Ethan's house. Tyler escorted Okzu into the house and into Ethan's lab.

Cole appeared, but his run into Mia's arms was halted by her outstretched hand. "Later." she smiled as she joined Ethan and the others in the lab. She closed the door as Tyler pushed Okzu into the seat. Ethan engaged the magnets in the chair.

"Do you need myself and Chloe for anything else? We could keep a lookout," Tyler said.

"Can you get Cole to help? He'll feel left out," Mia asked before turning to Lucy. "Unless you want to play with him."

"I'm staying here," Lucy said and promptly took a seat next to Okzu.

Mia locked the door after Chloe and Tyler. Despite a crushed arm in a sling and a damaged neural lace in his skull, Ethan strolled around his lab like he was about to present a lecture for the millionth time. It was all a distraction whilst Okzu's data was downloaded to Ethan's server. He stopped directly in front of the restrained Okzu.

"How can we sort this out? I don't want to kill you," Ethan said.

"You'd better not," Lucy said, as she placed a hand on Okzu's thigh.

Mia had asked Lucy to show him some affection to soften him, but that was back at Tushi World before he smacked her across the face. "It's okay, Lucy."

"I think he deserves a right to explain himself," Lucy said, squeezing Okzu's thigh.

Okzu explained how he'd arrived at the plan and why he created the alternative option. "The plan was for a seamless transition as opposed to the direct option of releasing 500,000 mini drones to target all those harming the planet."

Ethan slowly shook his head. "You're a genius with authority and power, but you're crazy. You're behaving like you're a God."

"He means well," Lucy said, bringing sneers from both Mia and Ethan. "He's trying to help the planet."

"Did you forget the babies he's been killing?" Mia snapped.

Ethan put his hand out wide. "Your intention is honorable, it's just the execution."

Mia turned away and sighed.

"The planet needs fixing," Okzu said firmly. "There are too many people."

"The planet is already being fixed. Air quality is improving every day. The government has brought forward the obsolescence order on combustion engines. They've increased levies on polluting industries–" Ethan said.

"It's not enough!"

Mia had stood close enough to Okzu to read his lace. "He's released the never 2B protocol. As soon as the power is back on at Tushi, killer drones will take to the skies."

"What are our options?" Ethan asked.

"Let it happen," Okzu answered.

Lucy sat astride Okzu and placed her hands on his face as she stared into his eyes. "You need to stop it."

"Where are the mini-bots?" Ethan asked. "We can stop them launching."

"They're split into twenty industrial units around the country," Okzu answered.

"Wouldn't that many orders crash the server," Ethan asked.

Mia read from Okzu's thoughts. "It's in waves of a thousand from each unit, so it doesn't crash the server. We need to get back there to halt the process."

"Are you going to help us fix this?" Lucy asked Okzu.

"For you. I will," he answered.

Lucy quickly kissed him and jumped to her feet. With the download complete, Ethan released the magnet. Lucy grabbed Okzu's hand and pulled him with her as they followed Mia and Ethan to the VTOL.

Tyler, Chloe, and Cole were not far behind, eager to offer any help they could, but would they be too late? The server would surely have been restarted already.

Chapter 39

Were they too late? As the VTOL sped with the four of them, a dark cloud moved over the highway. Cars swerved and crashed as drones exploded through windscreens of the cars emitting fumes. The carnage unfolded before their eyes, as an aeroplane plummeted from the sky. The resultant fireball added to the growing devastation.

"How did a drone get to a plane so quick?" Lucy asked.

Okzu stared forward and spoke without emotion. "The Tushi network. It includes some pilots of jet planes. It's their own fault. They should have switched to electric." Okzu looked at Lucy, his hands opened wide as he shrugged. "It's cheaper." Okzu shook his head, forever puzzled by the poor decisions people made.

The emotionless face of Okzu spoke volumes about how he'd tried to improve the environment, but like a kid trying to protect his sandcastle from the incoming tide. A time comes to level it yourself to avoid having to watch it crumble.

Okzu directed them to the nearest landing spot to the server room. No sooner had the VTOL landed. Okzu said, "I can end this." He climbed out and pulled Lucy along with him, with Mia and Ethan following.

The server room cleared the moment Okzu burst in. Okzu

entered his verification to access the system as Tyler joined them. Okzu's frenetic tapping of the keys didn't stop the virus. Mia read his mind, "he's not trying to stop it." Tyler pulled him back from the keyboard and threw him to the floor.

Mia's fingers were like a blur as she took charge to change the commands. Her focus remained strong, she didn't hear the incessant Lucy repeatedly asking for a progress update or Ethan offering to help.

Mia stepped back from the keyboard, still staring at the screen. "It's not possible to stop the drones already released, but I've canceled further releases."

"Great news," Lucy said, rubbing Mia's back.

"The first wave of 20,000 are out. There's no way to stop them or protect their targets," Mia said.

"They'll have already hit or be primed for defense of key locations," The unrepentant Okzu muttered.

"If you've stopped the others, you've saved 480,000 lives, that's not bad." Lucy tilted her head and smiled at Mia.

Mia's heart sank for those innocent people going about their daily routine, unaware they wouldn't make it home to their families. Ethan put his good arm around her. She rested her head against his chest as they both stared at the floor.

Okzu sat in a corner with his head in his hands as his body shuddered. Lucy crouched aside him and rested her hand on his shoulder.

Okzu lifted his head and frowned. "Don't pretend you care for me," Okzu said, before spitting on the floor.

Lucy stepped back and glanced at Mia. "Didn't think he'd buy it." She returned her attention to Okzu's drained expression. "It's over."

"It's far from over." Mia said. "Every network connected

droid has a new objective to save the planet."

"That's good though, right?" Lucy asked.

"It depends on the rules. Doesn't it Okzu?" Mia's fierce stare had Okzu cowering.

Lucy locked her eyes back on Okzu. "What do you mean, what rules?"

Ethan replied for Okzu. "50,000 Tushi have just received orders to protect the environment, by whatever means necessary. That will include reducing the population."

Lucy's act to show care for Okzu had gained a grain of truth but she snapped and lay into him. She shouted with each punch, "that's for each baby you killed!" She stepped back to deliver kicks, "and that's for all the moms."

Okzu hardly winced with Lucy's assault, but his knuckles whitened with the grasp of his head. The greater pain in his head made him squeal. Lucy stepped back when the squealing intensified like a stressed-out pig. Okzu looked to Mia and put his hands together for a last plea for forgiveness, but his constant squeal continued until his head imploded.

Lucy screamed as he slumped over with a mix of brain, blood and circuitry spilling onto the floor.

"That was for killing Ellie!" Mia said through gritted teeth.

Lucy noticed Mia's outstretched clenched fist.

Lucy's brow creased to see the power in the hands of her friend. "What have you done? Are you ready for that kind of power?"

Ethan placed his hand on Mia's arm and slowly brought it to rest by her side, before he asked, "Did you keep a copy of the virus to deselect the droids from the network? We need to get to the upload hub."

"I will lead the way." Tyler said. He opened the door to the outside and four mini-bots exploded against him knocking him to the floor. Mia screamed and Lucy moved quickly to re-close the door.

The dual blast shattered Tyler's head, with a further two gaping holes in his chest to complete his deletion. Mia fell to the floor aside a motionless Tyler. Memories of their time together flew through her mind at a rapid pace; Tyler protecting her from being burnt in the kitchen, how she saved him from her knife wielding mom, his upgrade, and the new level of love they'd shared.

Mia sobbed over Tyler's body. How could she go on without him? Ethan kneeled aside her and placed a comforting arm around her, but Mia was inconsolable. She eventually sat up and rested her head on Ethan's shoulder, silent in her grief.

Mia wiped her eyes and ran her fingers through her hair as she tried to collect her thoughts.

"This isn't over. We need to get to the upload hub," Ethan repeated. He stood and helped Mia to her feet.

Chapter 40

Mia, Ethan and Lucy left the bodies of Tyler and Okzu to charge through the corridors to the upload hub. It was a longer route, but safe from further mini-drone attacks.

As they reached the upload hub, four droids were guarding the room. Mia however had no intention of discussing their entry and with her telekinesis power thriving, they opened the door and stepped aside to let them through.

The face they saw before them stopped them in their tracks.

"Cole. What are you doing here?" Mia asked.

"I uploaded the virus to disable the network," Cole said with a smug grin.

Mia took him in her arms. "You're a clever boy."

He looked up with a cheeky grin. "I guessed you'd need my help, even if you didn't ask for it."

Mia let out a heavy sigh.

"I tried to contact Tyler a moment ago. He's not responding," Cole said.

"He didn't make it. A drone attack killed him." Mia's heart ached to share such sad news, but her brow creased at Cole's nonchalant response.

"I have a copy of his chip in my files. I thought you did to," Cole said.

Mia's head lifted, and color returned to her face. She turned to Ethan. "Can you build him the same?"

"Of course. I think we'll get processed together." Ethan smiled and looked at the sling holding his crushed arm.

*

The news twins reported the country had been victim to an attack by the usually peaceful 'Earth is First' campaigners. Six jets had crashed as a result, taking nearly 400 lives. Further drone attacks led to assassinations of thirty-eight ministers. The ministers had previously voted against updates to the environmental bill. They'd also campaigned for an extension to the license for combustion engines in order to preserve the automotive heritage of the country. The twins joked about how they had also wanted the return of Dinosaurs.

The delayed release of the virus to break up the decentralized network worked, and the Tushi returned to their previous instructions of being attentive partners.

*

Two weeks later.

Mia was at home with Lucy reflecting on the crazy few weeks and getting her up to speed on the extent of her new skills.

"You said you wanted to make a difference. Didn't think you meant saving thousands of people from certain death," Lucy said.

Mia gave her a wide grin. "It feels pretty awesome."

"What's next? Can't see you settling back into the coffee shop routine."

Mia stroked her chin. "Hadn't really given it much thought. I was in the coffee shop yesterday."

Lucy smiled. "You're destined for more than making lemon drizzle cake and pouring a few coffees."

Mia sat back and stroked her stomach. "I'll be happy to be a mom and run the coffee shop, unless someone needs my help."

"Have you told Kat yet? She'll be jealous you've taken the attention for once."

"Not sure she needs to know. She won't hear it on the news. I think the fewer people that know the better."

"If you want to keep it quiet, you'll need a superhero name and costume."

Mia raised her fist like superman and announced, "lemon drizzle girl to the rescue." She then fell into Lucy's lap in a fit of giggles.

They were still laughing when Tyler arrived home with Ethan. As Tyler stepped into the lounge, Mia jumped to her feet and dove into his welcoming arms.

"You looked like you are having fun," Tyler said. He returned her embrace, and they shared a long kiss.

A coughing from behind Tyler interrupted them. "Excuse me. Can you put her down? It's my turn." Ethan held his new arm aloft and gave Mia a fun-loving smile. Mia flung her arms around him and Tyler put his arms around them both.

"Can I join in?" Lucy said as she joined in the group hug.

*

Re-instated as Design & Engineering manager at the Tushi Corporation, Ethan took the additional role of Climate Change Champion to continue Okzu's work in a more ethical manner.

To celebrate, he invited Mia for a meal at the restaurant where they first met, the award-winning Italian restaurant, Giangolini's.

As the taxi came to a rest under the canopied red carpet, Mia asked Ethan, "Are you okay? Your lace is not working. I've been trying to use my telepathy to tell you how much I love you."

"It's fine. I switched it off. I want to have a normal night, just me and you."

"Okay." Mia switched off her lace and accepted Ethan's hand as he led her into the restaurant.

The brown, smoked glass windows brought back the memory of their first date, when she'd accepted the foursome date after being badgered by Kat to put past disappointments behind her.

The smartly dressed head waiter led them under the painted images in the restaurant, and once again she held herself tall and elegant to match the opulent surroundings. He led them to the same table, in a small alcove. The same picture hung at the end of the table, a golden leafed frame around two cherubs holding love bows whilst perched on fluffy clouds.

"I was so nervous last time we were here." Mia blushed at the memory.

"I was nervous too, but you looked so vulnerable." They took their seats. "You are very different now, but I love you more."

"Thanks. You're not too bad yourself." Mia tried to make light of his outpouring of affection.

The same waiter appeared with menus and Mia asked him, "how did you turn Kat's water to wine last time we were here?" He shrugged his shoulders and pinched his fingers together before he left with a wink and a smile.

Although he didn't repeat any magic tricks, the meal was

superb. Sweet and tender steaks with peppercorn sauce were followed with a light apple tartlet and gelato.

Ethan patted his stomach. "That was as beautiful as you." He took a sip of his wine as Mia blushed and tucked a stray hair behind her ear. She gave him a coy smile, and he returned a nervous smile. "You know I love you."

"Love you to," Mia said. She reached for his hand, but he withdrew it as a small waist coated violinist with slick hair sauntered up to their table playing romantic Italian music.

Ethan fumbled in his pocket and Mia's eyes lit up, but it dashed her hopes as he pulled out a handkerchief and wiped his mouth. With her eyes fixed on the hanky, he offered it. "Would you like it?"

Mia sat back and crossed her arms. "No, thanks."

Ethan unraveled the hanky, and Mia spotted a small blue box. She leant forward again and clapped her hands on her cheeks. "Mia." He opened the box. "Will you marry me?"

Mia's eyes filled as she stared at the ring.

A nervous Ethan added, "I'd give anything to hear a yes from you. I don't know what I'd do if you said, no."

Mia slowly nodded her acceptance before unleashing a booming, "Yes." She wiped her eyes and placed her hand in his for him to place the platinum half carat diamond engagement ring on her shaking finger. A salty kiss followed as tears of joy flowed. Applause rippled through the restaurant as the violinist played, "here comes the bride."

Ethan had finally found a woman he could truly trust, and Mia was everything he ever wanted.

After Mia's relationship ups and significant downs, she was now a strong and confident woman with the love of Ethan aside her. Welcoming their baby into the world would be her next challenge unless her skills were called upon again.

*

Mia moved in with Ethan, but Tyler and Chloe's eternal love and promise to protect them remained intact.

Cole grew to become a worthy assistant to Ethan.

It turned out that Alfie wasn't the player Luke had painted. Lucy forgave him for his minor indiscretion and their relationship blossomed again after he moved in with her.

Kat defended Mirek's actions as following orders to protect his family. She also announced her daughter Destiny was the smartest child to be born. What she wasn't to know was that Ethan and Mia's child would surpass any child that had come before.

*

The war wasn't won. There was no war. Dependence on technology was greater than ever. The difference between humans and robots became more difficult to identify and the merging into a transhuman race had begun. Humans couldn't compete with the ever-improving deep learning droids, merging their minds was the only way to keep in touch with the super race.

The softer side of life and the loveable Tushi droids were successfully restricted to love and protect their paired partners.

Tushi wives and their male counterparts didn't call their humans, 'pets,' despite it adequately describing the relationship. The droids fed their owners, encouraging exercise and provided nightly treats. A pet in all but name.

Other Publications in the Awakenings Series

Finding love in 2045

The start of Mia's journey and how she first met Ethan is revealed in "Finding love in 2045."

Mia, 25, strives to find a guy who will follow the traditional rules of courtship, but she's in the wrong era. Stuck in 2045, she's more vulnerable than ever as her craving for a deeper connection grows.

The popularity of AI sexbots provide a further challenge to find someone not intent on instant gratification.

Mia thinks she's found her man but is once again left deflated. Family issues also come to a head and dump her at rock bottom.

Who can lift her out of her malaise and bring her the love she desperately seeks?

Mia's transformation into a sexually confident woman begins, but she'll face more setbacks before she finds a love that will last a lifetime.

Time to Click (Available Winter 2021)

The full story of how Ethan lost his manhood is revealed in "Time to Click."

Ethan's thrilling adventure follows his quest for love and the mountain of confidence he gains, only to fall and lose his very manhood to a horrific act. Driven to avenge the atrocity he must first find a way home.

The story begins after he has been left for dead in the Scottish Highlands. Can he live long enough to find shelter in the sparse land? Will the memory of how he lost his manhood return to him? Will he be able to find the perpetrator and avenge the act? Will he be able to trust or love anyone again?

Printed in Great Britain
by Amazon

11210270R00163